SERVANT

by
K. Wiley Sider

ISBN: 069229662X
ISBN 13: 9780692296622
Library of Congress Control Number: 2014916928
Devilwood Press, Ellicott City, MD

A word was secretly brought to me,
my ears caught a whisper of it.
Amid disquieting dreams in the night,
when deep sleep falls on men,
fear and trembling seized me,
and made all my bones shake.
A spirit glided past my face,
and the hair on my body stood on
end.
It stopped,
but I could not tell what it was.
A form stood before my eyes,
and I heard a hushed voice:
"Can a mortal be more righteous than God?"
Job 4:12–17

THE MOTHERS

ONE

When it happened, Miriam just knew. When her big, fat, drunken slob of a husband rolled away from her, she knew. She knew by the ball of fire that started in her belly and spread its way south to engulf her. She knew when she felt that filling, that presence beginning deep within her. Miriam knew she was going to have a baby.

It had been foretold, you see. Miriam read her Bible, and it said that he would come again to judge the living and the dead, and she just knew she would be the one. Miriam knew she was going to be the mother of the second son of God.

***

The late summer sun beat mercilessly on the tin roof of the wood-and-tar-paper shack, turning the kitchen into an oven. Miriam sweated in front of a spitting frying pan that held their dinner, while her husband, Howard, sat at a peeling card table, nursing the lukewarm beer clenched in his fat fist. With nothing better to do, Howard stared at the faded newsprint that papered the walls of the small room.

Too poor for paint, Miriam made do with whatever she could find in the garbage cans behind the homes of the slightly less poor. Since Howard's disability check barely covered their food and his medicinal supply of beer and cigarettes, Miriam had grown very resourceful when it came to decorating their three-room house and clothing them—no easy feat since they both topped three hundred pounds. She was a faithful denizen of the Salvation Army and Goodwill stores and had no qualms about scrounging through other people's trash for much-needed items. She had even found a camera in one of them, which still worked if you didn't use the flash. Sometimes, when Howard wasn't looking, she stole enough of his beer money to buy film. She hid the money in the one place Howard was sure never to look, her treasured Bible.

Miriam dropped the plate of sausage and johnnycakes down in front of Howard, picked up her precious Bible, and clutched it against her heart.

A circuit preacher had given her the Bible when she was somewhat slimmer and her face still held a faded prettiness. The preacher had become quite smitten with Miriam when the young woman favored him with some forbidden pleasures in the backseat of his ancient Ford following a particularly frenzied revival that ended in the saving of young Miriam's soul. Miriam studied her Bible faithfully while waiting for the return of her preacher lover, who had resumed his life with his wife and seven children, returning to Miriam and the backseat of his Ford only when the revival circuit made its way through Merwin, Mississippi.

It was during the preacher man's absence that Miriam met Howard Dirkin outside a bar where he was restocking the cigarette machine. Miriam was quite taken by the beefy youth, as he was with her. With her sights set on Howard, a determined Miriam set aside her Bible and her preacher and went about the business of landing the unmarried young man. It took only a few unfinished encounters in her daddy's hay barn to convince Howard that they should marry. By then Howard was so feverish with unfulfilled sexual fervor Miriam had him agreeing to just about anything. As a parting gift, Miriam's preacher married the young couple then left Merwin for good.

2

Now, more than a year later, Miriam was no longer even remotely slim and even less interested in participating in any sexual antics with Howard. Oh sure, she submitted to her wifely duty when absolutely necessary, but it was no longer a labor of lust. Miriam returned to her Bible and faithfully attended every service at the small Pentecostal church up the road. It was there that she found herself listening for God. She knew it was only a matter of time before he'd send her the word, and, on that hot July evening, she got it.

There was a guest preacher up at the small Bible stand that stood as a pulpit in the tiny frame church. He was boring as dirt, and Miriam had to stifle a yawn. To pass the time, she surveyed the small group of worshipers, several of whom had actually fallen asleep while others sat and read their Bibles. One woman, Sarah Polk, even had the nerve to read a newspaper. Miriam knew there were people who went to church just to do their duty. They were the folk who simply went through the motions of worship and prayer without ever thinking about what they were promising. She could just picture them, full of themselves, thinking their measly act of faith ensured their ticket to heaven. But Miriam knew better; she knew the way to heaven was paved with suffering, real suffering. And Miriam knew a thing or two about suffering. Hadn't she submitted to every disgusting whim of that fat pig of a husband? And her still without a baby. Sure, she'd been pregnant plenty of times but never with Howard. And didn't she live in just about the worst house in all of Merwin? Oh, yes, Miriam knew a lot about suffering.

Now the preacher was droning on about how Jesus himself said that blessed are the meek for they shall inherit the earth. Everyone else thought that meant God would just love those who lay themselves down to be doormats. Miriam was smarter than that. She knew that Jesus wasn't blessing anybody; he was warning them. Jesus was telling them that if everyone didn't toughen up, they would get left behind at the time of the rapture. Those meek people sure would inherit the earth, while everyone else would get to go with Jesus. Miriam knew for darn sure she wasn't sticking around on earth while everyone else went to heaven. She had it in her mind to be the first in line.

Stifling another yawn, which earned her a dirty look from Sarah Got-Her-Nose-So-High-Birds-Nest-There-Just-Because-She Married-The-Doctor Polk, Miriam turned her attention back to the preacher, who was finally wrapping it up with an admonishment to all women to keep themselves pure. *What does he think we are, Catholics?* Miriam snorted. Well he could just stick it if he thought anyone was buying that particular piece of garbage. Miriam had read most of the Bible and knew there was plenty in there about adultery and the like, but even Jesus let a prostitute into his fold. Miriam watched as the young man returned to his seat. She was glad to see that particular sermon end. Maybe now something interesting would happen.

As if in apology, their regular minister, Reverend Ewell Tucker, took the stand and gave the small congregation his most benign smile. Then, with all the flourish of a seasoned revivalist, he snatched up the Bible and threw back a forelock rich with pomade.

"Brothers and sisters," he roared, waking old Mr. Meecham, who had been snoring audibly in the front row. Pastor Tucker stalked to the center of the small dais and stood, legs planted far apart as if bracing for the end to come. Miriam felt that delicious shiver run right through her body. He was a fine-looking man, with those sleepy dark eyes and thick black hair. Those tight pants he favored didn't hurt either. She liked Pastor Tucker...oh yes, she did.

"I said, brothers and sisters," he roared again, this time to a chorus of hallelujahs. "Are you listenin'?" More hallelujahs and cries of "Praise Jesus" answered him. In a dramatic whisper, he asked again, "Can you hear that?" Pastor Tucker looked around the room till his eyes rested on Miriam. Miriam squirmed in her seat, her heart racing. Under her Bible, she carefully placed a finger over the sweet spot between her legs. She could feel through her thin cotton dress the first hint of moisture.

If she weren't careful, she'd be likely to orgasm right then and there. She glanced over at Sarah Polk, who was staring at her with disgust. *That's right, Sarah, you cold fish. I'm gonna shake and shimmy right here,* Miriam thought. She knew plenty about orgasms from her friendly Bible-giving preacher, and she was fixin' to have one right now as she worked her finger back and forth over her sweet spot. Miriam looked back at Pastor Tucker, who was still staring at her.

"Can you hear that?" he whispered again. "He's talkin' to you right now. The Lord's got somethin' to say, and you better listen." Right then, Pastor Tucker slowly licked his full, red lips, and it was all over for her. Miriam began to shake uncontrollably.

"Let it roll, sister." Pastor Tucker raised his hand in praise as Miriam began babbling, her cries of pleasure drowning in the glories sung by the rest of the congregation. "Let the Lord speak through you." Miriam stood clutching her not-inconsiderable bosom, not caring that the wet spot on her dress was glistening visibly. It was then she heard the whisper in her ear.

"He's coming."

Miriam ceased trembling and stood stock-still waiting for the voice again. For one long moment, she heard nothing but the hum and murmur of the crowd around her. She had about given up when she heard it again. Right against her ear, as if Jesus himself had his lips pressed against her, she heard him loud and clear, *"He's coming. Bring him home."*

Then she fainted.

When she came to Pastor Tucker and several of the congregation, including Mr. Meecham, who was looking up her skirt, surrounded her. As she pushed herself up, Miriam delivered a swift kick to the old fart's ankle, which sent him scurrying back to his seat. Pastor Tucker made to help her up, which served as an excellent cover for a quick grope.

Miriam hardly noticed though, as she strained to hear more of what she now considered her heavenly message. Once she was settled in her seat, after more fussing and groping by Pastor Tucker, Miriam shooed him away and picked up her Bible. She barely heard him when he returned to the pulpit. Instead she closed her eyes and turned inward for a little prayer. As she asked for his word for her, Miriam, with her eyes still closed, opened her Bible at random and put her finger on the page.

Well, damn, sometimes it didn't work the first time. Miriam quickly glanced over the passage she had landed on...*Nothin', just some hogwash about false oracles and false prophets.* She sighed then closed her eyes to try again. When she opened her eyes and read the passage she had landed on, Miriam began to smile. There it was, in black and white, plain as day.

"For out of you will come a ruler who will be the shepherd of my people Israel."

Miriam's smile grew smug as she closed her Bible and hugged it against her chest. *Yesiree and Bob's yer uncle*, as her late mother used to say. Now it was only a matter of time. Miriam wondered what kind of fanfare would precede this particular conception. If her Bible was any indication, an angel was supposed to appear to Howard first, though Miriam was pretty sure no angel was going to waste his time talking to Howard.

Only faintly aware that the service was over and people were filing out of the small frame church, Miriam followed them out the door, giving only a perfunctory shake to Pastor Tucker's hand. This was met with surprise, as normally she would linger over a few minutes of heated flirtation. Tonight was different though. Tonight she needed to go home and see if Howard had been visited yet.

Miriam picked up the pace once she hit the gravel road that forked off the blacktop a half mile from the church. She practically trotted the quarter mile to the cluster of shacks that surrounded a lone maple tree on the bank of Pick Creek. Formerly slave quarters, Miriam's father had bought the very first one so that Miriam and Howard could have their own home after they married. She knew, though, that all he really wanted was to get them out of his house before Howard caught on to his dirty little doings with his own children. Miriam had made darn sure that Daddy bought her the best of the lot. Now she saw it for what it was...a hovel. Little more than a pile of wood with a roof, Miriam hated her home and was little surprised that the other shacks stood empty, the other residents having moved on to greener, or lesser, pastures. Tonight, however, she hardly noticed in her haste to find Howard.

Unsurprisingly, he was still sitting in the same spot where she had left him over an hour ago. Miriam studied him for any sign of a divine visit. Instead she saw a man halfway into his cups staring dully at the wall of comic strips in front of him.

Howard turned a bleary eye toward Miriam. Once a sturdy young fellow with clear blue eyes and curly black hair, Howard's drinking had brought about a swift and brutal decline. It began with an unfortunate accident during the delivery of a new cigarette machine. Poor Howard was on the receiving end of an inexpert unloading that resulted in a broken back. Inadequate care and inactivity took its toll on Howard, who gained over a hundred pounds in less than eleven months.

Howard pulled at the cigarette dangling loosely between his pale, fat fingers and squinted at Miriam through the smoke pouring out of his red, swollen nose. "What the great goddamn are you lookin' at?" he asked dully as he flicked ashes into the plate of uneaten food in front of him.

Miriam ran into the room, shushing him in panic, lest the angel hear and decide to go elsewhere. "Quiet," she spat at him. Miriam tossed her Bible and handbag onto the table and pulled a beer out of the ancient icebox. "He might hear you!" With a swift bang against the table, Miriam popped off the cap and slammed it in front of Howard.

7

Suddenly much more congenial at the arrival of a fresh beer, Howard asked, almost politely, "Who?"

Miriam pulled out the only other remaining chair and sat down. "The angel," she explained patiently. "You should be hearin' from an angel soon." Howard's face remained blank. Miriam sighed and rolled her eyes. "I got a message tonight that he's comin', and when I went to my Bible, it told me he was comin' through me!" she finished excitedly.

Howard stared at his wife, certain she had finally lost her mind. "Who's comin'?" he ventured to ask as he dropped the butt of his cigarette in one of the many empty bottles that littered the table.

Miriam slapped a hand to her forehead in exasperation. "Jesus, Howard."

"Well, dammit, woman. You don' have to curse at me. I juss asked you who was comin'. Good grief." Howard took a long pull at his beer then shot a dirty look at his wife.

"No, Howard. I ain't cursin'. I'm tellin' you Jesus is comin'...through me. I got the message tonight at church."

"You sure Ewell Tucker ain't pullin' your leg?" Howard smirked. "Wouldn't be the first time he's tried to get a leg over you." Howard laughed so hard at his own joke the chrome-and-red-vinyl kitchen chair groaned under his weight.

"Pastor Tucker didn't pass along the message, Howard," Miriam insisted. "God did...or maybe one of his angels...but for sure it wasn't any person." Miriam sat back in her chair and gazed at the timbered ceiling with a small smile on her face. "I just know it was divinely sent," she sighed. "Now we just have to wait for the angel to come visit." Miriam's gaze settled back onto Howard. "Bible says Joseph was visited first," she said as Howard finished off the bottle of beer she'd given him then belched noisily. Miriam shook her head. "Don't mean it's goin' to happen the same way again." Miriam stood and stretched until her back cracked. "Well I'd better clean up," she grumbled. "God won't want his begotten son raised in a sty."

TWO

God that woman is disgusting, Sarah thought as she drove her dusty car away from the small church. She could see the other woman in the distance, waddling home like a baby elephant. Sarah Polk loathed Miriam Dirkin though she would have been embarrassed to explain why. If asked she would cite the many reasons why most people in town avoided the Wooten family- the father's public drunkenness, the children sporting the occasional black eye or busted lip, the rumored incest among the family members, the father's sly ways of trying to get one over on everyone. The fact that his children hardly spoke certainly didn't help things either. If Sarah were feeling charitable, she might say the younger Wootens suffered shyness or were feeble minded, however Sarah wasn't charitable. She was perfectly happy to let the small town of Merwin go on thinking the children were as sly and calculating as the father was.

To be honest, Sarah had hardly given Miriam and the Wooten family a thought before the young preacher had rolled into town. Sarah had seen him first when he stepped up to the pulpit at their small church. He looked like a movie star and his voice was low and warm enough to melt butter. He'd certainly melted Sarah. At the end of the worship service, Sarah had made sure to introduce herself and worked to make an impression on the young man. At first he seemed just as interested in her, even going so far as to invite her to the local Dairy Queen for an ice cream. So as not to attract the amused glances of the town folk, Sarah and her intended sat in his car and enjoyed their ice cream and conversation. For her it was a magical moment. The sun was only minutes from setting and the sky had gone from boring blue to glorious pink and orange. Sarah was so overcome by the moment and the man sitting next to her that she even allowed him a few stolen kisses. And he was a perfect gentleman, even when Sarah rebuffed the hand creeping up her skirt. He had apologized immediately, agreeing to take their romantic exploration slowly and driven her home. When he took her out the next evening, she was so pleased she let him explore further and had not objected when he placed her hand on the front of his trousers. His own fingers were persistent and eventually made their way into her panties, simultaneously thrilling and terrifying her as they tried to enter her. Of course she ended their love play before things went too far and again the young preacher relented and drove her home.

Sarah had had her sights set on a future with the handsome young preacher when Miriam Wooten had put herself in front of him and given him certain favors that Sarah was unwilling to provide. Miriam was a whore, plain and simple, and she'd whored Sarah's intended right out from under her. Then to make matters worse, Miriam ups and marries Howard Dirkin out of nowhere. Sarah's preacher man disappeared after that and she'd later heard that he had a wife and children somewhere. She wanted to call it a lie. A man of God would never commit such a sin but the truth was Sarah was humiliated. People knew she'd been pursuing the young man and the fact of his marital status made her look like a fool. Sarah put her chin up and laid all the blame squarely on Miriam. If Miriam hadn't seduced the young preacher with her wanton ways he might have realized his affection for Sarah, nevermind the supposed wife and children. She affected a martyred air and resumed her daily life with a quiet nobility that caught the eye of the new town doctor. He wasn't a man of God, in fact Sarah was fairly sure he wasn't even a believer, but he was a doctor. And science was almost as good as God. So Sarah turned her eye to the young Dr. Polk before Miriam could interfere and before long they were married.

Now she was tied to a man she was certain despised her. Sarah's heart hurt whenever she thought of her husband. Their courtship had been brief and based on lies Sarah had told as she feigned interest in every single thing the young doctor enjoyed despite having no idea what he was talking about. He was too smitten to see that Sarah's country ways were a poor fit but his mother had Sarah pegged right away. She could still feel the burn of shame when upon meeting her, Samuel's mother pulled her son aside to question his decision to marry her. Of course it was done out of hearing and with the utmost concern for the welfare of both Sarah and her son but it was no less embarrassing to know that Mrs. Polk considered her low born and grasping for the Polk family wealth that, to be honest, Sarah didn't even know existed. She was shocked to arrive at their family home in Maryland and see that her entire childhood home could fit in their garage. Samuel's mother must have seen something on her face, a look of greed, or more likely satisfaction. Sarah always felt like she was destined for greater things and arriving at the massive home on the water, she knew it was true. Unfortunately, Samuel's mother disagreed and advised her son to set Sarah aside in favor of a more suitable match. Sarah's satisfaction grew when Samuel defied his mother and married Sarah anyway. Now, a year later, Sarah suspected he regretted his rebellion. The loss of his relationship with his mother was too great and Sarah was not the prize he thought she was. She knew the only way to redeem herself was to give him a child and so far she'd failed at that as well. She'd already had two miscarriages and she knew if she didn't give him a child soon, he would divorce her.

If only Miriam had kept her legs closed, Sarah would be married to her warm loving preacher man instead of the cold disapproving Samuel. Sarah pulled into the driveway and turned off the car. Samuel's car was gone and she knew he'd be gone until the evening. Though he hardly spoke to her, she strongly suspected the Wootens, and more importantly Miriam, had become his favorite patients. The thought fueled her hatred for the other woman. It was only a matter of time before Miriam took Samuel away from her too.

Sarah felt a cramp deep in her belly and sensed the wetness between her legs. The frown lines on her face deepened and her bitterness tasted like bile on her tongue. She had thought this would be the one. She slowly made her way into the house, hoping and praying that this time the Lord would bless her with a baby and her husband would love her again.

THREE

That night Miriam was so full of the spirit of the Lord, she hardly raised a fuss when Howard took it into his head to have relations with her. *What's the harm*, she figured, *seein' as no angels showed up.* It never dawned on her to question why the Lord would choose her when she was about as far away from pure as one could get.

When no angel showed up by the next night, Miriam began to wonder if maybe the Lord had found Howard lacking. A small seed of resentment that her big, fat slob of a husband might be the only thing standing between her and the glory of God began to creep into her heart. It didn't help that, once again, Howard was as drunk as he ever was and in the mood to fornicate. This time Miriam wasn't as amenable. In the back of her mind, Miriam thought that with Howard's seed present there might not be enough room for the Lord to make a baby in her. Even with Howard squirming around on top of her, though, not much was going on down there. Miriam pushed at his big, fat, naked belly until he slid off panting. She was relieved to find that as slippery as he left her, nothing likely made it inside. She felt a slight pang of worry at the thought that the Lord might have chosen someone else already. That small seed of resentment toward Howard nestled itself in the soil of her heart and began to grow.

It was difficult falling asleep, especially with Howard snoring audibly next to her. Miriam tossed and turned for hours until, finally, she dropped off. It was then that Miriam had a dream.

Behind her eyes, Miriam saw the underside of the corrugated tin roof that was the ceiling of their bedroom. Slowly, amid the shadows that clung like cobwebs among the timbers, a dark shape began to form then descend upon her. Miriam gave a great sigh of satisfaction. *At last*, she thought as it floated toward her. A sweet, fruity scent filled her nose, and she wondered if that's what heaven smelled like. As the shape came closer, Miriam felt a blanket of darkness come over her, crushing her. She gasped for breath but did not cry out, lest she frighten her visitor away. As the darkness smothered her, Miriam felt a burning begin from deep within. A small flame quickly grew into a great ball of fire, filling her with pain. Suddenly the shadow moved away, leaving Miriam panting for air. She could hear the bed squeak as Howard shifted his considerable bulk. In her sleep, Miriam began to smile. She knew...he had finally come.

The next morning Miriam was up before dawn giving the house a good scrub down. Every so often she would stop and lay her hands, red and swollen from the lye soap she was using, on her belly and give a great sigh of satisfaction. It was during one of these moments that Howard came in from using the privy out back. Miriam stood before the now shining cooker, lost in her musings, as Howard sat heavily in the dangerously frail chrome-and-red-vinyl dinette chair. He hardly glanced at her as he idly scratched at his fat, white belly, which undulated like a gentle wave with every movement of his hand.

As was her habit, Miriam took out bacon, flour, and eggs to make Howard's johnnycakes and poured clean water over Sunday's coffee grounds to make a weak but still caffeinated cup of coffee for herself. Howard grunted a request for his morning libation, which fell on Miriam's deaf ear as she was once again daydreaming in front of the hissing skillet. When his second grunt received no response, Howard turned in his groaning chair to put a flea in her ear.

"What's the matter with you, woman?" he hollered. "I've been sittin' here for just about ever, dyin' of thirst, and all you can do is stand there with yer dummy smile on yer face. Now git my goddamn beer!"

Suddenly, Howard's head snapped to the side as the back of the metal spatula Miriam was holding connected with the flat side of his face. Bacon grease and pancake batter smeared his cheek, now burned with the pattern of the hot utensil. Howard was so shocked that he sat speechless, his mouth hanging open like a choirboy. Miriam advanced on the stunned man, wielding the spatula like a tennis racket.

"You watch yer mouth!" she screamed. "Iffen I hear you one more time takin' the Lord's name in vain in front of his begotten son, you'll feel more than this!" Miriam stood before Howard, shaking in anger.

"What in hell are—" Howard began before the spatula met with his face a second time. "*Aaagh!*" he screamed as he held his cheek and made to grab at Miriam's hand at the same time.

Miriam swung it back out of his reach, high enough to do some serious damage should Howard decide to speak again. "I said watch yer mouth!" Miriam shrieked, her face mottled with rage and spittle flying from her mouth.

Howard remained silent, holding his swelling cheek. Miriam quieted as he stared at her with genuine fear. He waited until she put down the spatula to speak again. "You mind tellin' me what all that was about?" he asked politely. Miriam threw him a faded dish towel to wipe his face then fetched his beer. Instead of opening it, however, Howard held it to his throbbing cheek. Miriam dumped his now burnt bacon and johnnycakes onto a plate and dropped it onto the table before him. Fearing another backlash, Howard began to pick at it.

Calmer, Miriam sat down and took a moment to push away errant tendrils of greasy, red hair that were sticking to her sweaty forehead.

Then she gazed upon Howard with an expression of distaste as he made his way through his mostly inedible meal.

"I'm only goin' to tell you this once, so you listen good," she warned. "The angel came to me last night and blessed me with his seed. Now just because the Lord's found me worthy to bear his next son don't mean you still can't mess things up. So no more swearin', no more takin' his name in vain, and you best clean yerself up lest he decide you ain't good enough to be around his baby."

Howard stared at his wife for one long moment then erupted into great guffaws of laughter. Tears began streaming down his face, which had now gone beet red. Howard had to hold on to the flimsy table to keep from sliding off the chair. Miriam just sat and watched dispassionately, certain that Howard had lost his mind.

"Oh, woman," he gasped. "You really have gone 'round, haven't you?" Miriam simply sat quietly with a steely glint in her eye. Howard was so lost in his mirth he didn't notice her expression growing stony.

Howard pulled up the tail of his shirt and wiped his eyes. "What in the he—I mean tarnation—makes you think the Lord would have anythin' to do with you?"

Miriam stuck out her chin and gave Howard a mulish look. "I just know," she stated flatly. "Just like I know you don't have to live here if I don't want you to. So you best watch yerself, or you'll be out on yer ear."

Howard ignored his wife's warning and, with a final chuckle, opened his beer. After a long pull at the now lukewarm bottle, he noticed that Miriam was still watching him. "Get about yer business, woman. Bring me another, and this time without the food."

Miriam got up and fetched another beer as Howard shook a cigarette out of the nearly empty pack and lit up. Peering at Miriam through the smoke, he sneered, "Ain't you got church this morning? Ewell Tucker'll want to know about yer heavenly visit."

"My goodness, yer right. I gotta go tell him," Miriam cried. Throwing down the skillet she had begun scrubbing, Miriam grabbed her purse and her Bible and left for church.

Outside the air was already steaming hot despite the early hour. A cacophony of cicadas rang in Miriam's ears as she practically ran down the road. She was glad Howard had mentioned church. Though services did not start for another hour, she knew Pastor Tucker would be there getting ready for the day. In fact, the doors now stood wide open as she approached. Miriam panted her way up the wooden steps and entered the shade of the small room that served as a chancel. She could hear Pastor Tucker humming while he set up the folding chairs that took the place of pews. As she entered the main room, Pastor Tucker looked up and gave Miriam a beaming smile. His light blue polyester jacket lay draped over the Bible stand, and he had opened the top three buttons of his pale-blue short-sleeved shirt. Miriam could see the gray and black hairs that peeked out at the top glistening with beads of sweat.

"Ah, Miriam! Now what brings you here so early? You here to keep a poor man company?" Pastor Tucker came forward as Miriam wiped the sweat from her brow and fanned herself with her fat, white hand.

"He's coming," she panted, which made Pastor Tucker pause in his tracks.

"Who is, honey?" he asked sharply, looking over Miriam's shoulder at the front door.

"Jesus is, Pastor," Miriam replied.

Pastor Tucker laughed in relief. "Well of course he is, Miriam."

"No, I mean, he's goin' to be born again, through me. I got the message here in church, and last night the angel planted his seed," Miriam explained.

Pastor Tucker considered Miriam for a moment then seized the announcement with gusto. "My goodness, Miriam, we have been blessed, indeed!"

Miriam was so relieved that he hadn't laughed like Howard did she almost dropped her Bible. Ewell Tucker crossed the last couple of feet between them and grasped Miriam in his arms. In feigned joy, he pressed Miriam's body against his and rubbed against her. In her happiness, she hardly noticed his burgeoning erection. When his pants were fixing to pop right open, he pushed her away and grabbed her arms, rubbing her nipples with his thumbs on the way.

"This calls for a celebration!" he cried as he pressed against her again. "But first let us kneel and give a prayer of thanks." Ewell Tucker pulled Miriam to her knees and pressed one hand against the small of her back and the other against her womb, his fingers resting on the mound between her legs. She could feel them working outside the fabric of her dress and began to moan as they made their way to that spot Howard never seemed to find. Ewell Tucker saw the flush rise in her cheeks and licked his lips.

"Oh Lord in Heaven," he began to pray. "You have graciously accepted this woman as your vessel, planted in her the child who will lead us all to salvation. We thank you for finding her worthy, and we pray that you give her the strength to bear and mother your most blessed son, our Savior."

Miriam threw her head back as her body began to tremble. Again Ewell Tucker licked his lips then grasped her hands to his chest before thrusting them into his lap. Closing his eyes he continued his prayer.

"Oh Lord on high," he panted. "You have blessed us all that we may enter into the presence of your son. Make us worthy of your child. Make us...oh..." Ewell Tucker moaned then shuddered as he rubbed Miriam's hands against himself. Neither Miriam nor Pastor Tucker noticed that they were no longer alone. Both were brought back by a deliberate cough.

Pastor Tucker's head snapped up, and Miriam fell onto her backside as he suddenly let her go.

"Sarah!" he cried as he jumped up and grabbed at his jacket. Rushing forward, Pastor Tucker extended his hand, which Sarah Polk looked at with revulsion. At her expression, Pastor Tucker looked at his own hand then shoved it within the folds of his jacket. Behind him, Miriam gathered herself together and stood unsteadily.

"Miriam and I were prayin'," he stammered nervously. "She's brought us great news!"
"As have I," said Sarah quietly. "I'm going to have a baby."

"No!" Miriam gasped, startling both Sarah and Pastor Tucker. All the color went out of Miriam's face, and she had to grab on to the back of a chair to keep from falling.

"Yes," Sarah replied, "though I don't see that it has anything to do with you."

"Oh but it does!" cried Pastor Tucker. "Miriam is with child as well! His child...the Lord's, I mean."

"Really," said Sarah, dryly. "The Lord's child."

Miriam gazed at Sarah with horror as a thought occurred to her. What if he had chosen Sarah instead? Miriam felt as if a fist had been thrust into her belly. She sat down on the chair she had been holding on to. Ewell Tucker moved to fan her with his coat, until the sight of the stain on the front of his pants made him think twice. Instead he ran out of the room, mumbling something about water, leaving the two women to stare at each other.

After a long moment, Sarah spoke first. "What makes you think our Lord would choose *you*, one of his worst sinners, to bear his son? What on earth makes you think that *you*, of all people, are worthy?"

"Who are you callin' a sinner?" Miriam cried, fearful that the Lord or one of his messengers was nearby and listening.

"You are," Sarah replied reasonably. "What else would you call a married woman who masturbates her minister?"

"We was prayin'!" Miriam shrieked.

"I think the Lord knows better," Sarah said with a small, knowing smile. Before Miriam could answer, Ewell Tucker returned with his jacket on and fully buttoned so that if he stood slightly stooped, only a small crescent of the stain on his pants showed. He handed a jelly jar filled with water, cloudy with rust, to Miriam and made a great show of wiping his hands on a kitchen towel.

"Well, Sarah!" he boomed heartily. "We have been doubly blessed! I think we need to give a prayer of thanks for both you and Miriam!"

"I think I'll wait until the others show up," Sarah replied, her smile thin. "In fact, I think I'll wait outside." With that, she turned and went back out into the glaring sunshine.

Ewell Tucker turned to see Miriam staring at the water with a sick expression. Lest he get into more trouble, Ewell kept his distance. "Uh, something wrong, Miriam?" he asked hesitantly.

"Maybe it's her..." she mumbled then began to retch. Ewell stood by helplessly as Miriam coughed and spluttered. Eyeing the door, he helped Miriam to her feet and ushered her toward the door at the rear of the small building.

"I think you should go on home, Miriam," he said nervously. "Yer lookin' a little peaked."

Miriam was halfway out the door when she realized Ewell was pushing her to leave. "No," she protested, shaking her head. "I gotta stay. I need to pray on somethin'."

Ewell Tucker dropped her arm and stepped back as the rest of his congregation began to arrive. "Well, Miriam," he proclaimed loudly, one eye on Sarah as she came in and took her seat. "If you're feelin' better, why don't you sit down, and we'll get started as soon as everyone else arrives."

Miriam stared at Sarah as she moved back toward the chairs. Sarah watched Miriam with a knowing smirk as her sister, Lottie Martin, sat next to her and whispered in her ear. From her expression, Miriam could tell that Sarah had told Lottie about the illicit prayer session she had interrupted.

Miriam sat down heavily and stared at the floor, her face burning. Rather than listen to Ewell Tucker's fumbling attempts at preaching while covering the stain on the front of his pants with the fully inadequate Bible stand, Miriam tried to pray, but the feeling of knowing eyes looking upon her made it impossible. Neither could she concentrate on her Bible. Miriam stared at her Bible, seeing it for the first time as what it was...payment for services rendered. Her eyes grew hot as she forced back tears of humiliation. She was still fighting sobs when she realized that Ewell had wrapped up his brief service and people were filing out of the small church. Miriam got up and followed the last of the congregation to the front doors where several groups had gathered to chat. Sarah and Lottie stood among them, silently watching as Miriam passed by.

"I wonder," Sarah began as Miriam made to move past them.

Unable to help herself, Miriam stopped and faced Sarah. "What?" she whispered.

Lottie snickered as Sarah looked Miriam straight in the eye. "I wonder if the Lord will send you to hell for your blasphemy...or just punish you now."

In that moment, Miriam's grief turned into an intense hatred for this woman who would steal her only chance at God's glory. Miriam fought the urge to spit at Sarah and instead ran out into the sunlight, Lottie's laughter pelting her like rocks.

Rather than going home and having to listen to Howard, Miriam walked the mile and a half past her shack to her father's farm. She had been avoiding this visit for weeks, despite living just down the road. Miriam was the oldest of eight children, the family being an even mix of girls and boys. The youngest, her brother Wade, was only ten. Miriam's beloved mother, Flora, died just minutes after his birth, and no one let him forget it.

As she approached she saw that all of her siblings save two were scattered about the porch and dirt yard. Where there should have been laughter and play, Miriam found only sullen regard. Two of her brothers sat silently tying fishing lures with ragged line, while her two youngest sisters scrubbed at threadbare clothes in an old washtub. Her sister Inez, who at sixteen was three years younger than Miriam, had taken her place as their father's playmate when Miriam left. Inez wore an old flowered dress of their mother's, her dirty feet wrapped around the legs of her chair as she sat snapping green beans into a cracked ceramic bowl that lay in her lap. She paused and stared as Miriam walked up.

"Where's Pa?" Miriam asked.

Without speaking, Inez jerked her head back toward the house. Miriam knew that meant her pa was inside, probably sleeping.

"Abel and Caleb?"

"Field," Jacob mumbled. "Bringin' in hay."

Miriam turned back to her sister, who had gone back to her beans. "Goin' to have a baby," she said quietly. Behind her Wade snorted. Miriam turned and looked at him.

"You ain't the only one," he laughed until Jacob, the older boy, pushed him into the dirt. Miriam looked back at Inez, who had put down her bowl and stood up. Miriam could see the gentle curve of her sister's swelling belly as she stretched.

"Is it his?" Miriam asked, though she knew the answer.

Inez nodded.

"Why didn't you take the cure?" Miriam asked, though she knew the answer to that one too. Often it was too late to use the closely guarded folk remedy. It took just the right blend of castor oil, black cohosh, and evening primrose to achieve the desired effect. Too little and it just made you sick as a dog for nothing...too much could kill. Miriam had been lucky in the past.

"Didn't work this time," Inez answered quietly.

The two young women looked at each other for a long moment. Miriam was about to speak again when her father kicked open the screen door behind Inez. Delbert Wooten was a small, wiry man whose face had been sunburned so many times it very strongly resembled a dried apple. What little hair he had left stood straight up from the top of his shining pate like wisps of black smoke. As he stood scratching his privates, Inez silently moved around him and went into the house, slamming the door behind her.

"That one tell you 'bout her bastard?" he sneered at Miriam. "Can't even tell me who the pa is." Miriam's father glanced back at the house. "Whore," he muttered then turned back to Miriam. "Ain't got no money, if that what yer lookin' fer," he warned then spat at the ground.

"Came with news," Miriam began then faltered, wondering why she was even bothering telling her pa anything.

"Oh, ayuh," Delbert replied, eyeing his daughter keenly.

"Havin' a baby," Miriam said quietly.

"That so?" Delbert sniffed as he worked his fingers from his privates to his backside. "Ain't got nothin' to do with me, do it?" he demanded.

"No," Miriam stated flatly then turned to leave. As she turned, her eyes met those of Inez through the dirty screen, and Miriam bid her a silent farewell. Halfway across the dirt yard, she heard Wade call out.

"Hey, Miriam!"

Turning, she saw her youngest brother with his pants down around his knees wiggling his little hips so his tiny, flaccid penis flopped up and down. Dorcas and Rachel, the two youngest girls, and Jacob all turned away as Wade laughed maniacally. Miriam walked up and slapped him hard across the face, shutting him up right quick.

"Don't you never let me catch you doin' that again, to nobody, or I'll cut it off and feed it to the dogs," she hissed, her finger inches from his nose. Too startled to cry, Wade turned beet red instead as his father burst out in great guffaws. Miriam turned and stomped off.

FOUR

Sarah's joy at announcing her pregnancy faltered at the news that Miriam was also expecting. The last thing she wanted was to share her joy at impending motherhood with a woman she despised. Samuel had greeted the news with little enthusiasm and Sarah knew it was because he expected her to miscarry any day now. But this time would be different. She planned on confining herself to her bed whenever Samuel wasn't home. Luckily her sister Lottie would be coming by daily to keep the house clean so Samuel didn't think Sarah was shirking her duties to the home. She would even take the pills Samuel had given her even though they made her sick to her stomach.

She was already feeling nauseated when Lottie arrived to give the house a quick cleaning before Samuel returned from his round of house calls. Sarah sat in the kitchen with a cup of tea while Lottie chattered about everything and nothing. Sarah wasn't listening. The image of Miriam and Pastor Tucker was burned into her brain and she seethed with jealousy that Pastor Tucker had been far more excited about Miriam's pregnancy than her own.

"Can you imagine Miriam Dirkin thinks she's having the next baby Jesus?" she said, interrupting her sister's flow of nonsense. She hadn't planned on saying anything but the idea of it was just too ridiculous. Luckily Lottie disliked Miriam Dirkin almost as much as Sarah did.

"The woman is plumb crazy if she thinks the Lord would bless her with his son," Lottie remarked. She'd been giving the kitchen a quick wipe down and threw down the sponge to take a seat across from Sarah. Sarah smiled inwardly. She knew Samuel hated gossip but he wasn't here and she was bored. Lottie was always good for a chinwag and her job behind the counter at her husband's grocery store often gave her a perspective that Sarah wasn't privy to.

"One of the younger ones came into the store the other day," Lottie continued. "Looked at us like we were going to set her on fire or something. And I swear she hadn't bathed in forever. Even her money smelled dirty." Sarah smiled but said nothing. Lottie continued. "And what about Ewell Tucker going along with it? Do you think he believes her?"

Sarah shrugged but her smiled turned smug. "I think he'll believe anything if it comes with a hand job."

Lottie sighed. "I hope you have a girl so she and Amberlee can be friends. They can even do pageants together."

"I hope I have a boy so I can tell Miriam Dirkin *I'm* having the Baby Jesus," Sarah countered and Lottie laughed then turned serious.

"How will Jesus come back?" she mused.

Sarah stared at her sister. "Well he'd have to be born from a woman, right? It's not like he can just show up."

"Why not? He's Jesus. He can do whatever he wants."

Sarah shrugged then heard the front door open. She jumped up and grabbed the sponge Lottie threw down in time to see Samuel step into the doorway. She feigned wiping the counter as he glanced around the sparkling kitchen. His eyes settled on Lottie and Sarah could tell by his expression that he was less than pleased to see her there.

"Charlotte," he said by way of greeting then turned and left to go into his office. Sarah was about to pour him a cup of coffee when she heard the door close with a finality that she knew meant he didn't want to be disturbed.

Lottie looked at her sister, her expression worried. "Should I leave?" she whispered and Sarah nodded. Lottie jumped up and gave her sister a hug then fled.

Sarah sat down at the table and frowned. With Samuel home she would have to do the laundry herself. She sat quietly listening for signs of life but only felt the heaviness of disapproving silence. When Samuel's door finally opened again, she wasn't surprised to see him walk past the kitchen doorway without a single glance in her direction. She sighed then got up to finish the housework herself.

FIVE

By the time Miriam reached the group of shacks she called home, the sun was burning hot right above her head and sweat was streaming down her face and back. Her thin cotton dress clung to her wetly as she made her way to the lone maple tree next to the creek. A half a century ago, lightning had split the sapling in two. Over the years it had grown into a large, leafy letter *v*. Now only one part of the *v* remained, the other having been cut down to a stump forming a natural bench under the canopy of its twin. Miriam sat down to catch her breath. Pick Creek, now little more than a trickle, provided little comfort as Miriam kicked off her shoes and soaked her aching feet. With a sigh, she closed her eyes and leaned against the trunk of the tree. Her respite lasted only moments though, as Howard came stomping out onto the front porch, leaning heavily on the cane the hospital gave him when he broke his back. Howard didn't really need the cane and only used it when he was too drunk to walk straight.

"You on vacashun er somethin'?" he slurred. "Gi' abou' yer bizness, wummun, an' make me some food."

Miriam ignored him as he peered at her for a moment then turned and stumbled back into the house. She knew not to bother herself about Howard when he was this drunk. A few more minutes and he'd be passed out snoring, either in his chair in the kitchen or in bed. At least she hoped he'd make it that far. It wasn't long ago that Howard passed out on the floor just inside the door and Miriam had to go in and out the back till he woke up a whole day later. At least she missed the worst part. Just before his blackouts, Howard turned mean, vicious in fact. She had learned to stay away when he was reaching that point. Every once in a while, though, it caught her by surprise, and she'd come away from the encounter with a black eye or missing a chunk of hair. Sometimes she gave as good as she got, and Howard bore the scars to prove it.

Miriam waited a few more minutes then went inside. Sure enough, she could see Howard through the opening into the kitchen. He sat in his chair, head back, dead to the world. Miriam watched him for a moment, until a giant spit bubble formed at his mouth then popped. *Ain't dead yet*, she thought regretfully then went through the "parlor" to the back bedroom.

With her hands on her hips, Miriam surveyed the small room. Though the house had a pitched roof, it was only one level, and with only three rooms, there wasn't enough space to put a child up. Oh, sure, the baby could sleep in a cradle in the bedroom with them, but once he moved to a big bed, they would have to find room elsewhere. Though Miriam grew up sharing a bed with various family members, she figured God's son deserved better. Miriam looked up and tried to picture how much space there was above her. She guessed that whoever built the small house intended to put in a loft if not another level, for there was plenty of room up there. After a few more minutes of squinting at the roof, Miriam went into the kitchen to fetch something cold to drink then went out and headed down the road.

Her brother Jacob had said that Abel and Caleb were out bringing in the hay. Miriam figured they'd still be out there, since they were on their own without any help from their pa. It was Abel she wanted to talk to, for at eighteen, there wasn't anything he couldn't do with a hammer. Sure enough, Miriam found them loading up the back of the ancient farm truck with finished bales ready for delivery to the farmers' co-op near town.

Caleb looked up as Miriam approached and nodded at Abel. Both boys were shirtless and glistening in the heat. Their thin frames favored their father, and both were well on their way to tanning their skin into saddle leather. Miriam handed them the beers she had brought. Without a pause, Abel and Caleb downed them with a nod of thanks.

"So, whut's up? Ain't my birthday," Abel asked as he hoisted another bale up to Caleb, who had jumped into the back of the truck.

"Havin' a baby and I need yer help," Miriam answered. Both boys paused in their labors and looked at Miriam with an unspoken question. "Not his," she answered.

Abel nodded silent congratulations then resumed his labors. Caleb regarded Miriam for a moment longer then spoke. "You seen Inez?" he asked quietly.

Miriam nodded, her sorrowful expression mirrored in her brothers' faces. "Couldn't you stop it?" she asked.

"I warn't there," Caleb replied. "Abel tried." Miriam turned to her other brother to ask then froze at the sight of the welts that ribboned across his back as he turned to fetch another hay bale. Abel tossed it up to Caleb then stopped and stared at the ground, sweat, or maybe tears, rolling down the sharp angles of his cheekbones.

"What happened?" Miriam asked. Abel took a moment before answering. When he looked up, Miriam saw his eyes were red and swimming.

"Pa came home likkered up. He'd been all right for a time, but that last night, well…he'd gone for Rachel." Abel paused and rubbed the back of his hand across his eyes.

Miriam put her own hand over her eyes. "And her only eleven," she sighed.

"I put myself in front of her so's he couldn't reach her, just like you told me to," Abel continued. "Man alive, it pissed him off somethin' awful. Next thin' I know, he's beatin' me with his belt buckle. Bled like a stuck pig. Inez put herself between to make him stop, so he took her instead. I passed out before I could help her." Abel looked up at Miriam, his face twisted with grief. "I'm right sorry, Miriam. I tried...I guess I didn't try hard enough."

Miriam went over and put her arms around her brother. "You did just fine," she comforted. "He's a bad man, and there ain't nothin' you kin do 'bout that 'cept be a better man."

"Leastways he ain't touched any of 'em since he knocked up Inez," Caleb piped up. "Could be he's scared someone'll ask Inez 'bout the daddy."

"Let's hope someone does," Miriam said grimly, though family loyalty kept her from meaning it.

Abel wiped his eyes dry then asked, "What's it you need from me?"

Miriam smiled at her sweet, brave brother. "We ain't got enough room in our house for a little one. I was hopin' you could come and put in a loft for us."

"Sure," Abel replied. "Let me finish loadin'. Then Caleb can take back the truck, and I'll come look."

"You don't have to do it now!" Miriam smiled, shaking her head. "Baby won't be here for months and months."

"Ain't no better time," he said as he threw the last of the hay bales to Caleb then pulled on the white T-shirt that had been hanging from his back pocket. Caleb tied a tarp over the loaded truck then hopped in the cab and drove away with a wave.

Still shaking her head, Miriam set off with Abel back to her house. Little was said on the way. Miriam could tell that Abel was brooding over his failure to protect his sister. *Leastways he doesn't touch his boys,* Miriam thought with a silent prayer of thanks. There wasn't anything Del Wooten hated worse than homosexuals. Though he might diddle his daughters whenever he pleased, Del wouldn't do anything that would label him a "faggot." Miriam was glad for that. She knew deep in her heart that Abel never would have survived something as bad as that, and losing Abel would just about break her heart.

As they made their way up the path to the house, Miriam pulled Abel to a stop. "Best be quiet when we go in," she warned. "Howard's passed out, and I'd like him to stay that way."

Abel nodded, and the two went in. Sure enough, Howard still sat slumped and snoring over the kitchen table. Miriam led Abel through to the bedroom and pointed to the rafters. He looked up for a second or two then, with the aid of a small stool that stood in the corner, hoisted himself onto the nearest ceiling rafter. Using his height and shoe length, Abel measured off the size of the space above them then dropped down beside Miriam.

"No sweat," he assured her then, without another word, turned, and left the house.

Miriam followed him out the door and watched him make his way down the road back to the farm. When he was just a dot on the horizon, Miriam turned and went back into the house to finish up her cleaning.

Early the next morning, Miriam awoke out of a foggy sleep to a quiet tapping. Wrapping her threadbare robe about her, Miriam looked in on Howard, who slept soundly on his kitchen chair, reeking of urine, his face pressed against the sagging table, then went to the front door. Through the screen she could see Abel waving with one hand while clutching a load of lumber with the other.

"Hey, Miriam," he whispered. "I ain't aimin' to wake up Howard. I'll just pile this up out back."

"Abel," Miriam whispered back. "I told you before, you got plenty of time before the baby comes!"

"I best get started now, seein' as how I can only work durin' my off times." He grinned. "I'll just drop this off and come back later." As quietly as he could, Abel picked up the load of two-by-fours and carried them off.

Miriam closed the door behind him and went to the bedroom to check her Bible to see how much money she had put by. She was disappointed to find that over the course of a year, she had only managed to skim little more than forty-five dollars from Howard's disability checks. She didn't know how much lumber cost, but she was pretty sure forty-five dollars wasn't going to cover very much. Miriam sighed then took the cash out back to where Abel stood stacking the lumber neatly up against the side of the house.

Miriam held out the money. "It ain't much, but if you could give me some more time, I'll try and have the rest for you before you finish."

Abel looked at Miriam then at the money, shaking his head. "You keep that. Yer gonna need it when yer little one comes."

"I can't let you pay," Miriam protested as she thrust the fistful of dollars at her brother.

"Oh I ain't paying." Abel chuckled. "This here wood comes from the hay barn Pa was thinkin' of puttin' out in the back field. Bought it drunk and plumb fergot all about it." Abel smiled and thumbed his nose at their absent father. "Think of it as his baby gift." Abel gave the lumber one last kick. "I'll come back after supper, if that's OK with you. Caleb and me gotta work on that old tractor. I swear, if Pa would quit drinkin' up all his money, we could buy us a new one. Hell, we could buy just about anythin' we want!" He laughed.

Miriam laughed along with her brother then waved as he turned to leave. With a small sigh, Miriam went in to make breakfast.

That evening, Abel returned as promised, just as Miriam was cleaning up after their dinner. Howard had taken himself onto the front porch, where it was considerably cooler. Miriam's news of Abel's gift was met with little more than a snort and a demand for another beer. Miriam was happy to see him at least vacate the small house so that Abel could get started.

Abel made quick work of moving in all the lumber and ladders he would need for the evening, and before Miriam knew it, he had finished reinforcing the beams that would support the floor and had even built a set of ladderlike stairs along the back wall.

Miriam had high praise for her brother, and even Howard managed to lumber his way in and murmur polite words of approval before waddling off to the kitchen.

Abel was so talented that, with a little help from Caleb, it was only another couple of weeks before Miriam could go up and admire the new room, complete with a perfectly handcrafted cradle. She was so deeply touched at the sight of the small bed that her eyes swam with tears as she hugged her blushing brother.

"Oh, Abel," she cried. "It's so pretty! I don't know what to say!" A knock on the step had both of them turning to see Caleb coming up the stairs carrying a simple but beautiful bentwood rocker.

"Oh my," Miriam whispered. "How in the world did you manage to make somethin' so nice in just a week?"

"Don't be too impressed." Caleb laughed. "Abel made this fer Inez, but she told me to bring it here instead." Caleb's expression sobered.

Miriam caught the change in his mood. "Why?" she asked cautiously.

"Her baby ain't movin'," he answered grimly. "She's called in old Mrs. Pritchett to give her somethin' to take care of it. She's thinkin' she won't be needin' the rocker now."

Miriam made her way to the stairs and went down past her brother. "I'd better go and give some help."

Abel and Caleb offered no protest and, after placing the rocker next to the new cradle, followed Miriam out of the house.

SIX

At their pa's house, Miriam and the boys found the family patriarch sitting in the gloom of the front porch, sipping from an old corn-whiskey jug. From the smell of it, it was either moonshine or turpentine. Miriam ignored him and went past him into the house. Inside she could hear the sounds of retching coming from upstairs. She sent Caleb into the kitchen to fetch a pot of water and some clean towels then hurried up the stairs.

In the front bedroom, she found Inez curled up on the bed she shared with her two sisters, a basin filled with vomit lying on the floor next to her. Miriam's youngest sister, Rachel, held her hand as Mrs. Pritchett pressed her ear against Inez's swollen belly, which was much bigger than Miriam had originally thought. Their other sister, Dorcas, was at the head of the bed, wiping the sweat and vomit from their sister's face.

"How is she?" Miriam asked as she donned the apron she had brought with her from home.

The ancient midwife shook her head as she pushed herself up with a grimace. "Ain't hearin' nothin'. Ain't feelin' nothin', an' she's sicker 'n a dog. Bairn's dead. Lord have mercy on its soul." Mrs. Pritchett crossed herself before wiping her hands on her skirt then stooped to pick up a faded carpetbag.

Miriam moved to Inez and placed the back of her hand against her sister's forehead. "She's burnin' up. Maybe we should call Doc Polk."

Inez reached out and grabbed Miriam's wrist. "Can't..." she panted. "He ain't...one of us. He'll...know...then...they'll...all...know." Inez collapsed back against Dorcas, who gently cradled her head then looked up at Miriam with tears in her eyes.

"You could die," Miriam protested. "Don't kill yerself to protect him. He don't deserve that."

"Nooo," Inez moaned. Caleb came in at that moment bearing a large basin filled with water and a pile of clean sheets and towels. His face paled at the sight of his sister writhing on her bed. Miriam took the basin and linens from him and sent him from the room. Rachel took the linens and placed them on the chest at the foot of the bed, while Miriam carried the basin to a small table in the corner of the room. Turning, she watched as Mrs. Pritchett dug around in her bag then brought out a small jar filled with a brownish liquid, which she placed on the floor next to her. After a bit more digging, she brought out another bottle that Miriam recognized as castor oil.

"I don't think she's goin' to need that castor oil," Miriam said to the older woman. "She's about as sick as she's gonna get."

"It ain't fer now," Mrs. Pritchett replied. "She's gonna need that fer after."

Miriam looked at the old woman with grave reservations then turned to her sister for one last try at reason. "It ain't too late, Inez," Miriam pleaded. "We could send Caleb fer the doctor, or, better yet, let us take you over to the hospital."

Past speaking, Inez just shook her head weakly. Miriam sighed. She knew it was hopeless to argue. Despite the horrors Del Wooten inflicted on his daughters, they were all still extremely reluctant to involve anyone considered an outsider, which included just about everyone outside the small house.

Miriam ceased her musings and jumped as Inez began to vomit down the front of her nightdress. When she was done, Miriam pulled it off and cleaned up her sister as Rachel fetched her another gown. Inez began to retch again, but instead of vomiting, she doubled over with the force of the contractions brought on by the massive dose of evening primrose Mrs. Pritchett had given her.

"Ain't long now," Mrs. Pritchett sniffed as she donned a threadbare but clean apron. "Best get her in a squat so she can bear down."

Miriam and Dorcas moved to either side of Inez and brought her up into a sitting position. They waited a moment as another contraction seized Inez's body then, when it passed, helped her get her legs underneath her. Inez draped her arms over her sisters' shoulders and waited for another wave of pain to consume her. It didn't take long before her womb was once again caught in a tight fist of pain as it tried to rid itself of the dead child. A sob tore from Inez's throat, and Miriam cried out as if in response. Tears fell like a waterfall down Dorcas's cheeks, but the brave girl continued to bear the crushing weight of her sister. Miriam looked up to see Rachel silently crying in the corner, her eyes wide with horror.

Mrs. Pritchett turned to Rachel. "Best get over here, girl." Rachel slowly moved to the old woman's side and picked up one of the clean linens. Her lips were moving silently, and Miriam knew her youngest sister was praying.

Caught in the grip of another contraction, Inez began to moan. "Push now, girl," Mrs. Pritchett ordered then crouched down between

Inez's legs. Inez shuddered uncontrollably as blood began to pour from her. "Here it comes," Mrs. Pritchett cried almost gleefully. Rachel closed her eyes and turned away. With a feral cry, Inez bore down as the small, dead child her father sired upon her burst from her womb.

Mrs. Pritchett caught the stillborn baby and quickly wrapped it in a sheet, hiding it from sight. Inez fell back against the pillows, exhausted. Miriam and Dorcas both moved to clean her up. Everyone worked silently, each woman numbed by what they had just experienced. Not even its brevity could lessen its horror. Rachel continued to cry even as she assisted Mrs. Pritchett in clearing away the sheets and rags that were now covered with blood. Dorcas, though no longer crying, still rubbed her face now and then as if the tears were still falling. Miriam knew it would be a long time before she felt clean again.

After a few moments, Inez's weary voice broke through the silence like a gunshot. "What was it?" she asked.

Mrs. Pritchett shook her head as she placed the small bundle in her carpetbag. "Best not know," she replied. "I'll make sure it gets a proper Christian burial."

"Best not know," Inez repeated weakly then turned her face into the pillow and wept.

Mrs. Pritchett turned to interrupt Miriam's ministrations. "She's gotta pass the afterbirth," she warned.

"She's too weak," Miriam protested. "We'll have to do it fer her." Dorcas replaced the blood-soaked towels with clean ones as Miriam began to gently knead her sister's belly. Inez moaned in protest but was too weak to move. Thankfully, her contractions still persisted, and it was only moments before the placenta appeared, which Mrs. Pritchett again swiftly whisked away. Miriam knew it would be put to use, for, as everyone knew, there was a little bit of witch in the old midwife.

Though done with the delivery, Inez continued to moan intermittently, as if her body had yet to realize that it had already rid itself of the unwanted child. Miriam worried that Mrs. Pritchett might have given Inez too much of the cure, for though she was an excellent midwife, she was getting on in years and had been known to make mistakes. The old woman answered Miriam's thoughts as if she had spoken aloud.

"It'll wear off soon," she advised. "But she best sleep for another day or so, and no walkin' till tomorrow, at least. Girl's gotta rest. Ain't no different if the baby'd been alive." Mrs. Pritchett buttoned up her carpetbag and hoisted it onto her thin shoulder. "I'll let that sorry excuse for a pa you got down there know he ain't to touch her again. Next one just might kill her." With that, Mrs. Pritchett left the girls to tend to their sister.

Miriam washed the blood away from her sister as Rachel and Dorcas removed the stained clothes and sheets. Then all three moved Inez as gently as they could to change the bed linens. Miriam glanced at her youngest sister and noted without surprise that her eyes had changed. Gone was the expression of wide-eyed innocence that normally faced the world. Rachel now looked world-weary and sad, her eyes betraying the knowledge of a horror no child should ever know.

The three sisters paused and looked at each other as angry shouts floated up from below them. Miriam heard her pa yelling then the front door slamming. She knew the midwife had just been thrown out on her ear and most likely without payment. Without comment, the three young women removed the rest of the stained linens and left Inez to rest.

Outside the door, Abel had placed a chair where he could keep sentry over his sister. Miriam had no doubt about what the shotgun that rested on his knees was for. He looked like he'd been crying, and Miriam's heart went out to him.

"I ain't gonna let her down again," he said bravely. "Pa's talkin' like he's gonna come up here and teach her a lesson fer talkin' to Mrs. Pritchett 'bout his business. I ain't gonna let him."

Miriam looked at her brother for a moment then did something she had never done before. Without a word, Miriam went to her brother, put her arms around him, and hugged him tight. Abel laid his head on her shoulder and returned the hug. Miriam could feel his gentle sobbing against her neck and knew she would not let him go until he was done. Not to be left out, Rachel and Dorcas moved to either side of their brother and sister and wrapped their arms around them. Miriam put her arm around Rachel as Abel put his around Dorcas, and all stood as one. It wasn't until a noise on the stairs brought them all around that they parted. Miriam turned to see Caleb standing at the top of the stairs, looking like he'd missed Christmas. Rachel went to Caleb and wrapped her arms around his waist. With a smile that was both grateful and embarrassed, Caleb picked up his youngest sister and let her bury her face into his neck.

"Pa's lookin' fer you," Caleb whispered. "What do you want me to tell him?"

Miriam took the basket of soiled linens from Dorcas then propelled her sister toward Caleb. "Put them to bed, and then set yerself outside the door. Abel will stay here to watch over Inez. Where's Jacob and Wade?"

"Jacob's out in the barn, calvin'. Wade's most likely out there botherin' him," Caleb replied then carried the yawning Rachel into the room he shared with Abel. Dorcas followed, rubbing her eyes in fatigue. Moments later, Caleb returned to the hall with a small stool, which he set in front of the now-closed door. Miriam waited in front of Inez's door while Abel fetched another shotgun for his brother. She knew that even without a gun, she was a formidable barrier, topping her father's weight by about a hundred and seventy pounds. *If worse comes to worst,* she thought, *I'll just crush him with my backside.* Abel returned quickly, and Miriam went down to confront their father.

It took a good bit of looking, however, before she found him. She had assumed that he was still on the front porch where he had been when she had first arrived. Instead she found him in the kitchen nursing the same jug of corn liquor at the modest wooden table, as if he were waiting for his waitress to serve him up some grub. He looked up as Miriam walked in carrying the linen basket.

"Where the hell is Inez? I ain't had nothin' to eat fer a whole goddamn day! If that girl's layin' around agin, I'm gonna whip her right good." Delbert Wooten took a pull from the jug then leered blearily at his oldest daughter. "Why don' you come here an' sit on yer pa's lap fer a while?" Delbert moved to slap his knee but missed and nearly toppled onto the floor. "Give ya a dollar if it goes all the way in."

Miriam ignored the offer. "You ain't gonna see Inez fer a while," she stated flatly as she dumped the bloody bedclothes into a washtub. "She's gonna need to rest."

"What's wrong with her?" Delbert demanded. "She actin' like she's sick agin?" Delbert sniffed then scratched behind one sunburned ear. "She sure got that Pritchett wummun snowed. Said I was to stay out of her panties. I told that wummun she was crazy. Bitch don' know what she's talkin' 'bout."

Miriam poured water and soap powder onto the linens then grabbed a bar of Fels-Naptha. Ignoring her father, she began to scrub at the bloody stains. Soon the sink was foaming with bubbles stained pink from her exertions. When she was satisfied she ran the water over the linens and rinsed them until the water ran clear. Hanging them would just have to wait until the morning. Miriam stacked them neatly on the drainboard then turned to face her father.

Del Wooten had sat silently nursing his jug the entire time Miriam scrubbed the linens. It wasn't until she was finished and regarding him with intense disgust that he turned and leered at her in return.

"See somethin' green?" He burped then laughed at his own joke.

"Yer done, old man," Miriam warned.

"Yeah?" Del answered, his laughter gone. His eyes narrowed at Miriam's tone.

"You ain't to touch Inez agin. An' you ain't gonna start on Rachel nor Dorcas neither." Miriam crossed her arms over her chest. "You best make friends with that hand uh yers, 'cause you ain't usin' yer girls no more."

Del put his nose up in the air and looked away. "I don't know what yer talkin' about. That bitch Pritchett's got you brainwashed too. I always thought that dyke liked girls better than boys."

Miriam ignored that remark as well. "You know damn well what I'm talkin' 'bout. You touch a hair on their heads and you'll pay, old man. We ain't gonna cover fer you no more."

Del turned and stared at her openmouthed. "You'd do that? You'd bring that kinda disgrace to yer own family?" he asked, his face incredulous. "To tell such lies 'bout yer own pa! And after all I done fer you, buying you that nice house and all. Why you wanna hurt me like that?" Del gave his daughter the side eye, his expression a mixture of hate and worry.

Miriam wasn't buying it for a minute. "Inez almost died tonight, and all because yer too ugly to get it anywhere else and too cheap to buy it." She knew she'd pushed a button, for her pa was just about the vainest man in the entire state of Mississippi. People in town whispered that the Wootens had slave blood in them, but it was their Portuguese grandparents that gave them their coloring. Delbert took after his father and at one time had been very handsome, until the cigarettes, sun, and drink took away his looks. She watched dispassionately as his face turned bright red with rage at the insult. His rage building, he sat speechless, his mouth opening and closing, sending spittle flying this way and that. Miriam knew he was going to explode, and she couldn't care less.

When he could finally speak, Delbert's voice rose to a shriek. "GET OUT!" he screamed as he leaped from the table, upsetting the chair and knocking over his jug. "YOU GET OUTTA MY HOUSE RIGHT NOW!" Despite his fury, Delbert was smart enough not to touch his daughter, for deep down inside, he knew she posed a much bigger threat to him than he did to her. Instead, he screamed obscenities at her as she made her way to the door.

On her way out, Miriam glanced at the stairs to see Caleb on the landing, his shotgun aimed at their pa. She shook her head at him then waited until he went back upstairs. She then gave one last look at her still-screaming father then turned went out into the night.

Bone-tired, she hardly had a thought in her head as she made her way home. Once inside the blissfully quiet shack, she noted dully that Howard had managed to haul himself off to bed. As quietly as she could, Miriam undressed in the dark and, after a moment of groping around, managed to locate her nightdress. So as not to wake Howard, Miriam carefully slid under the quilt.

"Everthin' all right?" Howard asked from the darkness.

It was a good long while before Miriam could speak. "It ain't ever all right," she replied softly then went to sleep.

SEVEN

Miriam spent the next two weeks caring for Inez as she slowly recovered from her ordeal. Like Rachel, something had changed in her sister. Though she'd never gone through a stillbirth, Inez had had plenty of deliberate miscarriages and had always bounced back, physically and even emotionally, somewhat. This time was different though. Even accounting for all the blood that she'd lost, Miriam had figured Inez would at least be able to walk a couple of days after. But even three days later, Inez still needed help to the privy and could hardly stand on her own. A week later, she was still pale and listless and wouldn't eat any of the kale and spinach Miriam prepared to replenish her blood.

It was now two weeks gone, and Miriam was back at the house, not at all surprised to see Inez propped up in a chair on the front porch, wrapped in blankets despite the searing heat. Dorcas stood behind her, tears streaming down her face as she brushed clumps of hair from her sister's head. Miriam knew in that minute that no matter what her family thought about modern medicine, she needed to call in Doc Polk.

Out of the corner of her eye, Miriam was surprised to see her father standing just inside the barn door, glaring at her. He'd kept a low profile since that awful night, and Miriam knew it had a great deal to do with the armed vigil her brothers had kept over their sisters. She also knew it was only a matter of time before their pa's need for sex would send him sniffing around his girls again. She only hoped that her brothers' shot-guns were enough of a deterrent to prevent something terrible from happening.

Ignoring her father, Miriam went up to her sister and pressed the back of her hand against Inez's forehead. It was cold and clammy, and up close, Miriam could see her sister's complexion had turned ashen, her lips blue. And while Miriam and her sisters were as plump as their brothers were thin, Inez had shrunk as if she'd shed more than just an unwanted baby. Miriam looked at Dorcas pointedly, who held up the hairbrush she had been using. It was full of Inez's long, red hair.

With the corners of her mouth turned down, Miriam knelt next to Inez's chair and took an ice-cold hand between hers. "Honey," Miriam spoke quietly. "You ain't getting any better. We gotta call Doc Polk to come an' look at you."

Despite her weakness, Inez shook her head and managed a quiet "Nooo."

"Inez, I promise I won't say nothin' 'bout Pa," Miriam entreated. "We could say it was some boy who took liberties with you. Someone you didn't know."

Inez shook her head again then sank back into the chair, exhausted. Miriam sighed and dropped her lifeless hand. Looking up at Dorcas, Miriam asked, "She still bleedin'?" Dorcas nodded. Miriam looked at Inez's pale skin. She could see the blue of the veins in her cheek as if her skin had gone transparent. After another moment of watching her sister, Miriam stood and left the porch in search of Caleb.

Like Miriam, Caleb was one of the more pragmatic members of the Wooten family. She often found herself using him as a sounding board when she was at a crossroads. Now she needed his approval before she could feel right with herself about going against Inez's wishes to keep her ailing health a private matter.

Unfortunately Caleb was nowhere to be found, and Wade, the only brother she could find, was less than helpful when questioned. Miriam knew her father had been filling his head with spiteful words, and Wade would believe every lie. Those two were nuts off the same tree. Wade was just about the only one in the family who worshiped his father, and Del Wooten aimed to keep it that way. He'd even put it into Wade's head that there was nothing wrong with a brother making use of his sister for, as Del put it, "satisfyin' them manly urges." Wade took Del's advice to heart and cornered Rachel in the barn one afternoon, furiously working at his small penis, demanding his needs be looked to. Caleb put a stop to it, however, and, though he might worship his father, Wade feared his brother more.

Miriam stood and listened to Wade's tirade until she just couldn't listen anymore. After a smart smack against the side of his head, which sent him off screaming for their pa, Miriam left after making sure Inez had company to keep an eye on her.

On the way home, Miriam stopped again at the old tree and settled herself down for a long spell of thinking and praying. Though she was almost certain the Lord had chosen her to carry his child, she couldn't help but wonder if Inez's troubles were some sort of punishment for Miriam's past sins. And as much as she hated to admit it, Sarah Polk had been right to say that Miriam's relationship with Pastor Tucker was less than holy. Miriam was overcome with shame at the thought that the Lord knew Pastor Tucker had touched her where he shouldn't have and that she had enjoyed it. Now Inez was paying for it, and maybe she was too. Maybe the Lord *had* passed her by. Miriam shook her head, as tears began to fall, and then prayed for forgiveness.

EIGHT

Across Merwin, in a neighborhood that was substantially better than Miriam's, though still modest, Sarah Polk sat in her spotlessly clean kitchen chatting with Lottie on the telephone.

"And do you know, Delphinia told her husband she was going to a choir convention in Salt Lake City, you know, where those Mormon people sing, and really she was losing all their money in Reno, Nevada. That's why George had that heart attack. He told Samuel he couldn't take the news that they were flat broke and he'd have to come out of retirement and go back to work at the quarry." Sarah listened as Lottie made the appropriate sounds of shock and dismay. "Well, these are the kinds of things you hear when you're a doctor's wife," she said smugly as her husband came in through the back door. Samuel Polk disapproved of his wife's relationship with her sister and gave Sarah a withering look as he made his way across the room to the door that led into his study.

"I've got to go," Sarah interrupted Lottie in the middle of a sentence and hung up the phone. She sat chewing her lip for a moment then filled a cup with the coffee that she kept freshly brewed for Samuel. After a moment's hesitation at his door, she knocked quietly, paused to listen, then let herself in. Samuel sat at his desk making notations into the folder that held the medical history of his latest house call. Sarah placed the coffee near his hand then moved it aside when he glared at its close proximity to his paperwork.

Sarah watched as he scribbled indecipherable yet very precise notes with the fountain pen he'd inherited from his grandfather.

"I wanted to let you know that my back is starting to bother me," she began, "it's—"

"I'm sure you'll be fine," her husband interrupted. "Perhaps it would feel better if you spent less time sitting in that chair gossiping."

"Lottie just called to get my recipe for Waldorf salad," Sarah replied. "I was only sitting for a few minutes before you walked in." Sarah made a great show of kneading her lower back as if it might provide some relief. "I think the baby is pressing against my backbone."

Samuel finished with his first patient notes then pulled another from the hutch that sat on his desk. "The baby is too small to cause you any significant discomfort right now," he stated flatly as he reinked his pen. "Any pain you might be having is more than likely in your imagination. Why don't you go to your church and pray for relief? Perhaps you could also pray that your Lord lets you have this child. Or you could take the pills I gave you and actually carry this pregnancy to term."

Somewhat chastised, Sarah stood silently wondering what to say to get Samuel to pay attention to her. Then she hit on it. "Speaking of church," she said with a smile, "Miriam Dirkin thinks she's having the Lord's baby."

Startled, Samuel's head popped up, and he stared at his wife. Sarah was pleased to see her husband finally interested in her.

"Miriam Dirkin is pregnant?" Samuel asked.

Sarah nodded. "Oh, yes, and she's got Pastor Tucker convinced that she's giving birth to the next baby Jesus. Can you imagine that?"

Samuel stood and opened the black leather satchel he had carried in moments ago. Sarah watched as he filled it with all the necessary equipment to make a gynecologic examination.

"Where are you going?" she asked, though she already knew the answer and rued her mistake.

"Miriam needs to be examined and informed of the importance of good prenatal care." Samuel snapped the satchel shut and left the room.

Sarah stood and stared at the untouched cup of coffee that jumped slightly when Samuel slammed the back door. Her expression bleak, Sarah picked up the cup, carried it to the kitchen sink, and dropped it, shattering the porcelain and splashing coffee everywhere.

NINE

Miriam was still sitting under the maple tree when Doc Polk arrived. It was his firm but polite rap on the screen that brought her out of her reverie. Turning at the sound, she was not surprised to see him since he'd been the subject of her prayers for the last half an hour. Miriam chalked it up to her special bond with the Lord. With a hand to her aching back, Miriam wobbled her way over to the doctor.

"Doc Polk!" she called out. "Mind yer knockin', lest you wake Howard. Iffen you wanted to see him, then go right ahead."

Samuel Polk made his way across the dirt yard to meet Miriam halfway. "No, I came to see you. I hear you are expecting," he said as he offered Miriam his arm. She accepted gladly, and together they made it to the front porch where he sat Miriam down then took the chair next to her. "Are you having back pain, Miriam?"

Miriam shook her head. "Naw, Doc, baby's too small to do nothin' to me right now. It was my backside went to sleep on me whilst I was parked under that there tree. It'll pass." Miriam stamped her foot on the floorboards a couple of times to get her circulation moving again then watched as the doctor opened his satchel and removed various doctor things she hardly recognized.

"I came to do a prenatal examination and discuss proper care for you and your unborn child." But before he could begin, Miriam waved him away.

"Ain't necessary," Miriam said. "Baby makin's in the Lord's and Mrs. Pritchett's hands. I'll call on you iffen there's a problem. I got more important things to discuss with you." Any reservations Miriam might have had about bringing in an outsider vanished at the appearance of the doctor.

Samuel Polk knew better than to argue. Even with modern medicine available to them, few women in Merwin trusted him with "women's business." Midwifery still reigned, and he would only be involved if something occurred outside of Mrs. Pritchett's abilities. This turned out to be one of those times.

"Inez has takin' bad."

Samuel Polk regarded Miriam gravely. He knew from experience that the Wootens never called in a doctor unless it was a life-or-death situation and sometimes not even then. As Miriam gave him a highly abbreviated account of what had occurred, he returned his things to his satchel and stood.

"I'll go see her now."

Miriam pushed herself out of her chair and stomped her feet a couple more times for good measure. "I'll take you there. They ain't likely to talk to you if you show up by yerself."

"Are you sure you're up for the walk?" the doctor asked as he took Miriam's elbow.

"Oh sure," she answered. "I been goin' back and forth ever' day for the last couple of weeks now." With a final stomp and a quick stretch, Miriam and the doctor set off.

Both were panting when they arrived at the house. Miriam was concerned that no one was about, for the house turned into an oven in midsummer, and, despite the fact that Inez couldn't get warm, anyone who might be with her would simply bake in the heat.

Miriam led Doc Polk up the steps and opened the screen door. "Inez?" she called into the house. "Rachel?" No one answered.

Miriam motioned for Doc Polk to stay put by the door then went up the stairs to the girls' room. There she found Inez wrapped in blankets, sleeping, with Dorcas and Rachel napping at her feet. Miriam went over and shook Dorcas awake. "Up now," she said as she moved over to Rachel and shook her awake as well. "Get yerselves downstairs, and see to Doc Polk. He's come to look at Inez."

Rachel rubbed her tired eyes as Dorcas pushed sweat-soaked tendrils of hair away from her forehead. "Inez ain't gonna like that," Dorcas yawned.

"Inez ain't in any shape to complain, and anyway, I prayed on it and there he was, right at my front door. So the Lord made the final decision."

Dorcas gave Miriam a funny look, though Rachel seemed to accept Miriam's statement at face value. Both girls left their sister to Miriam.

"Mind you fetch some lemonade for the doc," Miriam called after them.

Moments later Doc Polk peered around the door uncertainly. "In here, Doc," Miriam said.

Inez stirred weakly under the covers then blearily opened her eyes. "Miriam," she whispered, peering as Doc Polk moved toward her. "Who's that with you?"

"Doc Polk's here to see you, Inez," Miriam stated flatly then waited for the protest. When none came, she assumed correctly that Inez was more out of this world than in it.

Doc Polk seemed to understand that Inez wouldn't be much help in describing her symptoms, so instead he set out to do a full examination. Miriam stopped him, though, as he moved to pull back the blanket covering Inez.

"Uh, no thanks, Doc," Miriam warned. "Midwife kin check her there. Ain't proper for a man to be lookin' at her privates."

Doc Polk began to protest but stopped at the sight of Miriam's set expression. He knew better than to do battle against ancient prejudices. So, after listening to her heart and taking her blood pressure and temperature, Doc Polk looked into Inez's eyes then sat back with a sigh.

"Well, without doing a blood test or gynecologic examination, I can't really say what might be wrong with her," he said. "However, her blood pressure is very low, and, from your description of the events that led up to this visit, I'd say that she probably lost too much blood and will take quite a while to recover."

Well, I coulda told you that much, Miriam thought to herself. She had been expecting some sort of special trick the doctor might know that Mrs. Pritchett didn't.

Doc Polk returned his instruments to his satchel then stood up. "At any rate, she doesn't appear to have an infection, which would be very serious."

Miriam shook her head. "Naw, she ain't feverish nor choleric in color. Just pale and cold."

Doc Polk turned back to Inez and regarded her for a moment then laid his hand on her head. Miriam was touched by the gesture and gave the doc his moment. With a heavy sigh, the doctor gently squeezed Inez's small, limp hand then followed Miriam out of the room.

Downstairs, he politely declined Dorcas's offer of a glass of lemonade then turned to Miriam. "Right now Inez is most likely anemic. I'll stop by tomorrow with some iron supplements for her. Keep encouraging her to eat, especially beef broth and maybe some creamed spinach. Go slowly at first since her stomach has been empty for a while. We don't want her to vomit."

Miriam nodded throughout his recommendations then thanked him. Doc Polk waved away her offer to pay and left.

Rather than returning to her own home, Miriam settled herself in a chair in Inez's bedroom doorway after sending Rachel and Dorcas into the boys' room to rest. With all that had happened to Inez, Miriam had had little rest herself, and she needed some quiet time to think on her own situation. Miriam looked down at her belly then gently laid a hand over her still-tiny baby.

Though she had yet to feel anything, Miriam was certain she was pregnant. There was no doubt in her mind about that. And yet Sarah Polk's comments still rang sharply in her ears. She had prayed earlier to be chosen to carry his son. She knew she wasn't thinking wishfully. Miriam had always thought she was destined for greatness despite her humble beginnings. *Like Abraham Lincoln*, she thought. And the Lord had almost always answered her prayers, as if she were special—not just in general but special to him personally. In fact, the more she thought about it, the more certain she was that he had forgiven her and that she indeed carried his child. For the first time in weeks, Miriam felt completely at peace. She knew Sarah Polk was wrong. She knew the angel had come. She knew she carried his son. Miriam closed her eyes and, with a small smile, fell asleep.

TEN

Samuel Polk made good time as he walked the two miles back to his home, though he arrived lathered in dust-covered sweat. Sarah was wiping down the sink when he walked in.

"So how is Miriam?" she asked with a cheerfulness she certainly did not feel.

Samuel moved past her into his office. "I did not examine Miriam," he said from the other room. "She took me to see her sister Inez instead."

Sarah paused and turned toward the office door in confusion. "Inez? But why would she take you to see Inez?"

Samuel appeared at the doorway and gave his wife a frosty look. "Now that would be none of your business, wouldn't it?"

Sarah turned away and furiously scrubbed at the faucet. She felt more than heard Samuel return to his office. With a final swipe at the gleaming chrome, Sarah threw her towel down and moved to pour Samuel another cup of coffee. Carefully she carried it into his office and placed it at the edge of his desk.

Sarah tucked an errant strand of hair behind her ear. "I was just going to say I hope everything is all right," she mumbled.

"Sarah, you know I won't betray the trust of my patients just to satisfy your curiosity," he replied coldly as he set his reading glasses on the bridge of his nose and turned his back on her. Sarah stood there for a moment wishing for some way to remove herself from the room with dignity. Instead she stood staring at her toes and mumbled something about getting herself a cup of tea. Samuel turned from the notes he had been writing and looked at her silently and dispassionately. Humiliated, Sarah blushed to her roots, turned, and left the room.

ELEVEN

Miriam thought she was dreaming when she awoke with a start. Through the windows at the front of Inez's bedroom, she could see that it was full dark already, which meant she had slept for quite a while. Painfully she pushed herself out of the chair and hobbled over to the table next to her sister's bed. Turning on the light she saw that Inez had thrown off her covers. Miriam leaned over to draw them back and saw that Inez had bled through the rags that Dorcas and Rachel had given her to use as a rudimentary sanitary napkin. She paused and stared at the bloodstained sheets before laying her hand on her sister's brow. It was cold. Not clammy cold like earlier either. Miriam pressed her ear against Inez's heart...and heard nothing. Her own heart clutched as if in a fist. Her sister was gone. Miriam took Inez's hand and began to pray. Tears fell as she whispered words of entreaty to the Lord, asking him to take her sister's soul into his kingdom.

Suddenly an angry shout interrupted her grieving. Miriam ran to the other room to find Dorcas asleep and Rachel gone. Turning, she fled down the stairs and out into the yard, where she heard shouts and screaming coming from the barn. As she headed across the yard, she ran into Rachel, the younger girl fleeing from the darkness inside the barn. Rachel threw herself into Miriam's arms and sobbed. Miriam had moved to comfort her when a single shot rang out causing both of them to jump. Rachel stopped crying, and both sisters stood quietly for one long moment then jumped again when Abel pushed the barn door aside.

"I didn't let it happen this time," he said shakily to his sister. "He won't be hurtin' Inez nor Rachel no more."

"Inez is dead," Miriam said quietly. Abel's face crumpled at the news, and Rachel began to cry again. Without a word, Abel turned and went back into the barn. This time Miriam didn't jump when she heard the second shot.

**

In town, Sarah Polk was lying next to her sleeping husband when she heard what sounded like a gunshot. For a fleeting moment, Sarah bitterly hoped Miriam Dirkin was at the business end of that barrel then quickly whispered a prayer for forgiveness for such an uncharitable thought. When she heard the second shot, she fell asleep with a small smile on her face.

TWELVE

Dawn found Miriam exhausted as she readied her sister for burial. She and Caleb had spent most of the night arguing over what to do about their father. Finally, in an uncharacteristic move, Abel decided to build Inez's coffin with a false bottom to accommodate their father as well. Miriam and Caleb could do nothing but agree since neither wanted Abel arrested for murder. They decided to put out the story that Del Wooten took off in grief over the death of his daughter. Abel set to work on the coffin, while Miriam ushered Rachel back to the house and Caleb cleaned up the mess in the barn. Thankfully, Jacob had taken Wade camping, so there was no need for them to know any more than what they would be told. Wade especially could not be trusted, so Miriam made Rachel promise she wouldn't say a thing to him or anyone else. She then explained to Dorcas what had happened and exacted the same promise from her.

By the time the coffin was finished, it was full morning and Wade and Jacob were due back any time. Caleb went out to the barn where he and Abel loaded their father into the false bottom then covered him with a layer of planking. Miriam watched as Caleb and Abel brought the coffin into the sunlight and carried it across the yard to the house. She went out and held the door for them so they could bring it into the front room where they placed it on a table she had cleared for it. Abel's face was pale and grimly set as he went up the stairs to fetch Inez. Wade and

Jacob walked in just as he was carrying her down wrapped in the white sheet Miriam had sewn around her.

"What the hell is that?" Wade asked rudely as Abel gently laid his sister in her crude coffin.

Miriam spun around, glared at him, then moved to strike, but Caleb cut her off and took both boys outside.

Miriam stared after the boys, debating whether or not she should go out and put a flea in her youngest brother's ear, but turned to Abel instead. "You go on up and sleep, Abel," she said gently as she pushed him toward the stairs. "Sleep for a good, long time." Abel simply nodded and went up, his steps heavy on the stairs.

Caleb came back with Jacob, who waited while his older brother wrote a note. "Take this to Pastor Tucker," Caleb said as he handed Jacob the folded piece of paper. "Tell him to come today for Inez's burial." Jacob nodded then left at a trot. Caleb turned to Miriam and sighed heavily.

"We gotta get them in the ground as fast as we can. Abel and me wrapped Pa in some old tarps and packed hay all around him to keep him from leakin', but that'll only last for so long. The sooner we get this over with the better." Caleb rubbed at his tired eyes till they were red. "I'm gonna head over to the co-op and then the Stop 'n' Save and make like Pa's run off 'cuz of Inez. Hopefully nobody will catch on."

Miriam agreed then went to fetch Caleb a thermos of coffee to keep him awake lest he drive right off the road. After he left, she settled herself in her mother's old rocker to wait for Pastor Tucker.

It didn't take long before Miriam heard him huffing and puffing his way up the front steps. Wearily she rose from the chair and opened the door to find Pastor Tucker leaning against the frame, panting for air. At the

70

sight of his sweaty, pouting face, Miriam revisited her shame at the liberties he'd taken with her in the past. In an instant Miriam felt an intense dislike for Pastor Tucker and the embarrassment he had caused her.

She was all politeness, though, when she opened the screen door for him and led him into the front room where Inez, and their father, lay in state.

"Oh, Miriam," Ewell Tucker gushed as he moved to embrace her. "I'm just so deeply sorry for your loss." Miriam stood stiffly as he tried to comfort her then backed away as soon as he let go. Ewell Tucker said nothing at her lack of response, but his confusion was apparent in his expression.

"Yes, well, thanks an' all for comin'. We was hopin' you could do a service for Inez's burial this afternoon, iffen you ain't too busy." Miriam could not bring herself to look him in the eye and stared at the floor instead.

"Well...sure, I can do that. But don't you think we should wait until tomorrow, at least? I'm sure there are others who would like to attend Inez's burial service. Other family members perhaps?"

Miriam shook her head. "There ain't no one else but what family is here...'sides, it being summer an' all, it be best to get her in the ground fast."

"Well, you know best." Ewell Tucker wiped at the sweat that rolled down his cheeks. "I'll just put something together for her and be back by, what, six o'clock?"

Miriam nodded. "That'll be fine."

Ewell Tucker looked at Miriam for a long moment, as if waiting for her to say something else, then pulled out a dingy handkerchief to wipe at his face. He moved to say something then caught himself and went out the door instead.

Miriam watched him walk down the steps and out into the yard. Normally she would have offered him lemonade and cookies and a little heavy flirting, but all that had changed. Sarah had shamed her something awful, and with the Lord's baby growing in her, she wasn't going to let anyone, least of all Ewell Tucker, mess it up for her. She was going to stay pure if it killed her.

Miriam put both Sarah Polk and Ewell Tucker out of her head and tidied up the house a bit instead. Then, after a quick word to Dorcas about Inez's burial, she set off for home.

Sweat was streaming down her back by the time she reached the front porch of her shack, where she found Howard sitting on an old wheelchair she'd found at the Salvation Army store just after he broke his back. Howard had squeezed himself in between the arms so tightly that rolls of fat rested where his arms should be. As usual, a bottle of beer was clasped tightly in his right fist, and a cigarette hung between two fat, nicotine-stained fingers.

"Good grief, woman," he said, his words already slurring. "Thought you might have moved out on me and forgotten to say somethin'."

Miriam, out of breath, slowly trudged up the steps. With her last ounce of energy, Miriam fell into the only other chair on the porch, a scarred ladder-back that Abel had made long ago. It was a few minutes before she could speak.

"Inez passed on," she panted. She hesitated then added, "Pa's gone."

"You gonna make me some breakfast or what?" Howard asked churlishly.

Miriam stared at her husband then asked, "Did you hear me? Inez died last night."

Howard stared right back and said, "I heard you. Whatta you want me to do about it? Bury her?"

"That's right, Howard; I want you to bury her," Miriam snapped. "I want you to drag yer sorry three-hundred-pound bee-hind the mile and a half to my pa's house and bury my dead sister."

Howard stared at Miriam, his eyes narrowed. It was a dangerous look. One that meant very bad things for Miriam, but she chose to ignore it.

"I want you to get up off yer fat ass and be a man for once!" she shouted then got up from her chair and went into the house, slamming the screen door behind her.

Howard stared after her. "Do that again, and you'll be sorry," he muttered.

Miriam spent only a couple of hours at the house making Howard breakfast and lunch and picking up the mess he'd made during her absence. When she was satisfied, she returned to the porch where Howard still sat.

"I'm goin' back," she said flatly as she passed him. "Food's in the kitchen. I won't be back till later, after her burial."

Howard said nothing, so Miriam left.

THIRTEEN

Telephone lines across Merwin were burning up with the news that Inez Wooten had died in the night and her pa had taken off in grief. The first call came from Lottie, who had been in her husband's Stop 'n' Save showing off her little girl, Amberlee's new pageant dress.

Caleb had stopped there first to put out the word that Del Wooten was gone and would anyone give his kids a holler when he showed up. Since Caleb had always been an honest, hardworking young man, lending a hand wherever a hand was needed, his word was taken at face value. It wasn't even a full minute after he left, though, before Lottie got on the phone to Sarah with the news, and from there it spread like wildfire.

As she hung up the phone, Sarah rubbed her hands together in excitement. She couldn't wait for Samuel to come home from the tiny hospital across Merwin so she could be the one to tell him. She'd use anything, even the death of someone like Inez Wooten, to get her husband to pay attention to her.

Unfortunately, Doc Polk had already heard and was on his way to the Wooten farm, bypassing his home completely. His older Buick sent up plumes of dust as he slowly made his way up the winding gravel road, where he came upon Miriam sweating from her exertions.

"Miriam!" he called as he pulled alongside of her. "Please...let me take you the rest of the way." Breathless, Miriam nodded and got in. Doc Polk eyed her warily as she sat sweating and panting, her normally alabaster cheeks aflame.

"I heard about Inez," he said quietly, his words punctuated by the metallic pop of a rock against the undercarriage of the car. "I'm very sorry."

Miriam was still so out of breath she couldn't answer, so instead she nodded.

Doc Polk turned and stared out the windshield as the house came into view. Dorcas and Rachel sat waiting on the front porch as Wade bothered Jacob, who was mending an old fishing pole. Miriam eyed the boys nervously. She didn't know what Caleb had told them about Inez and their father. And she didn't want them saying anything in front of the doctor. When Wade spoke, though, she knew she needn't have worried. Caleb hadn't told them anything more than what he was telling everyone else in town.

"Hey, Doc!" Wade cried as he hung from a rope he'd thrown over a low-hanging branch he'd been trying to pull down for most of the summer. "Yer too late! She's already dead!" Wade laughed at his own joke then stopped suddenly as the branch finally broke sending him down to the ground with a heavy thud. Doc Polk looked over at him with distaste but said nothing as Miriam led him into the house.

Even though all of the windows were open, no air circulated, and the smell of death hung heavy in the warm room. Doc Polk crossed to where Inez lay in her makeshift coffin. He gazed at her for such a long time that Miriam began to wonder at it. Finally he spoke.

"Was there any indication of how she died?" he asked quietly.

"Bled out," Miriam answered.

Doc Polk nodded and pulled a stethoscope from his coat pocket. He placed it in his ears then gently placed the drum where Inez's chest lay under her shroud.

"Ain't gonna work, her bein' dead an' all," Miriam said warily.

Doc Polk returned the stethoscope to his pocket and gave her a vague smile. "I just wanted to make sure since she died here at home and not at the hospital, which leads me to you, Miriam. I won't pry into the details of what led to Inez's death, which I will assume was due to a complication from childbirth. She's beyond my help now. But you're not. I want you to keep me informed of your progress. There's no need for you to fear coming to me if you have any problems."

Miriam shook her head. "No, sir. Like I said before, birthin' is woman's work. Iffen I need anythin', I kin call on Mrs. Pritchett. Iffen I'm dyin', I'll let ya know."

It was Doc Polk's turn to shake his head. "Miriam, you're going to have to let me know earlier than that. There are many things that Mrs. Pritchett might not be able to diagnose properly, like pre-eclampsia or a placental abruption. I want you to promise me that you'll come to the hospital the minute you feel something strange is going on. Bring Mrs. Pritchett if you need to." Doc Polk stepped up to her and took her hand between his. "I'm going to keep tabs on you, especially now. There are several very good drugs that can ensure a healthy pregnancy, and regular prenatal care can help us determine if you need them. All right?"

Miriam nodded just to end the discussion. She had no intention of letting Doc Polk do what Mrs. Pritchett was more than capable of. But he seemed satisfied, and that was all she intended.

"Again...I'm so sorry about Inez," he said quietly. Miriam nodded again, touched by his sincerity. With a final squeeze to her hand, Doc Polk followed her outside. At his car he pulled a binder out from behind his seat and wrote out a death certificate. He asked for the date and time of Inez's death then handed it to Miriam.

At he got into his car, he looked at Miriam one last time. "Promise me, Miriam," he said as he turned over the motor.

"I'll let ya know," she answered ambiguously. Doc Polk didn't notice but nodded and drove off.

Miriam turned to see Wade standing there with his pants around his ankles. "Miriam's got a boyfriend!" he sang as he swung his naked bottom around in a bizarre bump and grind.

Quick as a flash she went up to him and shoved him down into the dirt, where she held him with one hand. "Rachel, fetch me the scissors," she said over her shoulder.

Wade began to scream as Rachel ran into the house. Miriam squinted at her little brother as he tried to squirm out from under her hand, to no avail. "You sound just like a little girl," she sneered as Rachel returned with the scissors. Miriam took them and caught Wade's tiny, little penis between the blades.

"I'm gonna talk real slow so you kin understand me. I tole you this once before, and I'm gonna give you one more chance. You take this out again, an' I'm gonna cut it off an' make you a girl."

Wade had stopped screaming and stared at Miriam in horror. "I'm tellin' Pa," he whispered.

"Pa ain't in any position to help you no more. Yer dealin' with me now. Understand?" Wade just stared at her, not answering. "You hearin' me, boy?" Miriam closed the blades slightly, which made Wade squeak in terror then nod frantically.

Miriam's eyes narrowed, and she watched as sweat broke out on Wade's forehead. He looked so much like their father that Miriam was tempted to go ahead and cut off his insignificant little member before it could give anyone any grief. A dawning came into Wade's eyes as if he'd read her mind.

"Noooo...noooo," he whispered as real tears began to cut trails through the dust on his cheeks.

Miriam was not touched. Without an ounce of pity, she leaned over until their hot breath mingled and closed the blades of the scissors slightly. "If I ever see...or even hear that you've been botherin' Rachel or Dorcas...or any other girl...I'll make *you* a girl. You got that?"

Wade was shaking so badly he couldn't answer. Miriam closed the scissors yet again, and he began to sob.

"Say, 'yes, ma'am,'" she ordered.

"Y-y-yessss, m-m-ma'am," he stuttered.

Miriam gave him one last look of disgust then stood up from the ground and handed Rachel the scissors. Wade stared at her in horror, afraid to move, as she brushed the dust off her skirt.

"Get goin'," she ordered. "You kin go help Abel with his work. Make yerself useful."

Wade rolled over and scrambled across the yard while pulling his pants up. Miriam watched as he headed to the barn then looked over at Jacob, who was watching his brother with grim satisfaction. Jacob then turned and gave Miriam a rare smile before returning to his fishing pole.

The rest of the day was quiet as Miriam helped Rachel and Dorcas tidy up the house. Inez's linens were washed again then hung out to dry, and her room was turned out. Dorcas lit a small branch of thyme and walked slowly about the room casting wisps of smoke into the room's four corners. Miriam and Rachel watched the ancient ritual silently, each lost in her own thoughts. When the branch went out, they stood quietly for a long moment then filed out of the room and down the stairs to prepare for Inez's burial.

As the sun fell behind the trees, Caleb and Abel came into the front parlor to nail the lid on Inez's coffin. Both boys were dirty and sweaty from digging her grave in the family plot. Dorcas fetched them a basin of water and some towels so that they could wash before they set off to carry Inez to the graveyard.

Ewell Tucker arrived, panting, just as they were hoisting her coffin onto their shoulders.

"Evenin'," he gasped as he moved over to where Miriam was standing. As the new head of the Wooten family, Miriam simply nodded, and then all set off for the short walk to the small graveyard where four generations of Wootens were laid to rest. Everyone was silent, even Wade who trailed along behind them, pale and subdued. Jacob had to prod him a few times to make him keep up.

Despite the earlier heat of the day, the graveyard was blessedly cool, surrounded as it was by tall locust trees. Caleb and Abel carried Inez to the grave they'd dug near their mother's. They laid the coffin onto two ropes, and then all four of the boys took a rope and carefully lowered it into the ground. Wade had trouble with the weight of the rope, so Dorcas moved over and helped him. Miriam and Rachel stood by watching dully as Dorcas and the boys stepped back from the grave.

Ewell Tucker took his place next to the small wooden cross Abel had fashioned and cleared his throat. "Dearest friends," he intoned hollowly, and Miriam stopped listening. Ewell Tucker's voice turned into an incomprehensible drone as Miriam's mind blocked out everything but the sight of the small cross etched with the name of her sister.

Considering all they'd been through, Miriam hardly blamed Inez for wanting to die. Since the death of their mother, life had been hell for the Wooten girls. Miriam had tried to protect them the best that she could, but Del Wooten's appetites were just too much for them. Now Inez was dead and Rachel and Dorcas were changed forever. Miriam remembered grimly that, thanks to Abel, their pa was dead too, but instead of relief or joy, Miriam still felt his presence, like a weight, upon her. She knew she'd never feel free from him as long as there was a chance that someone would find out what Abel had done.

She was roused slightly as Rachel stepped forward and pulled a small bouquet of black-eyed Susans out of her pocket. She dropped them onto Inez's coffin then stepped back and leaned heavily against Miriam.

"Would anyone like to say anything?" Ewell Tucker asked as if from far away.

Miriam looked over at her brothers and sisters, who looked back at her, their faces blank. Then she turned to Ewell Tucker and shook her head. She barely listened as he concluded the burial rites and stepped back to allow Caleb and Abel to fill in the grave. Abel was about to start when he turned and tossed his shovel to Wade, who caught it awkwardly. Wade looked at it stupidly for a moment then, with a furtive glance at Miriam, stepped forward and began to fill in his sister's grave.

Back at the house, Miriam offered Ewell Tucker some lemonade and cookies, which he refused. She nodded when he nervously said his good-byes then watched him hasten down the lane. After a few minutes, he was out of sight.

As the sun went down, Miriam went out onto the porch where Dorcas and Rachel sat fanning themselves, for the dusk had brought no relief from the heat. Jacob sat near them on the steps and stared sightlessly into the dirt. Miriam took a chair and watched as long shadows crept along the sides of the dusty road.

In better times, when a person died, people would come to show their sympathy accompanied by some sort of offering. Men usually brought liquor, while the women would bring food. When Miriam's mother died, the house had been full of people offering their condolences. It was different now. The whole town knew Inez had died...but no one came.

***

As she sat sipping her lukewarm cup of tea, a small smile drifted over Sarah Polk's lips as if she were witness to the disgrace of the Wooten clan. In a way she was, for she'd spent the better part of the day phoning everyone she knew to make certain that no one was going to visit Miriam in her time of grief. If nothing else, Sarah was certain of her position as the wife of the town's only doctor. Even though several had questioned her reasons for wanting to shun the Wooten family, no one wanted to get on her bad side. Sarah saw this and, for a little while, relished the feeling of power it gave her. As she sat, alone, she amused herself with the picture of Miriam waiting futilely for someone to give a damn.

FOURTEEN

Miriam awoke to a morning that had dawned hot and steamy. Instead of getting up, though, she lay there and stared at the new ceiling, listening to Howard snort and fart in his sleep. She couldn't tell who was louder, Howard or the locusts that were already buzzing in the heat. Despite the darkness of the room, the air was still, and Miriam could feel beads of sweat lying like dew on her forehead. She pushed herself over to stand then doubled over when a wave of nausea engulfed her. Miriam put her hand to her mouth and made a beeline into the kitchen and out the door, where she began heaving into a cluster of weeds that grew next to the house.

She sat down heavily on the steps and raised a shaking hand to wipe her mouth. A second later, Miriam leaned over and began retching again, but this time she brought up the bitter, yellow bile that was all her body could find. When she was done, she felt well enough to return to the kitchen where she pumped until clear water ran into the sink. Miriam filled a glass then sat at the table and sipped it carefully until she was sure her stomach had settled. Then she smiled.

**

Miriam's smile would have been bigger if she had known that Sarah too was spending her morning headfirst in her seafoam-green commode. Sarah, unfortunately, wasn't as overjoyed by the clear and irrefutable evidence of her pregnancy. Instead, her moans echoed hollowly in the toilet bowl as her stomach continued to churn up everything it held.

Samuel Polk was down the hall in his office, preparing the files and equipment he would need for the day. At the end, he added a speculum with the thought that Miriam might allow him to examine her. Then he snapped his case shut and left the room.

On his way down the hall, he paused at the bathroom door and looked in at his wife, who hung limply on the toilet, her cheek resting on the seat. His expression turned to distaste as she thrust her face into the bowl and began to vomit up the remnants of her breakfast. When she was done, Sarah glanced up at the washcloth that lay on the sink just inches away from Samuel's hand. He followed her look but did nothing.

"Try to use another towel," he said coldly. "My mother gave us those." Then he left.

Sarah watched him move away from the doorway then listened to his footsteps echoing on the tile of the kitchen floor. By the time the door slammed, she was again retching into the bowl. She didn't dare tell him about the blood. She knew he would see it as another failure.

FIFTEEN

Despite her rocky start, Miriam was productive the rest of the morning. Howard slept well into the day, so Miriam was able to get much of her housework done before making the trip over to her pa's house. *Won't ever be able to call it anythin' else*, she mused as she kicked up plumes of dust along the road.

When she arrived at the house, she found Rachel and Dorcas cleaning up the breakfast dishes. Jacob, Caleb, and Abel were bent over the kitchen table, looking at some plans Abel had drawn up for a new barn. Wade was nowhere in sight, which at that moment Miriam thought was a blessing.

As she moved to the sink to help dry, Dorcas looked up and gave her a sweet if tired smile. Miriam looked from Rachel to Dorcas and noticed that, despite the horrors of the previous week, their eyes were beginning to lose that haunted look. Miriam unconsciously offered up a prayer of thanks then accepted a dripping plate from her sister.

Later that day, as she sat fanning herself on the porch, she wondered again where Wade had gotten himself off to. No sooner had that thought occurred to her, though, than a flash of dirty white T-shirt caught her eye. Miriam's heart gave a lurch as she spied a familiar figure standing in the shadows just inside the barn door. With his scrawny frame and wiry, dark hair, Wade looked remarkably like their father as he scowled at her from the gloom.

Her eyes narrowed as she watched him watching her. They stared at each other for several minutes before Wade gave up the game in boredom and retreated into the darkness.

I'll have to set Caleb on him if he keeps that up, she thought grimly then turned away from the barn as her attention was diverted by the sound of a car approaching.

It was the doctor, and Miriam figured his visit wasn't social since he was carrying his doctor bag.

"Afternoon, Miriam," he called out as he made his way up the steps. Miriam nodded a greeting and watched as Doc Polk sat down in the rocker next to her. "I stopped by your house earlier. Howard told me you were most likely here."

"He's awake then," Miriam said, though it was not a question.

Doc Polk nodded. "Yes. I believe he was just finishing up the breakfast you'd left him when I arrived." He set his bag down between his feet and took out his handkerchief, which he used to wipe the sweat from his brow. "I stopped by with the hope that you would let me examine you."

Miriam was shaking her head even before he finished his request. "Naw, Doc. Like I said before, birthin's women's business. I'll call on you iffen I have trouble Mrs. Pritchett can't handle."

Doc Polk sighed as the screen door slammed behind him. He turned to accept the lemonade Dorcas had brought out and took a long drink. "I was afraid you'd say that." He sighed again as he handed the glass back to Dorcas, who took it into the house. Doc Polk wiped his brow again then tucked his handkerchief into the breast pocket of his jacket.

"Well, I had to try," he said, leaning over and picking up his bag. "I've got to go make my rounds." He stood and went down the steps then turned back. "I'll be back to check up on you."

Miriam shook her head but said nothing.

"Thank Dorcas for me," he said by way of farewell then turned and walked to his car. He gave Miriam a smile as he climbed into his dusty car. Miriam waved as he drove away.

SIXTEEN

While her husband was attending to his reluctant patient, Sarah Polk lay on the floor of her bathroom, her face pressed against the cool tile. Despite the heat of the day, she was shivering uncontrollably, yet she was happy, for the horrible need to retch seemed to have passed. Sarah's eyes slid upward to the glass that sat invitingly in its holder on the sink, next to the toothbrushes and the bottle of pills Samuel had given her. For a moment she wondered if she wanted to risk the possibility of another round of vomiting for a drink. A wish fluttered from her and alighted soft as a butterfly on the glass she sought. For the briefest moment, Sarah imagined Samuel was there with her, bathing her forehead, holding a glass of cool water to her lips.

As her fantasy began to play itself out, Sarah's stomach began to churn again, even as she was picturing Samuel coming into the bathroom to gently hold her hair away from her face. She smiled dreamily even as her throat burned from the bitter acid that was all that was left in her.

SEVENTEEN

Over the next few months, life returned to as close to normal as it could. Miriam's time was spent caring for both Howard and her brothers and sisters as the year-end came and went with little fuss and no fanfare. By spring, Dorcas was of an age to begin taking over a good portion of the running of the Wooten house and Miriam was able to spend more time getting her own house in order.

Miriam was standing at the stove frying up Howard's johnnycakes when the first contraction moved through her like a wave. With her hands braced on either side of the stove, she rode it out then waited another moment to make sure it had fully passed. Then she finished up with Howard's breakfast and cleaned up the kitchen. At Howard's request, Miriam went to the icebox for another beer, where she felt a little pop like the snapping of a rubber band.

"Oh dear," Miriam groaned as water began to pour down her legs.

"Good grief, woman," Howard cried in disgust. "Get yer ass outside 'fore you flood us all!"

Miriam gathered up all the dish towels and tried to stem the tide of fluid streaming from between her legs. She looked desperately at Howard, who looked away in disgust. There was no way she would be able to convince him to go fetch Mrs. Pritchett. With formidable resolve, Miriam set off for the two-mile walk into town.

***

As Miriam was struggling along the dirt road, Sarah Polk too felt a crushing weight in her lower back that forced her to sit suddenly at the kitchen table she had been wiping down. When the pain had passed, Sarah looked toward the doorway that led into Samuel's office. Though she was sure he'd left for his daily round of house calls, she still held a glimmer of hope that something had delayed him long enough that he might be there to help her.

"Samuel?" she called out. Only a hot, pregnant silence met her call. Sarah bent over as another wave of pain moved through her, and a feeling of wetness spread across her backside. When she opened her eyes there was a circle of blood staining where her dress lay in her lap. Panicked, Sarah quickly moved to the phone to call Lottie for help.

EIGHTEEN

At the same time his wife was frantically dialing her sister, Samuel Polk was driving to Miriam's on the off chance she would allow at least one examination as she was so close to her due date. He was surprised to come upon her on the road so far from home. He pulled over quickly, creating a massive cloud of orange dust that surrounded Miriam where she stood, slightly hunched, holding a handful of what looked like dish towels against herself.

Samuel quickly moved to her side. "Are you OK? Are you having contractions?"

Miriam let him guide her to the car. "Yeah, water broke and everythin'. I'm just tryin' to get to Mrs. Pritchett."

Samuel settled her in the backseat. "You're not going to be successful. I just saw her at the Arnette house, helping with a twin birth." He'd tried to offer his assistance there, hoping that with the Arnettes being from town, they would be more progressive in their thinking. But he'd been turned away by Myrtle Beale, Shirleen Arnette's mother.

Miriam closed her eyes as another contraction flowed through her, this one considerably stronger and accompanied by intense pressure on her privates. "Well, Doc," Miriam grunted. "I guess it's yer show then."

With quiet satisfaction, Samuel Polk silently slid behind the wheel and drove Miriam to the hospital.

NINETEEN

Sarah sat in grim quiet while Lottie found a wheelchair just inside the delivery/emergency entrance. It took great effort to move from the car to the wheelchair, and when she was settled, Sarah saw that blood had soaked through to the seat of Lottie's car. "I'm sorry, Lottie," she began, but her sister waved away her apology.

"Don't worry, honey. That seat's leatherette. Nothing's going to stain it." Lottie pulled the wheelchair away from the curb and pushed her into the hospital.

With only two delivery rooms available, Sarah and Miriam ended up right next to each other. Samuel Polk had arrived shortly after Sarah and, after settling Miriam into her delivery room, went to examine his wife.

Sarah's eyes lit up when he entered her room with a nurse and the hospital's only junior resident, a young man from Jackson who was spending time in Merwin to study rural medicine before going on to his own practice elsewhere in the state.

"When did your contractions start?" Samuel asked as the nurse, whose name Sarah didn't know, pulled rubber gloves over his hands.

Sarah's smile faltered at the lack of affection. She looked over to Lottie, who smiled encouragingly.

"A little less than an hour ago," she answered quietly, "but there's a lot of blood." She winced as Samuel lifted and spread her legs to examine her. The nurse stood by impassively, but Sarah was mortified when the junior resident leaned in to observe her with great interest.

"This should be a good case for you," Samuel said to the room. For a moment Sarah hoped he was speaking to her, but she soon realized he was addressing the young man riveted by the event going on between her legs. "It appears the placenta has formed very close to the cervix and may be rupturing. This is the likely reason for the presence of blood. She is approximately six centimeters dilated." Samuel removed the bloody gloves and tossed them toward the trash can.

"Set her up for some gas for the pain," he said to the nurse. Samuel glanced at Sarah then turned to the young man. "I'll leave her to you, Dr. Evans. If you need anything, I'll be next door with Mrs. Dirkin." Without a word to his wife, Samuel Polk left the room.

"You know that slut next door thinks she's having the next baby Jesus," she said to the nurse prepping the gas tank next to her bed. The nurse and Dr. Evans looked at each other then down at Sarah.

"It's true," Lottie chimed in. "She told everybody at church that God told her he was giving her his son to bring back to the world."

Even in her pain, Sarah smirked, but then her expression sobered. Miriam might be a dumb hussy who masturbates her pastor, but right now she had the full attention of the only man in the world who mattered to Sarah.

***

When he entered Miriam's room she was sitting upright pushing away the gas mask the nurse was trying to put on her. "I said I don't need that!" she insisted as the nurse tried again to apply the mask to Miriam's face.

"You won't feel any pain if you take the gas," the nurse explained patiently.

Miriam gave her a look. "How am I s'posed to know when ta push if I cain't feel nothin'?"

The nurse looked over as Samuel Polk approached the bed. He waved her aside then gave Miriam his most patient smile.

"So, how about letting me see how far along we are?"

Miriam ignored him and turned to the nurse. "Ain't you Margie Adrieux's sister...Martine?"

The nurse glanced over at Dr. Polk then nodded silently.

"Could you call Margie and ask her to run over to my pa's house and tell them I'm here?"

Martine Adrieux looked over at Dr. Polk, who nodded. "Um, sure," she answered and moved over to the phone.

TWENTY

With the gas going, Sarah no longer felt the pain of labor nor the shame of having some strange young man poking around in her nether regions. Even the ache of her husband's absence failed to hold its grip on her. She knew that he had abandoned her to assist that fat slut Miriam Dirkin. Through her daze she saw what looked like the rest of the Wooten family passing her door, minus the dead one, of course.

Sarah turned to stare out the window and wondered if it was snowing outside. It had gotten so cold in the room, but she was too tired to ask for a blanket, even though there was one on her already. From far away Lottie asked her a question, but Sarah couldn't hear her. Even the frantic beeping seemed like it was coming from outside.

***

Dorcas and Rachel entered the room with Caleb and Abel and set about getting Miriam ready for delivery.

"Doc, you can stay iffen you want, but Mrs. Pritchett's comin' along soon as them twins is done," Abel said kindly. Birthing being women's work, Caleb waited for his brother at the door.

Miriam waved Rachel and Dorcas over to hold her up as she attempted a squat on the hospital bed. Martine Adrieux stood by, helpless without a doctor to assist.

"I ain't got time to wait for Mrs. Pritchett. This baby's fixin' to walk out iffen I don't start pushin'," Miriam grunted. "Martine, I'm gonna need you to catch if this baby comes out soon." She waved her brothers out of the room then moved to the end of the bed.

Samuel Polk stepped forward. "Miriam, I really think you need me to help at this point."

"Naw, we'll be fine." Miriam grunted again as another contraction ripped through her. As the urge to push came over her, Miriam bore down, with Rachel and Dorcas struggling under her weight. Martine moved to the end of the bed, and Samuel moved aside. When the contraction passed, Miriam settled back to relieve some of the pressure on her sisters. "I got the Lord's help on this one, Doc. It bein' his baby an' all."

Moments later another wave of pain came over her, and Miriam braced herself to push again. Martine checked underneath the sheet over Miriam's knees.

"Baby's crowning," she murmured and pulled over the water and towels as Miriam had had a bowel movement during the contraction. Samuel moved to intervene, but Miriam put up a hand to stop him. Her face turned beet red as another contraction rolled across her body. Miriam bore down for as long as she could then fell back to rest.

From the other room they could hear a commotion, what sounded like an alarm going off and furniture falling over.

Miriam felt another contraction coming on and moved forward again, her arms around her sister's shoulders. Martine pulled the soiled drawsheet away and got her hands under Miriam as the baby's head slid out.

"Keep pushing," Martine urged, and Miriam bore down harder, her sister Rachel stumbling a bit under the weight. When she couldn't push another second, Miriam felt the pressure ease immediately as the baby's body slid out of her. Exhausted, she fell back, and her sisters gently laid her against the pillows.

Everyone turned as the door flew open. The nurse from the other room stood in the doorway, covered in blood. "We need you," she said to Samuel Polk then ran back to the other room.

Before leaving Samuel turned to Miriam. "Well done. I'll be back to check on you."

Miriam gave him a weak smile. "No hurry."

TWENTY-ONE

Next door was chaos as the young doctor attempted to staunch the blood flowing from Sarah Polk. He looked around in a panic when Samuel Polk walked in. Lottie stood in the corner, her eyes wide, her fists pressed against her lips.

"I believe the placenta has pulled away. Her uterus is ruptured," Dr. Evans panted. Sarah lay pale and unconscious.

The nurse pulled a fresh pair of gloves over Samuel's hands then handed him a surgical tray. Without a word, Samuel pulled the scalpel from the tray as the nurse bathed Sarah's genitals with iodine. When she stepped back, Samuel swept the scalpel midline along her perineum, opening up the birth canal enough that the baby, placenta and all, fell into Dr. Evans's hands. He moved away quickly so that Samuel could locate the source of the bleeding and try to clamp it.

The nurse took the silent baby from the young doctor and left the room, pulling Lottie along with her.

Just minutes later, the nurse returned to find the two doctors standing in a pool of blood, Mrs. Polk lying dead in front of them.

Samuel Polk stared at his wife and wondered why he didn't feel anything.

TWENTY-TWO

Martine cooed as she cleaned up the baby who regarded her with dark, solemn eyes. Behind her, the two sisters of Miriam Dirkin cleaned up the detritus of childbirth while Miriam rested. Martine had just finished swaddling the baby when Miriam called to her.

"Let me have my baby. I want to see my boy," she said weakly.

Martine turned and handed the baby to Miriam. "Your boy looks an awful lot like a girl."

Miriam started. "What do you mean? He's pretty? Of course our Lord would be beautiful."

"No." Martine smirked. "I mean your Lord is a girl."

Miriam sat openmouthed as Dorcas and Rachel stared at her. "It can't be. The Lord's messenger told me, 'He is coming.' Why would he call him a he but send me a her?"

Martine, who was a Catholic, had very serious doubts about Miriam's conversation with any messenger but felt generous in light of the woman's firm belief in God. "Our Lord Jesus was born of Mary who was without original sin. To be our Lord's mother, you would have to have been born without original sin."

Miriam considered this as she gazed at her baby, tears filling her eyes. "Then it weren't me who would be the mother of our Lord…it's gonna be her. She's gonna be Mary."

***

Samuel Polk regarded the child that lay in the newborn warmer, her mother dead in the bed behind him. She was as fair as the child next door was dark but just as silent as she regarded him in turn. He was surprised to feel something for this baby despite the deep dislike he had felt for her mother.

He had made a terrible mistake marrying Sarah. He had thought it would help the townspeople accept him if he married one of their own and had sought an intelligent woman among the eligible ladies. But Sarah was not intelligent. Rather she was crafty and full of prejudices that were born out of her self-perceived elevation in society for having married him. Samuel's mother had pointed this out during their one and only visit to his family home in Maryland. He had been fooled until then. He had thought Sarah a perfectly nice young woman, if a little socially backward. It wasn't until later that he bore witness to her cruelty. His mother had been right to disown him. He had defied her by leaving behind his family legacy to marry a woman unworthy of his family name. Bitterness over what he'd sacrificed for Sarah filled the last bit of his heart that might have felt compassion for the dead woman.

As if perceiving something distasteful, Samuel's daughter scrunched up her tiny nose and looked away but did not cry. The expression was so much like his mother's that Samuel was filled with love for his child. He leaned over the warmer and gently lifted her into his embrace. He heard one of the nurses walk in, and Martine appeared at his elbow.

"She's beautiful," she murmured, and Samuel nodded in agreement. "What's her name?"

Samuel regarded his lovely daughter for a moment. "Olivia," he answered, giving his daughter the name of the woman he loved most in the world, his mother. "Her name is Olivia."

THE DAUGHTERS

TWENTY-THREE

Though they were born at the exact same time, Miriam's and Sarah's daughters could not have been more different. In a lone act of defiance, Martine refused to write Mary on the baby's birth certificate, so Miriam compromised, naming the baby Marianne instead. Mother and daughter went back to the hot shack next to Pick Creek, while Olivia, for a brief time, came home to the small but well-appointed house in town.

With Olivia lacking a mother to care for her, Martine Adrieux left her position as a nurse to care for Olivia full time. Samuel and, more importantly, his mother approved of this arrangement as Martine was both educated and spoke fluent French thanks to her French Canadian parents.

In time, however, Samuel felt Olivia, whom Martine had taken to calling Lovey, would benefit from an education identical to his own and sent her east, with Martine as her nanny, to live in Maryland with her grandmother while her father stayed behind to continue his important work among the unfortunates of Merwin, Mississippi. Having enjoyed the advantages of a privileged childhood, it all ended when Lovey's grandmother passed away mere days after Lovey's graduation from prep school, leaving her granddaughter everything.

Immediately following the funeral, Martine delivered Lovey to her father's house in Merwin then resumed her position at the hospital.

While Lovey was learning to assume her rightful position as her grandmother's heir and her father's caretaker, Marianne was learning how demented her mother really was. From the moment she was brought home, Miriam set out to raise Marianne as a proper mother of God. Always faithful to her church, Miriam became even more fervent in her beliefs, dragging Marianne with her to every church service and every revival meeting that came through Merwin. By the time she was a teenager, Marianne was an old hat at humoring her insane mother.

It wasn't until the two girls were much older that they finally crossed paths.

TWENTY-FOUR

It was the beginning of a brutally hot summer, and Marianne was already playing handmaiden to her father, who suddenly felt the need for cigarettes despite having been warned off them by Doc Polk. With her mother gone off to the family farm, it fell to Marianne to fetch smokes for her dad. She had set off a time ago and wasn't in any hurry when she found she'd already finished up her trek at the Stop 'n' Save. Marianne looked up to see a group of girls she had gone to school with filling up the gas tank of a dirty, gold convertible.

The Arnette twins, Verna and Irma, and their friends, Georgia DeWinter, Amberlee Martin, and Lovey Polk, acting like the society girls they were not, posed on the old convertible drinking Cokes and trying to look tough and rich at the same time, which only made them look ridiculous. On this, the hottest of days, they were all dressed up in sprayed-on jeans, white spiked heels, and lots of big plastic jewelry.

Lovey sat on the back with her feet resting on the seat below her. Marianne wondered why Lovey, who seemed so nice, was hanging out with such awful girls. She suddenly remembered that Lovey and Amberlee Martin were cousins and were thrown together despite the more than two-year difference in their ages. And out of the group, Lovey was the only one who could rightfully lay claim to being better, and richer, than any of them.

As she approached, Marianne heard Irma, Amberlee, and Verna giggling over a commercial on the radio. "'The heartland of America.' Well if they're the heartland what are we...the belly button?" Irma smirked. Georgia snorted, her Coke coming out of her nose.

Verna answered in her best announcer voice, "Merwin, Mississippi, belly button of America," then fell over laughing. Marianne wondered what they had in those Cokes.

"Armpit maybe, but definitely not the belly button." Lovey yawned.

"Don't you know anything about the human body?" Amberlee snapped. "We're so far south we're the butthole of America." Amberlee shoved Irma so hard she almost fell over the car into the dirt. Marianne watched her turn to Verna to give a slight nod in her direction. In unison they turned their identical, frizzed-up, Kmart-yellow heads to gaze balefully at Marianne as she reluctantly walked the last few steps to the front door of the store.

"What are you looking at?" Verna challenged, sliding down from the hood where she had been perched. Marianne looked to Lovey for help, but the other girl's expression was remote, her lips pressed into a grim line, her natural blond hair shining like gold in the hot sun. Despite the heat Lovey looked crisp and cool in her pink polo shirt and cotton shorts. Marianne knew from the other kids at the high school that Lovey's tennis shoes alone cost more than all the other girls' outfits put together, never mind the diamonds that winked in her ears.

Before Marianne could answer a voice piped up behind her. "Leave 'er alone. She don't need no crap from you. Go do yer tartin' somewhere else."

Marianne turned at the voice behind her and saw a young man standing at the entrance of the garage next door, wiping his grimy hands on an even grimier rag. He looked about twenty, with hair as light as hers was dark but cut so short you couldn't be sure there was any hair there at all.

He wasn't a handsome man, and he didn't look like a smart man either, but he was defending her, and right now that made him her new best friend.

"We got no truck with you, Joe," Amberlee Martin sneered, looking at Marianne. "We're just talking to our little friend here, aren't we, Verna?" Amberlee leaned against the car next to Verna and stared at Marianne.

Unable to read her look, Marianne took two steps closer to the door of the garage where her new friend Joe was standing.

"She don't look like no friend uh yers to me," Joe said, looking at Marianne in her oversized T-shirt and hand-me-down jeans from the Salvation Army. "Ain't trashy enough." Looking back at Amberlee and her following, Joe spat at the ground. Amberlee had to move her cheap, white vinyl stiletto to avoid the great gob of goo Joe sent her way.

Amberlee shot a menacing glance at Joe then gave up. "Fuck it," she said, giving one last glowering look to Marianne as she got into the car behind her friends. "Ain't worth breakin' a nail over anyway." With a cloud of dust that would make Pompeii proud, Merwin's only wannabe debutantes fishtailed then sped away.

Joe glared after the girls then turned away to walk back into the garage.

"Thanks," Marianne called after him.

Joe turned back to her. "No problem. You going into the Saver?"

Marianne nodded at the ground. "My dad needs cigarettes," she mumbled, suddenly shy.

"We gotta machine inside if you want to get them here. Cheaper than the Saver." Joe tilted his head toward the glass-windowed door next to the garage bay.

Marianne nodded then went inside where the oldest man ever sat behind the register doing a crossword puzzle. To her right was the cigarette machine, and Joe had been right. It was much cheaper than the store next door. Marianne wondered if she was charged more because she was a Wooten and a Dirkin. She used all her dad's change to buy three packs of his favorites then ducked from the gaze of the old-timer and pushed back out the door.

She was fixing to leave when she heard Joe call out. "You wanna pop?"

Marianne turned and saw him deep in the shadows of the garage leaning over an old, beat-up cooler.

She nodded then walked into the dark, where it was surprisingly cool. She tried to transfer all the packs to one hand, but it was too small to hold all three without crushing them, so she pulled up her T-shirt and dropped them down the front. Joe handed her a sweating but cold bottle of Coke. He popped the top for her and then his own. Marianne smiled and drank it down.

"You goin' to the carnival tonight?" he asked.

Marianne shook her head. "I'm not allowed. My ma and me are going to the revival there though."

Joe nodded. "You go to them?"

"All of them." She sighed then handed him the empty bottle. "Thanks."

Marianne made her way back down the dusty road, wondering about the young man. If she'd looked back, she would have seen him watching her.

TWENTY-FIVE

Lovey sat trying not to sweat as the other girls did their peacock dance around Amberlee's new car, a ridiculous five-year-old Mustang that someone had painted a weird gold color. Amberlee's father had given it to her as a graduation present, even though she'd barely made it through community college. Amberlee loved to point out that Lovey didn't have a car at all and offered to drive her everywhere as long as Verna and Irma could come along. Lovey didn't have the heart to tell her that a brand-new Jaguar XJS waited in her garage back home in Maryland, a gift from her grandmother before she'd died. Georgia was probably her closest friend in Merwin, but even she knew nothing about the extent of Lovey's wealth.

Now they were parked out in the hot sun in front of the Stop 'n' Save, waiting for someone to come by and be suitably impressed. The seats were so hot that Lovey opted to sit on the headrest instead, while the other girls preened. It was a colossal waste of time since anyone who might be remotely interested was either inside where it was cooler or at work like a normal human being.

But it was her last summer in Merwin before going off to college back east, and she wanted to enjoy it as much as possible, even if that meant spending it listening to Verna, Irma, and Amberlee joke about some stupid commercial on the radio.

Lovey was about a minute from going inside to see if her uncle needed any help in the store when Marianne Dirkin slowly walked up the road. Or was she a Wooten? Lovey wasn't sure. With her dark hair and nearly black eyes she had the coloring of the Wootens, but where the Wooten women were tall and fat, Marianne was tiny like a porcelain doll.

Lovey liked the Wootens. They worked hard, were unfailingly polite, and harbored no illusions that they were any better than anyone else, and she respected that. She knew Miriam was a little crazy with her fundamentalist Christian beliefs and the whole "Marianne's going to be the next mother of God" stuff, but for the most part she had always been very kind to Lovey for being motherless. Lovey truly appreciated the effort, knowing how awful her mother had been to the Wootens.

She could tell from the look in her eyes that Marianne was not the kind of audience Amberlee and her friends were looking for.

"What are you looking at?" Verna challenged the poor girl.

Lovey was about to speak up when a voice came out of the garage.

"Leave 'er alone. She don't need no crap from you. Go do yer tartin' somewhere else."

Lovey looked over to see the mechanic stepping out of the shade onto the concrete pad just outside the garage. He looked older, closer to Amberlee's age, and Lovey wondered if he was the reason they were sitting there baking.

When Amberlee answered him, Lovey knew she was trying to put on a show for the young man and enjoyed the fact that he wasn't even remotely interested in any of them.

Lovey smiled inwardly as the two exchanged insults then slid back down into the seat next to Georgia when it was apparent that Amberlee was going to drive off in a huff. The wheels spun on the gravel as the car rocketed away from the Stop 'n' Save.

As they drove away, Lovey glanced back to see Marianne looking down, her face forlorn, alone in a cloud of dust.

TWENTY-SIX

Marianne came home to find Miriam getting ready for the revival. At the last minute Howard decided that he wanted to go too, so Marianne ran the distance to the Wooten farm to see if Abel could give them a ride. Never one to turn down his niece, Abel drove Marianne back to pick up her parents, while Caleb took the rest of the Wootens in the old truck.

Since Howard was too large for the cab, he rode in the bed while everyone else crowded into the front.

Abel drove to the other side of town where the carnival had been set up on a barren field of county land. The carnival itself was a small one, with only a handful of rides but many opportunities to lose money at one of the games or gambling booths that lined the midway. Instead of cheerful calliope music, lively spirituals burrowed into the ears of the carnival goers. Off to the side in its own alley was a scattering of freak-show tents that charged outrageous admission prices and, rumor had it, even offered a nudie show.

The huge revival tent was set up near the front ticket booth and boasted a lively program condemning all the vices known to man, including the games of chance featured in the carnival. Such denouncements were not unusual, and carnivals and traveling shows were often targeted as sinful by the fundamentalist groups in the area.

The people of Merwin might have been surprised to know that this carnival and revival were hosted by the same group, a situation that would bear further investigation if law enforcement were to find out. One needed only to look at the line of brand-new RVs at the back of the lot to wonder how much money they were really raking in.

Despite the line of cars trying to park, Abel got as close to the revival tent as possible so Howard wouldn't have too far to walk. Marianne ducked her head as people walking past began to stare at her family. Her father was pushing four hundred pounds by then and could only go short distances before his knees gave out on him. Luckily he wasn't interested in the revival, so Abel helped him to a bench that had been set up just outside the tent.

Miriam bypassed Howard altogether and pulled Marianne inside so they could get a good seat before the crowds showed up.

With Miriam's reputation as a fundamentalist nut, the people of Merwin gave her a wide berth, and Miriam and Marianne had the front row to themselves. In no time the tent filled to capacity, yet the Dirkins still managed to keep their place of honor. Marianne had resigned herself to the fact that no one wanted to be associated with them when someone slid into the seat next to her. She was startled to see the boy from the garage sitting there staring straight ahead as if he'd been there all along. Miriam certainly noticed and leaned over to glare at him.

"Who is this?" she asked her daughter.

"He works at the garage in town," Marianne said by way of an answer, hoping her mother would be satisfied. She was not.

"What's yer name, boy?"

Joe leaned over Marianne and put out his hand. "Joseph, ma'am."

Marianne looked on in horror as her mother's face stretched into a beam of a smile. Miriam looked thrilled as she reached over and firmly shook the boy's hand. Marianne could see the wheels turning behind her mother's eyes and knew for her it was all falling into place the way it was supposed to.

"I don't recognize you," said Miriam. "Are you from here?"

"No, ma'am," Joe answered. "I'm from Fairhope...in Alabama. My grandpa took me in to help at the garage."

Miriam sat back and regarded the young man. "Yer Emmet Buckley's grandson?"

Joe nodded. "Yes, ma'am."

"Where are yer folks?" she asked, her eyes narrowed.

"Gone, ma'am," he answered.

Marianne hoped her mother would accept such a short answer. Luckily the revival was about to start, so her mother had no choice but to take him at face value.

"You have good manners, son. Yer welcome to sit with us," Miriam said, and her daughter sighed with relief.

"Thank you, ma'am," Joe replied then turned his attention to the preacher who'd taken the stage.

Most revivals ran long, usually well into the night, but this one was mercifully short. The crowd didn't know it, but the preacher wanted nothing more than to send his penitents out to sin among the games, promising that he could forgive their sins when they came back and hoping to guilt them into increasing their donations to his cause and his pocket.

Miriam pushed Marianne and Joe in front of her as the crowd left the tent. Marianne reluctantly led Joe to the spot where her father sat sweating in the heat while Caleb and Silas wandered over with Jacob, Dorcas, and Rachel behind them. Wade was nowhere to be seen and was most likely checking out the nudie show, though his four-year-old son, Junior, held tight to Rachel's hand. Marianne was mortified that her whole family was on display. While all the Wooten men were wiry, all the women were hugely fat. And though Dorcas and Rachel were the nicest aunts a girl could ever hope for, no one was going to look past their tacky, ill-fitting T-shirts and tight Kmart jeans.

"I'm gonna sit with yer pa awhile," Miriam panted in the heat. "Why don't you two go get some lemonade?"

"Get me some too," Howard said, beads of sweat dotting his forehead. Marianne was standing there wondering how on earth she was going to pay for lemonade when Miriam pulled a five-dollar bill out of her pocketbook and handed it to her. Marianne hurried away before her family could embarrass her further.

As they walked along the midway, Joe often stopped to watch people trying to win at the various balloon, bottle, and basketball games. Several booths had card tricks and cup games, all offering the chance of winning big money.

"Did you want to play?" Marianne asked, and Joe snorted.

"Them things is all rigged," he said in derision. He stopped at the basketball tent. "See this one? Them balls have too much air in them, so they bounce more. And the rings ain't round. They been hammered flat where you can't see it, so the ball can't go in no matter what."

Joe led her to the next booth. "And see them balloons? They ain't all the way full. You couldn't pop it if you sat on it, let alone with one of them dull darts."

"What about the fish game? Lots of people win at that one," Marianne asked, stopping at the popular booth.

Joe snorted again. "You pay them two dollars for three chances to win a fish you can buy at Kmart for five cents. And most times you gotta try more than that to win a mostly dead fish."

Marianne and Joe watched as parents paid their hard-earned money for chances for their kids to win the fish. Joe wordlessly pointed at the bags in the center. Marianne followed his finger and saw that several of the fish were already dead. She felt terrible that some poor child was going to win a dead fish.

Marianne moved on, mindful that her pa was waiting for something to drink. Marianne ordered three lemonades then blushed when Joe paid for them.

"Thank you," she mumbled, ducking her head shyly. Joe didn't answer but gave her an almost smile then picked up the lemonades for her parents.

As they were walking back to the revival tent, they passed a group of girls who had tormented Marianne all through school; Verna and Irma held court at the center of the group. As a unit the girls turned and watched as Joe led Marianne away from them.

"Why do they do that?" he asked as the group collapsed into a fit of giggles and insults behind them.

Marianne sighed then stopped and faced him, though she cut her eyes away to avoid seeing the inevitable disappointment in them. "I guess I should tell you now before you hear it from somewhere else, but...my family is kind of a joke here in Merwin. We are dirt poor. We live in a house that slaves didn't even want to live in, and everyone thinks it's because we have slave in us. My pa is the fattest man in just about anywhere, and my ma is fat *and* crazy."

Joe's expression was inscrutable. "Crazy how?"

Marianne wilted a little bit. "When she was havin' me, she thought she was havin' the next baby Jesus. Then when I was born and she found out I was a girl...well now she thinks I'm gonna be mom to the next baby Jesus. That's why I'm not allowed to do anything that might be sinful. I have to stay pure, so the angel will come to bless upon me the next son of God."

Joe regarded her for a moment then shrugged. "No big deal. I had to move here because when my pa went off to prison, my ma was wanting me to take his place in her bed."

Marianne stared as Joe walked back to where her parents were waiting. She'd never met someone worse off than her. In a terrible way, it felt good.

When the intermission was over, Marianne and her family filed back into the tent with Joe following. No one objected when Miriam pushed her way back to the front dragging her daughter with her. She was nonplussed to see a tall, thin young man already sitting smack-dab in the middle of the front row. He was dark and thin like a Wooten man but tall like a Wooten girl. Miriam glared at him as she sat down and pulled her daughter next to her. Joe took his place next to Marianne.

Marianne could tell the presence of the young man was bothering her mother but hoped that the band setting up would provide enough of a distraction to keep her from confronting him. A part of her hoped the preacher would pull out some snakes just to keep her mother from embarrassing her.

Marianne closed her eyes in mortification as Miriam leaned and shouted over the music. "Hey, boy."

The young man glanced over at her in surprise then pointed at himself.

"Yes, you. Who are you?"

"Silas," he shouted back. "Silas Pritchett."

"You related to Mrs. Pritchett?" Miriam asked, and Marianne groaned. Her mother had to know everyone's business.

"She's my grandmother," he answered then turned back as the preacher and the other speakers stepped onto the makeshift stage.

Miriam sat back, her expression thoughtful as the revival choir and band launched into a rendition of "Enemy's Camp."

Marianne settled in to enjoy the music. She never really understood the lyrics but enjoyed the liveliness of the song. So did everyone else, including the preacher and the other speakers. Marianne hid her smile behind her hand as the men in suits hopped and twirled along to the music. Several didn't seem to know the words and mouthed nonsense along with the singer. She glanced over at Joe and was surprised to see Lovey Polk sliding into the last seat in the row. Lovey gave her a polite smile then turned to watch the antics on stage with thinly veiled humor.

Marianne glanced over at Lovey, who sat cool and crisp in a dark-blue sleeveless cotton shirt and white Bermuda shorts, with pearls in her ears and at her neck. Marianne's heart sank. She knew Joe would never look at her again with someone like Lovey Polk sitting nearby.

She pulled her faded sweater over her T-shirt and ruffled denim skirt, knowing she looked shabby by comparison. She knew she was dirt, and people like Lovey were a constant reminder that no matter how hard she scrubbed, she'd never be anything but dirt.

Her heart soared when Joe reached over and took her hand.

TWENTY-SEVEN

As much as her father hated her comingling with the townsfolk, Lovey enjoyed being around them. Whether it was an act of defiance or a sincere desire to understand her mother's people, Lovey sought out opportunities to spend time in their company. And though she would never address it directly, Lovey considered her father to be somewhat of a hypocrite when it came to the town. Sure, he seemed to genuinely want to help them and cared for them to the best of his abilities, but when his daughter had arrived, she was promptly sent off to live with her grandmother in an environment her father felt more appropriate to her station in life.

And though she spent the occasional summer in Merwin, her father did not intend for her to settle there with him when she was done with her education at Smith College. She had made a token attempt to convince him to let her attend Ole Miss or Millsaps with Georgia but was informed in no uncertain terms that as a legacy it was her duty to attend Smith. She knew better than to argue. So since this was her last summer before going back east, Lovey intended to make the best of it. Even if it meant hanging out with girls she didn't particularly like.

Lovey pulled her father's old Chevy into the field and parked at the farthest end of the lot. Since Georgia wasn't allowed to go to the fair, she figured she'd meet up with Amberlee and the other girls. By the time she pulled up, it looked like the whole town was there. Lovey got out and walked across the field parking lot.

Though she was supposed to meet the girls by the Ferris wheel, Lovey was drawn by the music and wandered over to the revival tent instead. It was filled to capacity with the faithful of Merwin, Mississippi, but, curiously, a couple of seats still remained in the front row. Lovey knew her white shorts weren't appropriate attire for the conservative crowd but ignored the dirty looks shot her way and instead put her head up and made her way to the front to take a seat near the Wootens.

TWENTY-EIGHT

It was late, and everyone was drenched in sweat when the revival finally ended. The speakers had been OK, and as far as preaching went, it was pretty typical stuff. The music was really good, though the offering plate went around a few too many times. By the third go-around, the Wootens were out of money and Marianne was deeply embarrassed until Lovey Polk threw a fifty-dollar bill in the plate and told the usher to stop coming by. When she braved a glance in Lovey's direction, the other girl rolled her eyes and shook her head.

By and large it had been a successful evening for the faithful, with many saved, many healed, and many more lit with the fire of Jesus's love.

The Wootens were filing out behind the crowd when Marianne looked back and saw Lovey still seated but doubled over like she was hurting.

"Mama," she said to Miriam, who was in front of her, still humming the last hymn. Joe was at the front of the family, trying to make a path for them.

Miriam glanced back, and Marianne pointed to Lovey then walked back to the front of the tent.

"Lovey?" Marianne said quietly. "You OK?"

Lovey looked up, her face twisted in pain. "Terrible cramp all of a sudden."

Marianne looked down and saw that Lovey's white shorts were stained with blood. "Oh my goodness, you're bleeding. Do you want me to get my mother?"

Lovey shook her head. "I'll be OK in a second." She leaned over as another cramp moved through her then tried to push off the chair. When she looked down her face went white. "Oh no."

"Here." Marianne rushed over and tied her old sweater around Lovey's waist, hiding the growing stain, then held her hand out. "Can you walk?"

Lovey nodded, taking Marianne's hand, and had stepped forward when another cramp seized her. Marianne moved under Lovey's arm and held her up so she wouldn't fall.

"Can I help?" she heard from behind her. Marianne turned to see Silas Pritchett standing nearby.

"Something's wrong with her," Marianne said. "I think we need to get her to the hospital."

Lovey shook her head. "Home. I...can drive...home."

Silas stared at the blood that was now staining Marianne's sweater. "I think your friend's right. You need a hospital."

Lovey started to shake her head again but doubled over as another wave of pain ran through her. Silas moved quickly and lifted Lovey in his arms, and then, rather than trying to navigate through the crowd at the exit, he carried her to the space behind the stage where a flap was pulled aside for the band and preachers.

Marianne followed him through the flap and guided him back to the front, where her family stood looking for her. They were stunned to see Lovey Polk being carried over by a complete stranger.

"Something's wrong with Lovey," Marianne said. "I think she needs to go to the hospital."

"I'll take her there," Silas said and carried Lovey away.

Marianne looked at her mother. "Shouldn't we go with him? Lovey doesn't have anyone to look after her, and she doesn't know that Silas at all."

Miriam looked thoughtful. "We should at least make sure she gets there OK," she said then looked at Joe. "Can you take us?"

Joe nodded, so they set off to follow Silas to the hospital.

If the hospital staff thought it was strange for the Wootens to bring Samuel Polk's daughter to the emergency room, they were too well trained to comment on it. As Silas carried Lovey into the empty waiting area, the admitting nurse scowled at the group of Wootens congregating in her doorway then called for emergency staff over the PA system. A second later a doctor and nurse rolled a gurney into the room then as quickly rolled her back into the depths of the emergency department.

Marianne walked over to the window. "Her name is L—"

"I know who that is," the nurse interrupted, her tone both defensive and irritated. Marianne had put her head down and started to walk away when the nurse called her name.

"Miss Dirkin?" she said more gently, and Marianne turned back. "Thank you for bringing her." The nurse smiled, and her face transformed into the image that most people saw.

"Can I wait for her?" Marianne asked.

The nurse looked thoughtful. "It might be a while."

"That's OK."

"All right then. But everyone else can go home." Marianne's family heard their dismissal and readied to go.

Marianne thanked Silas, who brushed away her thanks then followed her family out leaving Joe behind.

"You want me to stay with you?" Joe asked.

Marianne shook her head. "I'm all right. It could be a long time."

"When you're ready to go home, just call the garage, and I'll come get you," he said, handing her a fistful of change.

Marianne looked at it in confusion. The pay phone only cost a quarter.

"Just in case you get hungry," he said, reading her mind, and then he left too.

Marianne pushed the change deep into her pocket then took a chair near the admitting window. All alone in the waiting room, she was uncomfortable at first but settled in to wait.

TWENTY-NINE

It took an IV of pain medication for Lovey to start feeling better. The staff found her father at one of his house calls, and he arrived shortly after the IV was in.

With Martine right behind him, Lovey's father came in and gave her a quick kiss on the forehead then checked her vitals and the exam report the nurse had handed him.

"I'll be right back," he said quietly and left the room, leaving Martine behind.

"Oh *ma chère*," she crooned as she smoothed Lovey's hair back.

"What's wrong with me?" Lovey asked, groggy from the IV medication.

Martine glanced at the door. "There's a tumor," she answered quietly. "They're looking at a sample of it right now, but they're probably going to send you to a specialist before they do anything else."

"A tumor...you mean like cancer?"

"They don't know yet," she said quietly.

Lovey's father stepped in with the young doctor who'd admitted her. "...I'll get them on the phone and make the arrangements," the young doctor said then left the room.

Samuel Polk crossed the room and sat on the edge of the bed. "Hello, sweetheart," he said gently as he took Lovey's hand between his.

"What's wrong with me?" Lovey asked.

Samuel glanced at Martine, who nodded slightly, then turned back to his daughter. "You have what appears to be a vaginal glandular tumor that is just outside your cervix. It's what's causing the bleeding. If I had to guess, I'd say it's clear-cell adenocarcinoma." Samuel looked away as if he were suddenly uncomfortable with the conversation.

"Can't you just remove it?" Lovey asked, though she already knew the answer. Though her father might be the chief of staff at Merwin Hospital, he was really a general practitioner, and the hospital wasn't set up for anything more complicated than broken arms and childbirths.

"You need a real biopsy and a consult with someone who specializes in oncology. We're arranging for your transfer to Sloan Kettering right now. Martine will be going with you."

Lovey stared at her father, knowing that he wasn't going to be there. His loyalty was to the people of Merwin, no matter how much he loved her.

Samuel at least had the good grace to know that he was sending his daughter away with nothing more than a family friend and again shifted uncomfortably. "You have a visitor waiting to see you," he said just to have something to say.

Lovey's brow furrowed. She couldn't imagine who might have come to visit. No one knew she was there. "Who?"

Samuel smiled then walked to the door and leaned out. A moment later Marianne Dirkin peered around the doorframe, a shy smile on her face.

"She came to see how you were doing," her father said, gesturing for Marianne to go in farther.

Lovey watched the girl slowly make her way across the room as if at any moment someone was going to throw her out. Samuel and Martine left, closing the door behind them.

"Hi," Marianne said timidly.

"Were you here the whole time?" Lovey asked, incredulous. She'd lost track of time, but she was sure it had been hours already.

Marianne nodded. "I didn't want you to be here by yourself. I know if I were here, I'd want my family around me."

Lovey smiled. "Thanks. Will you sit and talk to me?"

"Sure," Marianne answered, perching at the end of Lovey's bed. "Do they know what's wrong?"

Lovey tried to shrug. "It looks like I have a tumor in my...umm..." She waved at the general area between her legs, not knowing how to phrase her situation politely.

"Lady parts?" Marianne answered for her.

Lovey chuckled. "Yes...in my lady parts."

"Wow. A tumor? That sounds serious." Marianne's pretty face frowned. "I didn't even know you could get a tumor there."

Lovey smiled awkwardly.

"So I guess they're going to send you away again, huh?" Marianne said quietly.

Lovey nodded. "They're sending me to New York to see a doctor there. I was supposed to go away for school in the fall anyway."

This time Marianne nodded. "There's so much more for you out there than there is here anyway."

THIRTY

It was full dark when Marianne stepped outside the hospital. It was too late to call Joe, and she was reluctant to impose on him any more than she already had. Home was only a few miles away, so she set off on foot instead.

What Merwin had in rural charm it lacked in sidewalks, and it wasn't long before Marianne was on the blacktop. Usually people took shortcuts through the fields, but in the dark it was impossible to see, and Marianne knew rattlesnakes built nests in the bushes. It would be just her luck to step on one in the dark.

On the plus side, it was too late for traffic, so Marianne had the road to herself. The heat hung heavy on the street as crickets sang in the weeds next to her. Every so often a pair of eyes glowed from the brush, but Marianne ignored them. Otherwise the world was silent, the only sound her tennis shoes on the black asphalt.

She was lost in thought when a pair of headlights lit the road in front of her. Marianne turned to see an unfamiliar truck stopping behind her.

"You OK?" a voice called out. The shadow of a tall, thin man stepped out and walked to the front of the truck. The headlights revealed the young man from the revival, Silas, the one who had carried Lovey to the hospital.

"I'm fine," she answered then turned back to resume her walk.

"Can I give you a lift?" he asked. Marianne turned back and looked at him. His expression was hopeful and concerned at the same time. With his black hair and blacker eyes, he looked just like her uncle Abel.

Marianne looked doubtful.

"I won't hurt you, I promise," he said then smiled. It transformed his face, and Marianne felt a sense of comfort with him. "Besides, I want to ask you about that girl."

"Lovey?" she asked, and he nodded. Marianne considered his offer for another second then shrugged and got into his truck.

"What did you want to know?" she asked as he drove off.

"Anything, everything I guess," he answered, his eyes glued to the road. "What was wrong with her?"

Marianne studied him as he drove. His black hair was longer than most boys kept theirs, and it curled slightly, especially along the line of his jaw. His features in general were so fine he could easily have been mistaken for a really beautiful woman.

"She has a tumor," Marianne answered. "Her father is sending her away to a hospital in New York to find out how bad and to take care of her."

"Wow, New York?" Silas's eyebrows went up. "That's really far to go to see a doctor."

Marianne turned and stared at the road ahead. "She's not really from around here. Her mom was Sarah Beasley, and her dad is in charge at the hospital, Dr. Polk?" She glanced over to see Silas nod. "Her mom was from here, but she died when Lovey was born, so her dad sent her back to his home...somewhere back east, to grow up. I think they're rich or something."

"Are you good friends? You must be to spend all that time at the hospital tonight."

Marianne considered his question. "I like her," she said by way of an answer. "We were born on the same day...but...my family's not the kind of people her family would be friends with."

Silas was quiet as he thought about that. "Does she have a boyfriend?" he asked softly.

Marianne shook her head. "I wouldn't really know about that, but I don't think so."

The two sat in silence, both lost in thought, until Silas pulled onto the road to her house.

"You can let me off here," Marianne said, and Silas pulled to a stop at the top of her driveway. "Otherwise my mother's going to grill you about your family."

Silas smiled, and Marianne got out. "Thanks for the ride," she said then slammed the door.

"No problem," he answered before pulling away.

THIRTY-ONE

Lovey was back in Annapolis, wrapped in an ancient breadfruit-patterned quilt on the old screened-in porch at her grandmother's house...well now it was her house. She sat and looked out over the water that bordered the property. Though the Tudor-style home had been built in the 1920s by her grandfather, it had been updated through the years, and Lovey's grandmother had painstakingly maintained it until her death. The attorneys that handled the trust wanted her to sell it and all the other properties her grandmother had owned, but Lovey couldn't bring herself to think about letting go of anything. They'd left her alone during her treatment but had taken up again in the hopes that they could settle the estate once and for all. The millions her grandfather had made in shipping had only grown under her grandmother's management, and Lovey had inherited all of it.

Martine walked up and set a cup of tea, her pain pills, and a stack of mail down next to her. The breeze off the water was cold, so Martine walked back into the house and returned with a soft knitted hat to cover Lovey's hairless skull. She had made it through the surgery to remove the tumor and subsequent radiation treatment without incident, but as bad as the cancer was, it was the chemo that was going to kill her.

Lovey tried to drink the tea but set it aside as waves of nausea moved through her. She leaned back and looked out over the grounds down to the dock where a great blue heron stood at the end watching the water intently.

On the top of the pile of mail was an envelope from Smith College. Lovey didn't have to open it to know it was an acceptance to defer her admission to the school. It was almost September, and even after two surgeries, she was potentially facing a third that would remove the remainder of her reproductive organs. She thought she would feel hurt or anger that she would never have children of her own, but she only felt dead inside.

Lovey pulled the small radio over and turned it on. She scrolled through the radio stations then switched it to AM radio, where she found what she was looking for. She sat back and watched the egret staring at the water as the gospel music wrapped around her, offering peace and comfort.

Far in the distance she could hear the sound of the doorbell then Martine's footsteps as she crossed the hardwood floors.

Lovey assumed it was a deliveryman and closed her eyes to the breeze that blew off the water.

"Chère?"

Lovey started then looked over to see Martine framed in the doorway with someone standing behind her.

"You have a visitor." Martine stepped aside, and the young man from the revival stepped out on the porch.

Lovey was taken aback. Though people had called and sent cards and flowers, no one had ever come to visit her. Not even her father, who had only come during her surgeries.

"Do you remember me?" he asked.

Lovey nodded. "You're Silas, right? You're the one who took me to the hospital."

Silas nodded then gestured to the chair next to her. "Can I sit down?"

Lovey nodded again as Martine gave her a knowing smile then disappeared back into the house.

"What are you doing here?" Lovey asked, her hand going up to tug her stocking cap lower, self-conscious about her appearance in the face of such physical beauty.

Silas stared at her as if memorizing her face. "I don't know. Marianne told me how to find you and...I felt like I needed to come to see how you were doin'."

"That's a long way to come," Lovey remarked then pulled her stocking cap down over her ears again.

Silas reached out and pulled the cap off her head. "Stop doing that," he said quietly.

Lovey closed her eyes and turned her face away. She'd grown used to the stares. She startled when she felt his hand move over the fine patches of down that were all that was left of her hair. His hand was warm and gentle as it cupped the curve of her skull.

She opened her eyes to see him smiling at her. She couldn't think of a single thing to say.

"When you were in school, did you ever play with magnets? We had an experiment where you put two magnets near each other and counted how long it took before they found each other. The stronger the magnets, the faster it happened. I think people are like that," he said, taking his hand away. Lovey missed it instantly. Instead he reached down and took her cold, small hand in his then looked out over the water. Lovey stared at him, unable to look away.

Silas spent only that day with Lovey before driving back to Mississippi. She searched her brain for some reason to make him stay, but her doctors were waiting for her, and she knew he needed to go back home to care for his grandmother.

Lovey watched him drive away then turned to walk back into the house. "Martine?" she called out. "I think I'd like to go visit my father."

THIRTY-TWO

Summer had been brutal in Merwin.

With few jobs available, Marianne tried to contribute to her father's disability checks by working the farm stand just outside the Wooten property. Though most people refused to socialize with the Wootens, a few had no problem eating their cheap eggs and produce.

Marianne spent her days sweating behind stacks of tomatoes, beans, and, later in the summer, fruit and preserves her aunts made in the evenings.

Eggs were kept in coolers filled with ice, and it was on the coolers that Marianne sat and waited for customers to come by. At sunset, when her uncles came by to close the stand, Marianne would walk into town to see Joe.

At first her visits were awkward, until Joe found her a place to settle in while he ran the garage. She'd pass the time sitting on a pile of tires while Joe worked on the cars that people brought in.

From her vantage point she could see the townspeople coming and going, though they couldn't see her. She liked that feeling of watching the world and enjoyed her snapshot view of the petty dramas that went on in the town. She discovered that even though their daughters were friends, Lottie Martin and Shirleen Arnette did not like each other at all and that Shirleen only came to the Stop 'n' Save when she needed milk. But if Shirleen avoided the Stop 'n' Save, her daughters practically lived there.

Marianne suspected it had less to do with Amberlee and more to do with the young man who worked in the garage. When she came by herself, Verna drove her dad's old Ford and always seemed to need to have Joe look at it. As often as she came to the garage, one would think the car was falling apart. But Joe humored her, more for the money than the attention. For Marianne, watching Verna was like watching her own private soap opera.

At the end of the day, Joe would close up the garage and the two would retire to his room at the back of the station to watch TV. The first time Joe reached out to hold her hand, Marianne about jumped out of her skin.

Their first attempts at affection were also awkward and fumbling. Joe was shy at first then, emboldened by Marianne's lack of protest, braved an attempt under her shirt to touch her small, hard breasts. It wasn't until he tried to put his hands into her panties that she stopped him.

"I can't," she panted. "I promised I'd stay pure."

Joe sat back and nodded, his face remote.

They were well into fall when things grew more serious. They had been kissing, their caresses growing more urgent, when Joe pulled back. "I've got to stop, or I won't be able to later."

Marianne stared at him, this honorable man who wouldn't take her virtue from her. With new resolve, she stood up and started to unbutton her shirt.

Joe's eyes went wide as she pulled it off then unsnapped her bra. He started to protest when she pulled down her jeans and stepped out of her panties, but Marianne just shook her head and pulled his hand onto her breast. She loved this boy, and she aimed to keep him.

"We can do whatever you want. You just can't put it in," she said quietly.

Joe tore his clothes off then stood in front of her naked, staring at her hungrily. He was thinner than he looked with clothes on, and his erection stood straight up. Marianne was terrified and yet never wanted to touch something so badly in all her life.

Timid, she reached out and gently wrapped her fingers around it. Joe groaned as she tentatively moved her hand up and down then reached over and pulled her close. They fell together on his small bed, and Joe began to thrust against her hand. Unsure of what to do, Marianne lay still until Joe moved back and pulled her hand aside. She stared at him as he lay down again and pressed the full length of his erection along the cleft between her legs. She started to protest, but Joe pressed his lips against hers.

"Shhh, I won't go in," he promised, his hips moving urgently as he ground himself against her. Marianne could feel her skin part to reveal her most private spot, which was now rubbing directly against the length of him. She moaned softly, sending Joe into a frenzy. She felt an itch building between her legs as he rubbed against her faster and faster. Her body shuddered as the itch exploded into her first orgasm. Joe's followed, and he spurted across her bare belly.

"Oh my God, oh my God," he moaned then fell against her. Marianne clutched his shoulders and rode the wave of her orgasm.

They lay still, panting together as Marianne began to fill with shame. She might technically still be a virgin, but she was no longer pure. Tears pooled in her eyes.

"I love you," she heard Joe whisper. "Don't cry. I love you, and I'm gonna make you love me too."

Marianne's tears cut trails down her cheeks. "I already do."

THIRTY-THREE

As the weather turned cooler, instead of going to the garage, Marianne went home to accompany Miriam to church. She was feeling massive amounts of guilt over her wanton behavior with Joe and needed to atone for her sins in the only place she felt clean. She had been throwing up a lot lately, and she was pretty sure that, despite their precautions, she was pregnant.

She was agonizing over what to say to her mother when she came upon Joe's truck parked outside her house. Rather than going in the front like she usually did, Marianne quietly walked to the back of the house and stood near the kitchen door to eavesdrop on their conversation. Unfortunately they either were not in the kitchen or were speaking too quietly to hear anything. Marianne stiffened her resolve and went inside.

Joe and her parents were indeed sitting on the old, threadbare living-room set, and by the look on her mother's face, the news was good.

"Joe's here to ask yer daddy's permission to marry you." She beamed.

Joe stood nearby, staring at Marianne, his expression inscrutable as usual.

"Well go on, boy; ask her!" Howard said, his tone jovial for once.

Joe smiled a little then pulled a small box out of his jeans pocket and walked over and knelt in front of Marianne. "Will you marry me?" he asked, opening the box. Inside was a small diamond ring that was the most beautiful thing Marianne had ever seen.

She nodded, tears springing to her eyes, and her voice caught as Joe took the ring from the box and slid it over her finger.

Harold and Miriam clapped, and then Miriam got up to pour celebratory beer in the place of champagne.

"So when's the wedding?" she called from the kitchen.

Joe got up and hugged Marianne, who was still crying. "I have to go back home to get my birth certificate, so I thought we could get married in Alabama. There's no wait there."

"Then let's all go," Harold announced and tried to push himself off the chair.

"We ain't goin' now," Miriam scolded as she carried in four glasses of beer on a dinner plate. "It'll take all day to get there."

"It's about five hours or more," Joe told her. "We have to go to my mom's first, in Fairhope, and get my stuff then head up to Bay Minette to get the license. There's a judge there that can marry us if you want. Or if you want we can come back here and have a proper wedding."

Marianne glanced at her mother and knew exactly what she was thinking. Other than the Wootens, it was unlikely anyone would come to their wedding, not to mention the dilemma of having to pay for it.

"I'd just as soon get married there," Marianne announced as she dried her face. "If family wants to have a party when we get back, then that's OK with me."

Miriam seized on the offer. "Then that's what we'll do. Yer daddy and me will ride with you to Joe's family; then we'll all go up to get you two married."

Joe shook his head. "It'll just be us there. My ma won't want to come with."

Marianne didn't sleep at all that night. The excitement of her impending marriage and her fear over her pregnancy kept her mind from settling down. It was long before dawn when her mother made her way up the steep stairs to Marianne's loft.

"I kin hear you tossin' up here," Miriam whispered. "You OK?"

"Mama...there's somethin' I need to tell you." Marianne was terrified of disappointing her mother. Miriam moved across the room and sat at the end of Marianne's bed and looked at her daughter long and hard.

"I...uh...I think I'm gonna have a baby," Marianne said quietly.

Miriam scowled. "You didn't stay pure?"

Marianne shook her head. "I tried. I didn't even let him put it in, but I've been throwin' up an' all."

Miriam looked confused. "What do you mean you didn't let him put it in?"

A blush crept up Marianne's cheeks. "He kept his...dingle...uh, on the outside. It never went in."

"Did you bleed?" Miriam asked, and Marianne shook her head. "What about his spunk?" she asked, and Marianne blushed furiously.

"Well, it kinda went everywhere, but I know it didn't go inside."

Miriam's expression turned shrewd. "Then how do you know you're gonna have a baby?"

"My bubbies hurt something awful, and I've been getting sick in the mornings. But there's no fever or nothin' like I've got the flu, and my monthly hasn't come in a while."

Miriam scowled at her daughter then slowly smiled. "You've been blessed, baby. Maybe an angel didn't visit you, but you've been blessed just the same as Mary was."

Marianne knew there was probably a more likely reason but didn't want to argue with her mother. Instead she gave a tentative smile.

"We'll go to church as soon as we get back. We need to pray on this." Miriam gave her daughter a rare kiss then went back downstairs. Marianne watched her mother go then tried to get some sleep.

It was still dark when Joe arrived at the house to pick up Marianne and her parents. Still too big for the cab of Joe's truck, Howard settled in the back on a stack of cushions pulled from the couch then covered by a ratty, old afghan that had been crocheted by somebody's relative then donated to the Salvation Army.

It was a long drive, and Marianne kept glancing out the rear window to make sure her father was OK. She'd worn her nicest dress, and Joe had brought her wild flowers for a bouquet.

It was well into the morning by the time they made it into Fairhope. Marianne was curious to see where Joe grew up. The town was a mix of fine, expensive homes and trailer parks. Considering how his grandpa lived in Merwin, she wasn't surprised when they pulled up to a run-down house off a poorly maintained road.

It was a one-up and one-down duplex sorely in need of some paint. The second floor had an open space that looked like a large balcony, while the first floor had to make do with a cracked concrete slab for a patio. The yard served as both a lawn and a driveway and clearly hadn't been mowed in forever.

Joe stopped the truck just in front of the house and ran in the front door. Marianne and her family assumed they were to stay put but got out of the truck to stretch their legs after the long ride.

A few minutes later, a skinny blonde wearing nothing more than a long, dirty T-shirt stepped out onto the upper deck, a cigarette dangling from between her fingers. She squinted at Marianne through the smoke as Joe stepped out of the house, slamming the door behind him.

"Seems a boy should take care of his mother before he goes and gets himself a wife," she drawled, her hip cocked, her arms crossed under her nonexistent breasts.

Marianne blushed furiously, fully understanding the implication. Ignoring his mother, Joe stepped over to help a scowling Miriam back into the truck.

Joe's mother glared at Marianne then gave a bitter laugh. "You just remember, honey, I had him first."

Marianne climbed into the truck behind her mother, and then Joe sped off in a cloud of dust.

They went a couple of miles before anyone spoke. "She's young lookin', yer mom," Miriam said.

"She was thirteen when she had me so...yeah, she's pretty young," Joe said through gritted teeth.

Marianne could tell her mother wanted to say more but was grateful when Miriam left it alone.

They rode for another forty minutes into Bay Minette and reached the county office by nine.

They were a sorry sight climbing out of the truck. Howard had slept most of the way, and his hair stood straight up at the back of his head. It took both Marianne and Joe to help him scoot down to the end of the truck bed, and Marianne worried about him trying to walk. If he fell, there was no way any of them could get him up again.

Howard managed to stay on his feet, though, and the group followed as he slowly made his way into the Baldwin County Probate Office.

Marianne was annoyed that there were so many stares as her father walked up. *It's not like Bay Minette's a skinny town*, she thought. There were plenty of people standing around staring that could stand to lose a pound or hundred.

When they were finally inside, Harold settled onto a chair in the reception area to catch his breath, while Marianne and Joe went to get their license. It only took a few minutes, and then they waited an hour for the judge to become available. Joe had the foresight to make an appointment, but things moved at a snail's pace in the county offices.

It was almost two hours later by the time the clerk led the judge out to the reception area where they waited. Harold was too big to walk the distance to the judge's chambers, so they had to make do with the waiting area in the clerk's office. It wasn't the prettiest or most roman-tic setting, but Marianne was thrilled. For his part, Joe smiled at the floor as if too shy to look at her. Once the I dos were exchanged five minutes later, the judge signed their marriage license, and Marianne and Joe were husband and wife. The clerk and her staff all clapped as Joe gave his new wife a chaste kiss.

It was a long drive back to Merwin, and it was late afternoon when Joe dropped Miriam and Howard off back at their home then drove Marianne to the garage. She was almost shy as they entered his small room at the back. Joe stared at her as he closed the door behind them then crossed the room to kiss Marianne properly.

"I think I'm pregnant," Marianne said against his lips.

Joe looked at her in surprise. "Are you sure?" he asked as a bell rang in the garage bay. Even though he'd put the closed sign up, someone had pulled in.

Joe glanced out his door then gave a sigh. Verna Arnette had pulled her car all the way into the bay and had gotten out to pose next to it. She tapped her foot impatiently and made a big show of looking at her watch.

Joe's grandfather opened the door from the office and shuffled into the bay. "We're closed."

Verna glanced at him, irritated. "It's an emergency."

Joe opened the door and stepped out. Verna's face transformed from that of a petulant brat to a coy ingenue as she smiled at him.

"We're closed, Verna," Joe said.

"I know, silly. I saw the sign, but my car is making a weird noise, and I'm afraid something's really wrong."

Verna's smile fell as Marianne stepped out of Joe's room. "Why is she here?" Verna asked pointedly.

"Because we're closed," Joe answered.

"But why is she always here?" Verna's voice was quickly approaching a whine.

"She's my wife," Joe answered. "Where else is she going to be?"

Verna's shocked expression would have been comical if Marianne weren't worried about the trouble she might cause for them later. The Arnettes fancied themselves townsfolk, but they were just as spiteful and petty as any of the families they looked down upon.

THIRTY-FOUR

Georgia was away at college, so it was Amberlee and the Arnettes who sat on Lovey's porch while Martine wrapped a sweater around Lovey's shoulders. Her hair had grown in enough to not need a cap, but she still suffered lingering effects of the chemo.

Verna was recounting her disastrous visit to the garage. She'd already told the same story from various angles several times, and Lovey was getting tired of her voice.

"How could he?" Verna cried dramatically. "He was supposed to marry *me*. We were supposed to be together."

"I suspect he loves her," Lovey answered. "Besides, why would you think he was supposed to marry you? You weren't even dating. Just because you liked him doesn't mean he belonged to you."

Verna turned to glare at her. "What do you know about it? You're not even really from here."

Lovey gave her a long, level look. "I'm as much 'from here' as you are. I was born here, my mother was born here, and I'm pretty sure I've spent more time with Joe and Marianne than you have. He loves her, he married her, and you should probably leave them alone."

Amberlee tried to play mediator. "He probably had to marry her when he knocked her up. That's the only way girls like her can get a man."

Lovey was about to argue that comment when her father walked out onto the porch. He gave Amberlee a stern look. "Olivia needs her rest, Amberlee. Why don't you take your friends and go now."

Verna and Irma stared at Dr. Polk with their mouths gaping, while Amberlee jumped up and gave her cousin a quick hug.

"Sure thing. See you later, Lovey," she said then pushed the girls off the porch in front of her.

Samuel leaned over and kissed Lovey on the top of her cap of hair then turned and went back into the house. Lovey watched the girls quickly drive off then got up and followed him. She found him in his office, where he'd already settled in at his desk. He looked up when Lovey appeared in the doorway.

"I know they're your friends, Olivia, but I don't like those girls here. Why do you insist on having them over?" he asked as he pulled out a letter opener to cut open a stack of envelopes in front of him.

"They're not really my friends," she said by way of an answer.

Samuel paused in his task and looked up at her. "Then why are they here?"

Lovey shrugged. "I guess because they're friends with Amberlee and I have to be nice to her because of Aunt Lottie. And with Georgia gone there aren't a lot of girls my age here in town. Other than Marianne Dirkin...well I guess it's Buckley now."

Samuel looked at her curiously. "What do you mean?"

"Marianne married Joe Buckley. Amberlee said they're going to have a baby."

Samuel jumped up and moved past her. "If that's the case, I should go check on her. She needs good prenatal care right now."

"Can I go with you?" Lovey called out after her father.

Samuel turned and smiled. "Of course."

Samuel and Lovey checked at the garage first but were told by Joe's grandfather that the couple could be found at the Wooten farm, so they set off for the drive. The Wootens lived past the back of beyond, but the day was cooler than usual, so they enjoyed the trip with the windows down.

"I want you to understand that I hold no ill will toward the Arnette girls and your cousin," Samuel said tentatively. Lovey nodded but remained silent. "It's just that they are not the kind of young women I want around you."

Lovey knew that but was still curious. "May I ask why?"

She watched his profile as Samuel's expression turned pensive. "I know it seems hypocritical for a physician to not like one person over another...but they remind me of your mother," he answered. "What drew me to Merwin was the critical need for health care, and I originally thought the population to be genuine...sincere. Imagine my disappointment to have married someone who so clearly defined herself by what she considered her elevated station in the community...and thus treated others accordingly."

Lovey nodded. Her father never spoke of her mother, and her aunt's version of the woman who'd given birth to her had been grossly sanctified by her death. She had always wondered where the truth lay.

"I don't particularly care for them either," she reassured him. "I find them to be narrow-minded and judgmental...even cruel toward people they believe are beneath them." She looked at his profile as he drove. "Is that why you like the Wootens and the Dirkins so much?"

Samuel looked confused. "What do you mean?"

Lovey thought for a moment. "*I* like them because they have no pretensions to be anything other than exactly who they are. There's some nobility in that, and I respect them for it. The Arnettes and Aunt Lottie seem to spend a lot of time assessing the value of others and ranking them in some sort of rural caste system."

Samuel chuckled. "Well said. And I agree." They sat quietly for a mile or so before Samuel asked, "Where do you place yourself? If the general population of Merwin knew your true worth in terms of education...and money...they would certainly place you at the highest of their perception of social value."

Lovey shook her head. "I disagree. I think at that point a reverse elitism would come into play, and they would avoid me altogether. But to answer your first question, I don't really place myself anywhere. I'm not like anyone here, and that's neither good nor bad. To put it simply, I want the people I like to be happy and the people I don't to become the kind of people I like."

Samuel smiled. "'I think you may judge of a man's character by the persons whose affection he seeks. If you find a man seeking only the affection of those who are great, depend upon it he is ambitious and self-seeking; but when you observe that a man seeks the affection of those who can do nothing for him, but for whom he must do everything, you know that he is not seeking himself, but that pure benevolence sways his heart,'" he said quietly.

"Charles Haddon Spurgeon." Lovey smiled.

Samuel turned and smiled back at her. "Exactly."

They checked at the Wooten farm first but were told by Rachel that the young mother was most likely looking at her new house with her husband, so Lovey and her father set off again. They reached the small cluster of shacks to find the couple surveying the dilapidated houses scattered around the Dirkins' small home. Despite its own run-down state, the Dirkins' home was by far the best of the bunch. The others had pretty much fallen down, while the last one standing looked like a mild breeze might send it over permanently.

Marianne turned then smiled as they drove up. Her hand rested on the nonexistent bump in front of her, and Lovey was absurdly happy for the other girl.

Abel and Caleb Wooten were there as well, with piles of wood and boxes spilling over with nails and tools. Lovey noted that Abel Wooten bore such a strong resemblance to Silas Pritchett that they could be father and son. She wondered if Silas might have been born on the wrong side of the blanket.

Joe and Marianne walked up as Samuel pulled to a stop. "I understand congratulations are in order." Samuel reached out and shook Joe's hand.

"Thank you, sir," Joe said shyly.

Lovey gave Marianne a gentle hug. "You look like you're glowing," she said, smiling. "I'm so very happy for you."

Samuel stepped over and gave Marianne a quick look. "You are glowing," he announced. "Will you be able to come to the office for a few checkups?"

Miriam had wandered over by then and answered for her daughter. "Now we've gone over this before, Doc. Mrs. Pritchett kin care for Marianne just fine."

"I don't know about that, Mama." Marianne shook her pretty head. "With Silas gone, she's getting too far in years to be walking around all over the place."

"Where did Silas go?" Lovey asked idly.

"He took a job on one of them oil rigs in the Gulf," Miriam answered for her daughter. "He's not likely gonna be back for at least a month...if ever. Them jobs pay a lot. I know his *grandmother* is missing him."

Lovey heard the slight sneer in Miriam's voice and wondered about it.

"Be that as it may," Samuel replied, interrupting her thoughts, "I hope you at least consider getting checked periodically until the baby comes"—Samuel put his hand up before Miriam could raise her objections—"even if it's just the nurse who takes a look."

Miriam pressed her lips together. "We'll see. Maybe that'll be OK."

Samuel knew better than to push it, so he said his good-byes. Lovey gave Marianne another hug then followed him to the car.

"Hey, Doc!" Joe trotted over to where Samuel had paused just inside the open car door. "I don't want anything goin' wrong, so I'll bring her. OK?"

Samuel nodded. "That would be great, Joe. I'll take good care of her."

Joe gave a rare smile then slapped the hood of Samuel's car.

Lovey returned Marianne's wave as they drove off.

THIRTY-FIVE

Marianne watched as the Doc and Lovey drove away, a cloud of dust billowing after them like a bridal train.

"It's gonna take some time," she heard her uncle Abel say behind her. "We got harvest comin' in. If Wade could help, we'd probably be able to get it done before the baby."

Miriam snorted. "I ain't gonna count on Wade to help with nothin'. We'll just have to make do."

Abel nodded then walked over to help Caleb get support poles up on the sides of the house. Not one for construction, Joe followed behind to learn.

Miriam turned an eye on her daughter. "Why's Lovey askin' after that Silas boy?"

Marianne feigned innocence then shrugged. "I guess 'cause he was so nice to her back at the revival. Maybe she wants to thank him. She's real polite like that."

Miriam looked back at the men working on the house, but her eyes weren't really seeing them. "There's somethin' about that boy. He's lookin' way too much like a Wooten to be a Pritchett, and I don't care what that old woman calls herself—she ain't no missus anythin'."

Marianne looked at her mother in dread. "What do you mean?"

"I mean I've known Agnes Pritchett my whole life, and I ain't never heard of her havin' any babies of her own, let alone grandbabies. That woman's hidin' somethin'." Miriam shook her head then looked at Marianne. "And I aim to find out what it is."

Marianne was hopeful that her mother would either forget or just decide to leave Silas and Mrs. Pritchett alone. He seemed nice enough, and Mrs. Pritchett was so old Marianne didn't want to cause her any more grief than they already had.

Luckily, Miriam was distracted by the pregnancy, which was confirmed as Marianne's thin body started to show early. True to her word, Miriam dragged her daughter to see Pastor Tucker, who made a big show of accepting Miriam's word that her daughter carried the Messiah. Much ado was made of Marianne's burgeoning belly, much to Miriam's satisfaction and Marianne's dismay.

They would end up spending a lot of time at the church.

THIRTY-SIX

Though she didn't go to the daily worship services, Lovey attended the small Pentecostal church on, at minimum, a weekly basis when she was home. She knew her father didn't approve, but she didn't know how to describe the feeling it gave her to sit in the small wooden church and immerse herself in the sense of community it afforded her. When she was away from Merwin, she would often turn on the Christian channels on Sundays to listen to the preachers, but they were a poor substitute for the man she considered her minister. Ewell Tucker might look like a caricature of a small-town preacher, and his morals were highly questionable, but his message was less of hellfire and more of love.

It also gave her the opportunity to see the Wooten/Dirkin family without being intrusive. While most people avoided Miriam and her family, Lovey made sure she always said hello and often sat near them during services. Pastor Tucker appeared to follow suit and made a point of engaging the parish in prayer over Marianne's burgeoning belly.

Lovey respected Miriam's steadfast belief that her daughter carried the next son of God, and her presence in support of Marianne's pregnancy went a long way toward convincing the other parishioners to reserve judgment or at least wait until Lovey and the Dirkins were long gone to engage in their petty gossip.

Verna and Irma were especially hateful but were too afraid of Lovey's social status to speak out against her. Instead they launched a smear campaign against Marianne that would have made Sarah Polk proud. They spread rumors that were contradictory, though no less inflammatory. Verna put out that it was her, not Marianne, that Joe was supposed to marry, but Marianne stole him away with her pregnancy. Irma implied to anyone who would listen that Marianne wasn't really pregnant and was just faking it to get attention.

Lovey watched Marianne suffer the abuse and her heart went out to the other girl. Verna and Irma would sit near her family and make pointed comments about Marianne, her mother, and Marianne's pregnancy, purposely speaking within hearing of the Wootens and everyone else in the congregation.

Lovey tried to ignore them, thinking eventually they'd run out of steam, but the sight of tears running down Marianne's cheek drove her to intervene on the other girl's behalf. Lovey stood and walked up to the Wootens' pew and sat down next to Marianne then turned and glared at the twins. Verna and Irma flushed with anger and embarrassment but bit their tongues and kept silent for the remainder of worship. Marianne looked over and gave Lovey a grateful smile. In return, Lovey reached over and squeezed her fingers.

After worship, Lovey made a beeline for the twins, who stood with their heads together, surrounded by family members. "He didn't want you," she said loudly, and Verna again turned an alarming shade of red that was almost purple.

The other members of the congregation all fell silent and turned to watch the little group.

"*He* didn't want *you*," Lovey repeated, "and you're just going to have to get over it. And if I ever hear you say another word about Marianne or Joe Buckley again, I'll make sure everyone knows about your little problem last summer that sent you to that clinic in Jackson. How is that scorching case of herpes, anyway?" Lovey watched as Verna turned apoplectic, and then, satisfied she'd gotten her point across, turned and walked away.

Shirleen Arnette descended on her daughter, screaming questions, while the twins' father gave embarrassed smiles all around.

Marianne thanked Lovey again when she returned to where her family was standing.

Lovey smiled grimly. "Don't let them be so hateful, Marianne. You can fight back."

"I feel like I should forgive them," Marianne replied, her hand moving protectively over her belly, "and if what Mama says is true... about my baby, then I need to be a good example for him. Just like Mary was."

Lovey's expression softened. "You will be a good example, Marianne. But even Jesus would expect you to defend yourself. Hopefully the Arnettes will be quiet now, but you can't count on it. And I won't be around much longer."

"Where are you going?" Marianne looked frightened at the prospect of Lovey leaving.

Love paused for a moment then said quietly, "I have more tests coming up, and my doctors are all in New York."

Marianne's pretty face looked concerned. "Is it the cancer? Are you sick again?"

"I don't know." Lovey's usual composure broke for a moment as grief constricted her features.

169

Marianne reached over and took Lovey's hand. "I'll pray for you," she said quietly.

Lovey smiled through the tears that threatened to fall and squeezed her friend's warm hand. "And I, you."

THIRTY-SEVEN

The baby was due any day now, and Miriam was taking the last of Marianne's things next door when Howard finally woke up. He'd been drooling on the cracked Formica of the kitchen table when a massive cramp bit through his lower back. Wiping the spit from his chin, Howard looked around for his wife.

"Miriam!" he bellowed then sat still, listening for an answer. She had left snacks and a warm beer next to his hand, and her Bible still sat in front of her chair, as if she'd just stepped away. With his bulk, Howard could no longer reach the radio that sat near the icebox. He cracked open the beer and drank it in one long swallow then opened the giant bag of chips that held permanent residence on the table.

By the time he finished them, he was bored and growing more irritable by the minute. For want of anything better to do than stare at the peeling paper on the walls, Howard pulled Miriam's Bible over and opened it. As he pulled the cover open a twenty-dollar bill floated to the table. Howard stared at the bill then began to turn the pages. Between every two pages Miriam had stashed money. Howard's face grew red with fury as a small pile of bills fell onto the table. "MIRIAM," he bellowed.

"What the hell, Howard?" Miriam appeared in the doorway. "What's wrong with—" Miriam stopped at the sight of her Bible opened in front of him. A pile of the money she'd squirreled away over the last twenty years sat in front of a man who wanted nothing more than to drink and eat it all away.

Howard slowly turned and glared at Miriam. "What the fuck is this?" He gestured to the stack of bills. "Are you *stealing* from me?"

Miriam felt her own rage bubbling up. "*Stealing*? You think I'm *stealing*?" She stalked over and snatched her Bible out of his hands. "*I* make sure we have a roof over yer fat, lazy head. *I* buy food to put in yer fat mouth, so you kin sit on that massive ass and do *nothing*. I keep our daughter pure, so the Lord will find favor over her, while you don't do anything but *sin*. I take care of everything, so you kin feed yerself till yer the size of a damn WHALE, and you accuse me of *STEALING*?!" Miriam had reached over to retrieve her money when Howard clamped his meaty hands around her wrist.

"THIS IS MY MONEY!" he bellowed.

"This is *not* yer money," Miriam said in a low voice, snatching her wrist back out of his hand. "This is the money you didn't put in yer mouth. This is the money yer daughter brings home after working all damn day and her full with a baby. This is the money I bring home from sellin' the shit I scavenge out of other people's trash. Don't you dare say that this is yer money when you didn't do *shit* to earn it. I work my ass off to keep this family in the Lord's favor, and I ain't gonna let you ruin it for everyone else...*sinner*."

Howard's eyes narrowed in the fat of his face. "You think you're so goddamn holy, don't you?"

Miriam stared as he shifted his massive bulk in the chair to face her.

"That your Lord would send his son to be raised by a slut thief like you?"

She backed away as fury brought Howard to his feet.

"You think I don't know the Bible?" he growled as he took a step toward her. Miriam backed up, hitting the edge of the doorframe. "You know what they did to thieves in the Bible?"

Miriam stared in horror as Howard grabbed her carving knife off the sideboard; then she tried to dart out of the kitchen. Despite his size, Howard was too fast and grabbed her wrist again. Then in one swift move, he pulled up her hand and stabbed the knife through her palm, pinning her to the doorframe. Miriam gasped as Howard leaned into her face. *"They crucified them."*

Miriam's pain was so great she couldn't make a sound. Panting, she fell to her knees, her hand still pinned to the doorframe high above her. She stared at the blood running down her arm in streams as Howard pulled the box of beer out of the icebox. He lumbered back to his chair and fell heavily into it.

Fury washed over Miriam, and then she blacked out. When she came to she could tell by the scant number of empty cans in front of him that she hadn't been out for long.

"Let...me down," Miriam gasped, her hand throbbing.

"Why don't you pray and see if your Lord gets you down?" Howard sneered as he neatly stacked the bills in front of him.

Miriam felt her face flush with anger again. She pushed up off the floor then reached over and pulled the knife out of her hand. The pain was so great she fell to her knees again as the world went dim around her. A moment later she was able to push herself off the floor again and grabbed a towel to wrap around her hand.

Howard glanced at her out of the corner of his eye. "Get me some dinner, or I'll nail you up again."

Miriam pulled her cast-iron skillet off the shelf and lit the stove. She set the skillet on top of the flames and stared at it, waiting for the smoke to start rising from its surface. Miriam ignored Howard's grumblings behind her and stood in silence while the skillet turned good and hot. She turned the flame up as high as it would go and watched in satisfaction as the curing started to burn off.

"What the fuck, Miriam?" Howard started in on her with undisguised irritation in his voice. "What's taking you so goddamn long?" With his back to the stove, there was no way he could tell what Miriam was doing, and he was too fat to turn around to look.

With her injured right hand, Miriam lifted the yellowing pan and turned to where Howard sat. "Here you go," she said then brought the skillet down on the top of his head with every ounce of fury in her. The hot iron seared the skin on Howard's balding scalp, sending the smell of burnt flesh wafting through the kitchen. Miriam felt his skull crack under the force of her swing, but for good measure she pulled the pan back up and brought it down again. Howard fell forward onto the table, if not dead, then at least dead to the world.

Miriam placed her pan back on the stove then gathered up her Bible and the cash on the table. She glanced around the kitchen before throwing a kitchen towel at the stove's flame. If she was lucky, the walls would catch as soon as the towel caught.

Miriam moved into the other room and took a quick look around. There was so little in their meager surroundings that there was nothing she needed to take with her. Miriam sat on the faded, threadbare sofa and waited to hear the sounds of flames crackling in the other room.

It was only minutes until she spied smoke escaping around the edges of the doorframe and the room growing noticeably hotter. Miriam stood up then heard the sound of Joe's truck making its way down the gravel drive. To stall for more time, she slowly walked to the front door then hurried to the front yard as Marianne screamed, "Mama!"

Joe had pulled to a stop in front of the house he and Marianne shared but ran over at the sight of his wife screaming in front of his in-laws' house next door.

"Oh my God, Mama." Marianne hugged her mother. "What happened?"

"Yer daddy's drunk...passed out...and the kitchen's on fire," Miriam panted, feigning shock.

Joe ran for the door and stopped at the wall of smoke in front of him.

"Joe...don't!" Miriam cried after her son-in-law.

Joe ignored her and went in, pulling his T-shirt over his nose. The smoke in the kitchen was almost black, and Joe could barely see his father-in-law slumped in his chair, empty and full cans of beer scattered across the table in front of him.

Joe moved over and shook Howard's shoulder with enough force he almost knocked Howard out of the chair. "HOWARD! YOU GOTTA GET UP! HOWARD?" But Howard was completely out.

Joe turned and glanced at the flames that flowed up the walls then pulled his father-in-law as hard as he could. Even sitting, Howard was far bigger than Joe, and it took all his strength to pull him off the chair. Howard teetered for a long moment then came crashing down on top of Joe, pinning him to the floor. With five hundred pounds of dead flesh on top of him, Joe couldn't even breathe.

Outside, Marianne and her mother stared at the door, waiting for Joe to show up. When he didn't appear, Marianne ran to the side of the house to see if she could see him through the kitchen door. She screamed when she saw that the walls on that side were completely engulfed in flames. She ran back and started filling buckets with water from the yard pump, but her mother stopped her.

"You gotta go to the farm and call the fire department," Miriam ordered.

Marianne shook her head wordlessly. "I can't run that far," she said, her hands going to her belly as if to protect her baby.

"Then take Joe's truck," Miriam said. "I'll stay here and get water on the house."

"But I only know how to drive a little bit," Marianne protested.

Miriam grabbed her daughter by the shoulders and shook her. "You gotta do this, baby. I know you can."

The sound of a large pop coming from the kitchen sent Marianne flying to Joe's truck. She struggled with the ignition but managed to get it started and into gear.

Miriam ran over to grab a bucket then stood and watched her daughter drive away. When she was sure Marianne was out of sight, Miriam dropped the bucket, crossed her arms, and watched the house burn.

Blind to anything but her need to get help, Marianne accidently bypassed the farm and drove straight toward town. The roads twisted beyond her ability to navigate them, and she found herself on the graveled shoulder instead of the blacktop.

Panicked, she turned the wheel too sharply, sending the truck off the road and into the culvert that ran alongside the road. The truck stopped violently against the bottom of the creek. Marianne stared as the windshield came up at her fast. Then everything went dark.

Marianne sat back in a daze, staring at the starburst that had appeared in the windshield. She could feel what she thought was the warm water of the culvert running down the side of her face. Her hand went to her head and came away red with blood. She slowly turned and stared at the ground next to her then pushed open the door and stepped into the freezing water. Mud sucked at her feet, making each step harder and harder. She finally made it to the hardpan and stopped to catch her breath then climbed up the embankment to the road. Just ahead of her was the garage and the Stop 'n' Save. She knew the garage was empty, so she stumbled to the door of the store, where she collapsed, panting, in the doorway. Mr. Martin ran up to her, his expression at first annoyed, then alarmed. "Girl, what 'r' you doin'?"

"Far," Marianne slurred, pain rolling across her belly. "Far."

Then the world went dark again.

THIRTY-EIGHT

Lovey stared out the window next to her bed. Her room was high enough that she could see over the tops of the trees next to the hospital. It was a much different view than her room in the New York hospital. New Jersey was much prettier than she'd thought it would be. A snowstorm had moved through, leaving behind a blank canvas upon which the sun could work its art. Ice had frosted the trees, turning them to glass. With the sun shining, the effect was dazzling and almost painful to look at.

She could hear her father in the hallway speaking with her oncologist. Her last surgery was scheduled to take place shortly. They would be taking everything this time, including her ovaries, an oophorectomy. Lovey thought it was a ridiculous word for something that would so profoundly affect the rest of her life.

She knew she would be facing more chemo and hoped that Smith College would allow her to delay her freshman year until next fall. If not, then maybe she could go to Ole Miss after all.

Lovey glanced over when the door to her room opened. One of the nurses came in, followed by the anesthesiologist and a handful of residents. Martine sidled in behind them, moved to the side of the bed, and took Lovey's hand.

"We're going to get you ready now." The nurse smiled. Lovey nodded then turned back to the window as the sun moved behind a cloud sending the forest into shadow and washing the landscape back to gray.

THIRTY-NINE

The hospital staff quietly cleaned the room of the bloodstained detritus of childbirth as Miriam stood nearby, her grandson in her arms. He was a carbon copy of his mother, who lay dead in the bed in front of him. Miriam stared at her daughter's body while her grandson blinked myopically at the world around him.

"We're going to move her downstairs shortly," the nurse said quietly. "The coroner comes in tomorrow. He'll do a postmortem exam to determine how exactly she died. Do you want us to call the funeral home for you?"

Miriam stared at the young woman. "We take care of our own."

The young woman looked startled. "Don't you want them to do a proper funeral?"

"We take care of our own," Miriam repeated.

The nurse shrugged then opened the door to find Abel and his sisters framed in the doorway. With a backward glance at Miriam, the nurse fled the room.

Abel stood watch at the door as his sisters moved to the bed to prepare their niece for burial. Dorcas gently rolled Marianne's body to the side and pulled off all the stained bed linens, while Rachel filled a basin with soapy water. Dorcas pulled off the drawsheet last, leaving Marianne on the plastic sheet that protected the mattress. Together, they gently bathed her body until all traces of the last few hours were gone. All that remained was a slight swelling at her hairline, which betrayed the injury that killed her, and the line of stitches where her baby had been excised.

The room was silent and thick with grief as Rachel and Dorcas dressed Marianne in a plain, white cotton gown then covered Marianne's body with a clean sheet of muslin. They painstakingly hand sewed the edges until she was enveloped in a shroud of white.

"She's done," Rachel announced quietly, coughing away the tears that choked her.

Abel silently moved from the door and crossed the room to Marianne's bed then looked over at Miriam. "You ready?" he asked her quietly. Miriam gave him a single nod.

Abel leaned over to pick up Marianne's body then carried her out of the room, with Rachel and Dorcas following. Miriam wrapped her grandson in another blanket then followed them out.

"Wait," the nurse called out. "You can't go. She needs to be processed by the coroner...wait!"

Abel, Rachel, and Dorcas ignored her on their way to where Caleb waited in the truck. Miriam stopped and turned to stare at the young woman for what was the longest minute in the nurse's young life then turned back and followed her family out the door.

The nurse moved to the glass door and stared as the truck drove away, not realizing she would be the last person to see the Wootens for a very long time.

***

The phone was ringing at the house in Annapolis. Lovey's father dropped the last of her luggage by the front door then stepped into the small office at the front of the house to answer it. Lovey picked up the extension upstairs at the same time. She was about to hang up when she heard the voice of June Dampeer, the head nurse from the hospital, on the other end. It was more than extraordinary that June would be calling them from Merwin, so Lovey listened in.

"Hey, Doc." June's voice sounded somber, but Lovey could hear a trembling of nervousness under her tone. "I just wanted to give you a heads up. The Dirkin house burned down last night. Appears there was a kitchen fire. Howard Dirkin and the boy from the garage both perished."

Lovey put her hand to her mouth to stifle the sudden sob that burst from her throat. Her anguish was so keen she almost missed what June said next.

"The reason I'm calling is the Dirkin girl was brought in by Gary Martin with what looked like a head injury. John Evans tried to stabilize her, but it was too late. He opted to save the baby, but we lost the girl."

Lovey closed her eyes against the sudden burn behind her eyelids. Her face constricted in pain at the loss of such a lovely girl who had been so kind to her.

"There must have been elevated intracranial pressure," Lovey heard her father murmur. "I'll take a look at the coroner's report when I get back."

"That's just it, sir." June sounded hesitant. "The coroner didn't get a chance to do a post on her. The Wootens came and picked her up before he could make it in. Howard Dirkin and the boy are both done though."

"Take him out to the house," Samuel suggested. "They'll probably have her laid out there. They're old-fashioned like that."

"We tried that, sir. In fact we just got back." Lovey heard June take a deep breath. "They're gone, sir...the whole family. It's like they disappeared."

"They can't have disappeared," Samuel protested. "They have to be somewhere."

"The house is empty, sir." June's voice got quiet, and Lovey had to strain to hear her. "Del Wooten's pa owned a bunch of swampland in the Atchafalaya Basin. If they went there, nobody's going to be able to find them."

Lovey heard her father sigh. "Keep me posted then. I'll be back in a few days."

"Sir?" June called out before Samuel could hang up. "I forgot to ask, sir. How is Lovey?"

"She'll live," Lovey heard her father answer. "Unlike poor Marianne."

THE SON

FORTY

Merwin looked little changed as Lovey drove through the town. Maybe there were a few more fast-food restaurants and an already-aging Wal-Mart, but for the most part the only things that had grown in last decade or so were waistlines and the poverty rate.

Lovey parked in front of her father's small postwar rancher. Little had changed there too. At some point her father had had the house painted from its original red to white, but that was long enough ago that the white had aged to more of an eggshell. Lovey felt terrible when she realized how long it had been since she'd visited her father. He usually came to her at the house in Annapolis, but his health was failing him, and now the mountain was coming to Muhammad.

Martine met her at the door. She looked tired but still lovely. Only the barest hint of gray threaded the dark brown hair she'd pulled into a messy bun. There were faint lines around her eyes and a heavier one between them, as if she'd spent the last few years frowning. Lovey knew the stress of caring for her father had taken its toll on Martine, who had never failed in her unofficial service to the Polk family. Lovey had made sure that she was compensated, and Martine didn't know it, but Samuel had long ago bequeathed his entire estate to her, including the money he'd inherited from his father.

"How is he?" Lovey asked as she gave Martine a hug.

Martine shrugged. "Some days are better than others," she answered, returning Lovey's embrace. "How are you?"

It was Lovey's turn to shrug. "I'm fine. Some days are better than others."

Martine chuckled then led Lovey to the back of the house where her father's bedroom overlooked the woods behind the house. The first thing to hit her was the overwhelming stench of urine underscored by a subtle note of decay. The second was her father's appearance.

Samuel Polk had changed greatly in the years since Lovey had been gone. Always thin, he was now skeletal, his body ravaged by the deadly combination of cancer and Alzheimer's. He'd been diagnosed with stomach cancer before his mind started to go, so the habit of taking chemotherapy was so ingrained that long after his doctors discontinued the therapy, he still insisted on taking his pills. Martine had taken to giving him placebos just to keep him calm. As the Alzheimer's progressed, even swallowing became a forgotten skill, and he now survived on a feeding tube. With the cancer now in his lungs, Lovey had come home to oversee the fulfillment of his final wishes. Once his mind forgot how to breathe that would be the end.

Lovey sat on the bed next to her father and took his hand. He didn't stir except to gasp at the ceiling like a fish out of water. Lovey held still until he settled again. "What is his respiratory rate?" she asked quietly.

"Twenty-six per minute," Martine answered.

Lovey put her fingers to her father's wrist and watched the clock. "His heart rate is about ninety," Lovey said. Martine nodded. "Any coughing?"

"Not yet."

Lovey gave her father a kiss on the forehead then left the room behind Martine. "Is it worth it to drive around town?" she asked.

Martine shrugged. "It hasn't changed much, chère. There's one of those tent revivals at the old church," she offered. "I remember how much you liked those."

Lovey smiled.

She pulled her suitcase into her old room and opened it. She'd packed light but had included clothing appropriate for meeting with her father's Mississippi lawyers the next day. She pulled out a lightweight shirtdress and some low heels and changed her clothes.

When she was done she stepped into the small bathroom attached to her room and pulled her hair into a low ponytail and added a pair of her grandmother's earrings.

Martine had resumed her place at Samuel's side, a book in her hands. She looked up when Lovey stopped in the doorway.

"I'll be back soon so you can get some rest," Lovey promised.

Martine smiled. "Take your time, chère," she said then nodded to the small daybed that had been set up in Samuel's room. "I can rest here."

Lovey looked at the other woman then crossed the room and fell to her knees in front of her. Martine startled as Lovey wrapped her arms around her in an uncharacteristic show of affection.

"Thank you, Martine," Lovey said quietly. "You're the best mother a girl could have."

Martine returned the hug then laughed as she wiped the tears that had come to her eyes. "Go on," she urged, "before you really get me crying."

Lovey gave her a quick kiss then left.

The small Pentecostal church had seen more recent improvements than Lovey's father's house, due in large part to the considerable donations she made on an annual basis. There was a small addition along the side, which looked like either offices or classrooms, and the parking lot had been freshly graveled and framed by railroad timbers. A recent coat of white paint made the small wooden church look almost new. A huge tent had been set up in the neatly trimmed field next to the church, and several tables stood nearby offering lemonade and baked goods. These tables were manned by smiling ladies that Lovey only marginally recognized. Several said hello as Lovey walked by. She smiled and nodded but kept walking toward the tent. There were a few people already sitting, enjoying their refreshments. Lovey found a chair at the end of a row somewhere near the middle.

Though the revival wasn't due to start for a few minutes, a band was already playing. From the parking lot it had sounded slower, more hymnlike, but as the minutes passed the music grew livelier and more energetic. The change was subtle enough that people weren't rushing for their seats, but it was a definite cue that the revival was about to start.

Lovey recognized a few faces making their way into the tent. Several were startled to see her but recovered enough to nod their hellos. Lovey smiled back then turned to watch the revival preachers take the stage at the front of the tent. She was surprised at the sheer number of speakers. She recognized one of them as a notorious charismatic exorcist. It was going to be a long night. She settled in as a singer opened the service with one of her favorites. The young woman had a voice like an angel, and the musicians were really good as they quietly eased into a version of "Yes, I Know."

People moved more quickly, and the seats soon filled with the bodies of the faithful. Lovey's eye was caught by the slow, deliberate walk of a heavyset woman on the far side of the tent. She was supported by a thin boy who led her to a seat at the end of the front row. Lovey was surprised to see the boy take a place on the stage near the preachers. She'd heard of child prophets, but she'd never seen one before.

The musicians stopped, and the crowd sat silently as another singer stepped to the center of the stage. Behind her a group of women crowded the stage and lined up along the edges of the tent.

This singer was even younger than the first, and the tent was remarkably silent for the number of people who had congregated under its massive roof. With a voice as clear as a bell, the girl began to sing "Down to the River to Pray." With each new verse, more singers would join in. Lovey had goose bumps, and tears threatened to spill from her eyes. By the end of the song, all of the women were singing, and Lovey felt a sense of peace and love fill her heart. The effect of all those voices singing a simple spiritual was overwhelming for her, and she fought the urge to get up and leave. She felt a tap on her shoulder and turned to see an ancient woman, seated behind her, holding out a tissue.

"The Lord comfort you in your time of struggle, dear," the woman said, her voice shaky with age. "He'll see your daddy home when it's time."

Lovey let the tears spill and smiled at the woman's kindness. "Thank you," she whispered, taking the tissue.

The older woman nodded then sat back as the first speaker took the stage.

As far as revivals went, it was fairly standard stuff. Some of the speakers stuck to traditional preaching, explaining the gospels and defining what was called the Great Commission, which Lovey thought was a grand way of saying evangelism. Some had adopted the prosperity gospel, which Lovey believed to be a deliberate misinterpretation of the Bible used to manipulate the faithful into giving up their hard-earned money in the hopes of earning God's favor and eventual monetary blessings. Lovey deeply disapproved of their message. Other speakers were fully invested in the supernatural side of their faith, with several attempts at healing and speaking in tongues.

After every preacher, the collection plate went around with exhortations over the loudspeaker using Bible quotes to remind everyone of their tithes. Lovey put in an initial donation then shamelessly passed on all the other plates. One of the ushers threw a quote from Proverbs at her. "'One gives freely, yet grows all the richer; another withholds what he should give and only suffers want,'" he scolded.

Lovey answered with a verse from the book of Matthew. "'Beware of practicing your righteousness before other people in order to be seen by them, for then you will have no reward from your Father who is in heaven,'" she told him, smirking as she handed back the plate. The usher scowled at her but mercifully avoided her for the rest of the evening.

The singers were performing when one of the preachers put out for an altar call. Lovey sat politely and watched the sick and penitent make their way to the stage for physical and spiritual healing. The sun was beginning to set, and moths were starting to circle the lights above them, several landing on the canvas ceiling only to take off and circle again. Lovey glanced at her watch and was making a move to leave when the singers stopped and the young boy stepped to the front of the stage. The crowd quieted in anticipation of hearing the boy preach. Lovey was curious enough about the boy prophet that she sat back down to listen

His dark eyes moved over the crowd then seemed to settle on some-one in the middle of the tent. Then he began to speak.

While other preachers ranted with words of fire and brimstone or sang their sermons with a formulaic cadence, the boy's voice was quiet, almost hypnotic. People leaned forward, their eyes wide as the young prophet cast his spell over the faithful.

"Every year Jesus's parents went to Jerusalem for the festival of the Passover. When Jesus was twelve they went to the festival according to custom. After it was over, Jesus stayed behind in Jerusalem. But his parents didn't know. They thought he was somewhere in the family, traveling with them, so they went on for a whole day. When they stopped and looked for him, they did not find him. So they traveled back to Jerusalem to search for him and found him at the temple, sitting with the teachers...asking them questions. His parents were upset. They said, 'Son, why have you treated us like this? We were scared when we couldn't find you.'

"Jesus answered, 'Why were you looking for me? Didn't you know I would be in my Father's house?'"

The boy paused, his eyes moving across the crowd. "As Mary and Joseph sought Jesus, Jesus sought the Lord. Jesus sought to learn from his Father. Not the father who was raising him, but the Holy Spirit that had brought him to earth to save the world. But before he could save the world, he had to learn...just as you're all here to learn."

The boy paused again, and the crowd seemed to hold a collective breath in anticipation of his next words.

"All of you are here because you are searching for something. Some are searching for meaning, and some are searching for hope, but all of you have come here because you need something. You think you need healing or a better job. But what you really need is love. God's love.

Some people here will tell you the only way to God's love is to give them your money."

Lovey hid a smile behind her hand. The other preachers frowned at the boy, who had paused again, as if searching for a way to finish his thought.

"But they're wrong. God does not care about your money. He doesn't care about what kind of car you drive or house you live in. You can give all of your money to the tithe, and God won't care. You can't buy your salvation, because Jesus has already died for your sins. You can't buy your way into God's love...because he already loves you. You can't become a friend to the church, because God is already your friend. You can't pay someone to tell you what God wants from you, because you already know. God has already put it in your heart. You only have to open your heart and listen."

One of the preachers stepped over and laid a fatherly but firm hand on the boy's shoulder and whispered in his ear, his other hand moving the microphone away, broadcasting a dull thud over the sound system.

"But I'm not done," the boy protested. The older man commandeered the mic then cued the music to begin, while another preacher led the boy off the stage. An usher came up and took the boy and the woman who'd accompanied him out of the tent.

"Let's hear it for Josiah Buckley, ladies and gentlemen," the older preacher announced with false cheer. It was ironic that the collection plate went around right at that moment. The singers launched into a rendition of "He Has Made Me Glad," but, unsurprisingly, the plates came back with less. Whether it was because of the boy's words or the fact that most people were out of money by then, Lovey didn't know or care. She made a mental note to speak with Ewell Tucker about the invited speakers.

She stood and made her way out of the tent then circled it until she saw the boy standing near a bench where the woman rested. At first Lovey thought the boy was only about ten, but she realized as she got closer that he was probably a teenager...a very young-looking teenager.

As she approached the woman turned and looked at her. Lovey was stunned to recognize Miriam Dirkin. Other than her size, which had grown considerably larger, and the threads of gray in her dark-red hair, she was remarkably unchanged.

"Mrs. Dirkin?" Lovey asked, even though she was sure.

"Well if it isn't Lovey Polk," Miriam's voice scratched. Her face may not have aged much, but her voice sounded like it had lived many lifetimes.

"May I sit?"

Miriam nodded at the bench next to her.

"It's been such a long time," Lovey began then paused, unsure of what to say next.

Miriam smirked. "We've been around."

Lovey smiled politely. "I mean since Marianne died."

Miriam's smirk fell from her face for a moment, revealing the depth of pain still present. She looked away but said nothing.

Lovey glanced up at the boy, who had laid a protective hand on his grandmother's shoulder. He was the perfect combination of his parents, with his father's bright, blue eyes and his mother's coloring.

"My name is Lovey. I very much enjoyed your preaching. I know you don't know me, but I was a friend of your mother's."

Miriam looked at her sharply but let the comment about the relationship stand. She could not dispute that Lovey had liked her daughter and had been kind to her during her short life. "I heard you were sick," she said instead.

Lovey nodded. "I had cancer. It's been gone for a long time now."

"And now yer daddy's sick."

Lovey nodded again.

Miriam looked away again. "I'm right sorry about that. Yer daddy's always been real nice to me."

"Yes, ma'am. He had a lot of respect for you and your family. He felt terrible that he wasn't at the hospital when Marianne was brought in."

Miriam's face clenched. "Too long ago to keep on about it."

"Yes, ma'am," Lovey replied, chastened by the other woman's desire to keep her daughter to herself. "Well I just wanted to pay my respects," she said as she stood.

Miriam said nothing but nodded somewhat in Lovey's direction. Lovey accepted the snub gracefully but held her hand out to the boy. "It was very nice to meet you, Josiah."

Josiah gave her a beaming smile. "Nice to meet you too," he replied politely. "I hope we see you tomorrow too. There's gonna be music."

Lovey smiled and nodded but didn't promise anything. With a polite nod she turned and left.

It was full dark by the time Lovey pulled up to her father's house. Only a single light shone through the front window, and Lovey knew that it came from a small lamp just inside the front door. Over the years, it had been left on, waiting for the last person to come home to turn it off. Lovey let herself inside and switched the light off then made her way back to her father's room.

The smell of urine had lessened, and Lovey assumed Martine had given her father a sponge bath while she was gone. Another small lamp was on in his room, and Lovey could see by its glow that Martine had fallen asleep in the chair next to his bed. She moved over and shook the other woman awake. Martine startled at first then smiled sleepily.

"Nothing happening here, chère," she yawned. "How was your church?"

"It was fine," Lovey answered. "Go to bed. I'll stay here."

Martine nodded then, after a quick check on Samuel, left the room. Lovey pulled her nightclothes out of her suitcase and stepped into her father's small bathroom to change out of her dress. When she returned she bypassed the chair and settled on the small daybed instead. Other than a lone cricket outside in the grass and her father's stertorous breathing, the world was silent.

Lovey closed her eyes and held her hands clasped in front of her. Though she appeared to be praying, she had long since given up talking to God. Instead she thought about the boy's message. She knew she was searching for something at the revivals and church services she frequented. But it wasn't until his words fell on her open ears that she realized she had been searching in the wrong place. She'd spent most of her life away from Merwin, but she always came back when she was troubled. And now she was truly troubled. And prayer had failed her.

She had prayed for knowledge and comfort, for acceptance, for love. But it was the thing she could never have that she most wanted, and the loss was keenly felt. She had been blessed with enough wealth and education to be able to do anything she wanted, except have a family. All because of a small bottle of pills.

Lovey opened her eyes and stared at her father, wondering if he had known the risks when he'd given his wife the drugs that were supposed to prevent miscarriage. She figured he probably didn't. His concern for his wife did not extend to ensuring that she was well cared for. He had done the least by her and, as a result, left his daughter to pay for the sins of her mother. Then he'd sent her away under the guise of some ill-defined desire for her to have better opportunities elsewhere, which belied his self-proclaimed egalitarianism.

Now he was dying, and she would never know why he'd really sent her away or if he was sorry.

Lovey closed her eyes and let her father's rhythmic breathing lull her to sleep.

FORTY-ONE

It was midmorning when Lovey returned from her meeting with the attorneys. She was satisfied that her father's wishes were in place and wouldn't be challenged when his time came.

She let herself into the house and walked to the kitchen where she found Martine preparing her father's nutrition bag for an early lunch.

"Did everything go well?" Martine smiled at her as she injected vitamins into the bag.

Lovey nodded. "Everything went well. Now it's just a matter of time."

Martine nodded at the teakettle. "I boiled you some water in case you wanted tea. If you can wait a moment, I'll get it for you."

"I'll get it in a minute," Lovey answered then sat quietly and watched the older woman. "Can I ask you a question?"

"Of course, chère."

"Why didn't you and my father ever get married?"

Martine was so startled she almost dropped the syringe. "Why would you ask something like that?" she stammered.

Lovey tilted her head and smiled at the woman who'd taken care of her since infancy. "I know when I left for prep school you stayed here... long before Dad started to get sick."

Martine started to interrupt, but Lovey put her hand up. "I know you kept your apartment but only for propriety's sake. Were you sleeping together the whole time?"

Martine looked away, visibly embarrassed. "Your father would be mortified if he knew you were aware of our...situation."

Lovey smirked. "I think our relationship would have been a lot healthier if it had been more open."

"That wasn't really my decision, Lovey." Martine looked sad. "I think your father was just trying to protect you."

"From what?"

Martine sighed. "He sent you away because he didn't want you to turn out like your mother. He was afraid that if you spent too much time with her family, they would have more influence on you than he would."

This was the first time someone had actually said it out loud. And even though she knew her father thought very little of her mother's family, it was still startling to hear the depths of his contempt. "Was she really that bad?" she asked.

Martine thought for a moment. "Your mother was...difficult. She wore different faces depending on who she was talking to. And she could be cruel to people she thought were beneath her." Martine paused, searching for words. "It...surprised him. And when it looked like her last pregnancy was viable...instead of rejoicing in it...your father felt trapped. I think he would have divorced her if she hadn't died. Of course I only know his side of it. Your mother cannot speak for herself."

"But that doesn't excuse how he's treated you," Lovey protested.

"Perhaps he was afraid of making the same mistake," she answered as she cleaned up the remains of his meal preparation. "And there was another woman at one point."

Lovey was surprised. "Really? Who?"

"I don't remember her name. She was a visiting physician at the hospital. It was about the time you left for school."

Martine stared down at her hands, and Lovey could tell the memory was painful.

"He was quite taken with her, and she really was a more suitable match for your father. So when it looked like it was becoming more serious, I left here and moved back into the apartment." Martine picked up the TPN bag. "I'll be right back. I don't want him to have to wait too long."

Lovey stared after Martine's retreating back. She'd known nothing about this other woman, and she wasn't happy to hear that her father had been anything less than considerate to the woman who'd raised her.

When Martine returned it was clear that she wanted to change the subject, but Lovey had one more question. "What happened to that other woman?"

Martine shook her head. "I don't really know firsthand. They seemed like they were going to get married; then suddenly she was gone. The next day your father came to my door and said that you were coming back for a short visit and asked me to come back. So I did. I didn't find out until much later that one of the nurses overheard your father and the woman arguing about you."

Lovey was surprised. "Me? I'm hardly a topic worth breaking up over."

"I don't know about that, Lovey. You're quite precious to some of us." Martine smiled. "Anyway....June said it sounded like your father wanted to bring you home, but the woman wanted you to stay away. Or even to send you to school in Europe. And I know your father would not allow you to go so far away."

Lovey doubted that but left that one alone. "Why did you come back to him?" she asked instead. "You could have had your own family...your own children."

Martine shrugged. "I did have my own child. Maybe I didn't give birth to her, but she was still mine." She reached out and took Lovey's hand. "We live the lives we're given, chère. There's only so much we can change before fate or God steps in and changes our path for us."

Lovey stood and moved around the counter to give Martine a long-overdue hug. "You were a great mother," she said quietly before letting the other woman go.

Martine laughed as she wiped tears from her eyes. "Then it was all worth it."

Martine resumed her vigil next to Samuel, so Lovey drove up to the church early enough to speak with Ewell Tucker before the other parishioners arrived. As she pulled into the parking lot, she noted that the only car there was a modest and practical Ford Explorer. At least her donations weren't padding the preacher's lifestyle.

Lovey walked into the small church and found it empty, so she wandered into the new section of the building where he'd installed meeting rooms and offices. A long hallway cut the addition in half, and she could hear the faint sounds of gospel music coming from an open doorway at the end. She followed the singing to a small, neatly kept office where Ewell Tucker sat behind a plain oak desk, writing something on a yellow legal pad in front of him. A dusty, unused computer sat near his elbow.

"You know it's a lot faster to do that on the computer," Lovey joked from the doorway.

Ewell looked up, startled. "Oh, ha," he laughed. "I can't quite get the hang of that thing. It's just a big, ole paperweight in here."

Lovey smiled then sat in the small wooden chair in front of his desk.

Ewell put a hand to his thinning, artificially black pompadour and gave her his biggest smile. "So when did you get in? I would have made a point to stop by and pay my respects." Ewell's smile faltered as he realized his faux pas. "Oh, and please accept my condolences for your father. How is he?"

Lovey's smile turned rueful. "He's dying, and we both know he wouldn't have welcomed you in the house anyway. But that's not why I'm here. I was at the revival yesterday, and I was surprised at the number of preachers who were spouting that prosperity nonsense. And when Josiah Buckley preached the truth of the gospel, they cut him off."

Ewell frowned. "Lovey, you know that every preacher is going to have his own message. I can't tell them what to preach."

Lovey leveled a look at him. "You and I both know that the people of this town would give up their last dime if it meant the possibility of everlasting wealth."

Ewell said nothing, but his expression turned stricken.

Lovey continued. "And the boy's message was in keeping with the goal of this church's ministry. It would be a shame if your funding were to be reallocated to a ministry that truly embraced values that best served the people of Merwin."

Ewell put his hands out. "What would you have me do?"

"You might not be able to tell them what to preach, but you can tell them what *not* to preach...and let Josiah Buckley speak. The people here need to hear his message."

Ewell rubbed his face, looking all seventy of his years despite the improbable black of his hair. "Today's a music day anyway, with only a little bit of message between singers. I'll see what I can do."

Lovey graced him with a smile. "I know how persuasive you can be. I have faith that today's preaching will be more appropriate."

Ewell gave her a strained smile as she stood to leave. "I'll see you outside," Lovey said over her shoulder as she left Ewell to finish his own sermon.

By the time Lovey made her way outside, most of the music groups were already there setting up the stage. Some of the parishioners had arrived, the men to take charge of parking and the women to set up refreshments and lunch items. Lovey nodded politely to the people who greeted her then took a seat inside the tent.

One of the musicians seemed to take note of the growing audience and started a piano version of what sounded like "O Could I Speak." Somehow the simple hymn made the sun shine brighter and the air feel clearer. When he was done, a small group of singers took the stage amid the men setting up equipment and started an acoustic version of "The

Old Rugged Cross." Lovey closed her eyes and let the music transport her.

Ewell Tucker had been wise to invite mostly folk and bluegrass singers and bands. Lovey preferred the simplicity of traditional hymns. She'd been to many revivals, both large and small, and the music was as varied as the preaching. She'd found that as well composed as contemporary Christian music was, it often lacked the heart of traditional revival music. The more modern music couldn't compare to "How Great Thou Art" or "His Eye Is on the Sparrow." She especially loved it when the children sang, their pure voices conveying an innocent faith that was often lost with the adult singers.

As the crowd moved into the tent, the preacher who was serving as emcee took a microphone and spoke to the congregation. Lovey ignored him, instead watching Josiah lead his grandmother to the same seat she'd sat in the day before. He was dressed in another suit and looked like a miniature version of the adult preachers on the stage.

Lovey noticed that several preachers were seated with the crowd instead and that they were, coincidentally, the same gentlemen who'd pitched the prosperity gospel. Ewell Tucker knew what side his bread was buttered on, and Lovey figured that since she was the donor that had most likely paid for the revival in the first place, he was going to do whatever she dictated.

The revival proceeded as planned, with long musical performances peppered with shorter and more general sermons and readings. The collection plate was suspiciously absent. Instead a donation box sat at the entrance to the tent, manned by one of the ushers from yesterday. He glared whenever someone passed the box without putting in a donation and was all smiles to whoever stopped.

Lovey sat through several preachers, waiting for Josiah. When they called an intermission, she wondered if they were going to skip him altogether. Miriam seemed to have the same thought and questioned the preacher serving as emcee. Lovey could hear her calling out to ask when they were going to let Josiah speak clear across the tent. She could see Ewell Tucker rushing over to intercede.

Lovey got up and moved over to where Miriam sat. Miriam glanced at her then resumed hectoring the preacher, while Josiah stood nearby, hovering protectively near his grandmother.

"We been waitin' all day, and you still haven't let him preach. You afraid of what he's gonna say?" Miriam's expression was mulish.

When it looked like the man was going to argue, Lovey put her two cents in. "I agree. I've been waiting to hear Josiah speak, and I want to know why you aren't letting him participate."

"Now, ma'am." The preacher put his hands up in a gesture of surrender, but his tone was stern. "This doesn't concern you."

Lovey's eyebrows went up. She was about to challenge that remark when Ewell quickly whispered into the man's ear loud enough that Lovey's suspicions were confirmed. She had, indeed, paid for the revival, including the honorariums the preachers charged to participate. She watched as the other man's eyes widened in surprise then narrowed with avarice. When he looked at her again, she knew he was seeing nothing but dollar signs.

"Well we can certainly make some time for young Brother Buckley," he said with false generosity.

"I think you can do better than that," Lovey answered coolly. "In fact, I think young Brother Buckley should preach for the remainder of the day. And since each preacher receives the collections after each sermon, the collections for the day will go to him."

"But...but...we can't work for free," the preacher stammered as his face turned red. "I mean we need to get out God's message."

Ewell looked like he was about to interrupt but stopped when Lovey put up her hand. "Perhaps you don't know your Bible as well as you should, but the Gospel is free. I believe we've heard your message loud and clear. You've already been paid, and I'm sure you have already distributed the collections from yesterday. I'd like to know how much went to Josiah."

The preacher had the good grace to look uncomfortable. "Child prophets don't usually get paid, no matter who he says he is," he lied. Miriam glared at the man.

Lovey appeared to think about that. "And how much of the collection have you paid to this church?" she asked.

This time he couldn't lie. "None."

"Then I think you're done," she announced as Miriam looked on triumphantly. "Josiah will preach for the rest of the day." Lovey looked at the boy. "Do you think you can do that?"

Josiah nodded.

Lovey turned to Ewell. "Please take possession of the donation box. Whatever's in there by the end of the day will go to Josiah's ministry." Ewell nodded then ran to do as he was bade.

Lovey turned back to find the preacher staring at her, his face turning an alarming shade of red. "You may go now," she said dismissively, watching with satisfaction as he stomped off dragging the rest of the preachers with him.

Ewell returned with the donation box and placed it on the stage then took the microphone to serve as emcee for the remainder of the day.

Lovey sat next to Miriam to wait for Josiah. "Does everyone always do what you say?" Miriam asked in wonder.

"Yes," Lovey replied simply.

Miriam sat and chewed on that while Lovey watched a family of teenagers perform. "I heard you was a doctor like yer daddy," Miriam said after a few minutes.

"I am a doctor but not like my father," Lovey answered. "After medical school I joined a medical mission rather than go into private practice."

"I don't know what that is," Miriam admitted.

"If something happened somewhere in the world, like a flood or an earthquake...I would travel with a team of other doctors and nurses to provide care for the people affected. And since my field was emergency medicine, I would be part of the first team to go. We would set up triage centers where we could treat people with the worst injuries."

Miriam looked horrified. "That sounds awful."

Lovey glanced at her. "It can be. But it's necessary."

They sat quietly for a bit and enjoyed the music. Then as the singers finished, Ewell got on stage and tapped the microphone. "Today we are blessed to have Brother Josiah among us. You may remember him from yesterday, and I am very happy to announce that he has graciously accepted our invitation to be the featured speaker for the day," Ewell announced, motioning for Josiah to come to the center of the stage.

Josiah walked confidently to the center and accepted the microphone with an adult grace, but instead of speaking, he stood quietly and looked over the crowd. People had been speaking during his introduction, and the hum of quiet conversations had underscored Ewell's speech. As Josiah stood there, voices fell away until complete silence filled the tent. Even the birds in the trees were silent.

"'The harvest is past, the summer has ended, and we are not saved,'" he began.

A collective intake of breath could be heard from the crowd, and Lovey felt goose bumps rise. It was strange and uncomfortable to hear a child recite such a serious verse. She unconsciously leaned forward to hear what Josiah would say next.

"The people of Jerusalem had disappointed God. They were disloyal...they were faithless...they put wealth over worship and paraded false idols before the God who had delivered them from slavery. They celebrated the blessings but not the benefactor. They rejoiced in their success but not in their sponsor. It wasn't until after they'd broken their relationship with God that they mourned his punishment. They turned their back on God and in their rebellion suffered his wrath. When they sought him for salvation, he was not there. Because it was too late."

Josiah took a breath, and the crowd took a breath with him.

"You must ask yourself, have you turned away from God? Have you been disloyal to him? Faithless? When good things happen do you pat yourself on the back...or tell yourself you must have good luck?

"When we live our lives, God must be first. When we wake up in the morning, we must praise him for his gift of life to us. When we eat our meals, we must thank him for our bounty. When good things happen, we must acknowledge his hand in our lives. We were given life. We were given a world in which to live our lives. And no matter how big or how small our lives are, we must be thankful that God has given us another day. Every day that we live in his glory we must rejoice in his grace...in his light...and in his love. Amen."

It was a gentle admonition made more powerful and compelling coming, as it did, from a mere child. The crowd was silent; even the music groups stood stunned by the quiet rebuke. Ewell seemed to remember himself and jumped up to motion to a group of children who stood waiting to perform. Josiah stepped down off the stage and sat in the empty seat next to Miriam.

"That was a lovey sermon," Lovey said. Josiah smiled his thanks.

The music continued. Lovey stayed for another of Josiah's sermons, this time a recitation of the beatitudes. When he was done, Lovey thanked him then turned to Miriam. "I need to be getting back to my father. I just wanted to say that Josiah did very well. You should be very proud of your grandson," she said. "He's quite gifted as a speaker."

Miriam nodded. "Thank you. Please give my best to yer pa."

Lovey smiled. "I will."

FORTY-TWO

Lovey's father lingered for another week, his condition worsening a little each day. Lovey and Martine remained by his side until the afternoon he took his last breath.

Though he may have set himself apart socially in the town, he'd treated just about everyone at one time or another. The news of his passing spread quickly, and it wasn't long before former patients and coworkers from the hospital began stopping by to pay their respects and drop off the requisite casserole or baked good. Lovey received them all with grace and took the opportunity between visits to finalize his funeral arrangements.

Long before his decline, Samuel Polk had made it very clear that he did not want a funeral, nor did he want to be buried next to his wife. Never a religious man, Samuel Polk had eschewed traditional funeral arrangements and had requested that his remains be cremated and scattered wherever Lovey saw fit to cast them. Despite his wishes, Lovey caved somewhat to the customs of the community and agreed to a memorial at the hospital where her father had spent his entire adult life but drew the line at displaying his ashes, which the gossips of Merwin declared to be scandalous.

She furthered the scandal by refusing to host a reception at the house and receiving condolences at the hospital instead. This was more out of respect for Martine than anything else, since the majority of the visitors were little more than busybodies looking to snoop into her surrogate mother's private life. The town was already speculating on Martine's fate now that Samuel Polk was gone. Lovey had already heard rumors that Martine was being kicked out of her father's house, that Samuel had secretly married her, and even the insane rumor that Martine was really Lovey's mother, despite the fact that the entire town had attended her mother's funeral just after her birth.

That's why it was such a surprise when the door buzzed late that afternoon. Martine and Lovey glanced at each other in surprise, and then Lovey got up to see who it was. She opened the door to see Miriam Dirkin and Josiah standing on the front step dressed in their best church clothes. Josiah held a bouquet of wild flowers.

"Miss Miriam!" Lovey said in surprise. "Come in!"

Miriam ducked her head then entered the house with Josiah in tow. She glanced around the small living room that had changed very little since Sarah Polk died.

"Please sit." Lovey gestured to the faded, green chenille sofa. "Would you like some iced tea or lemonade?"

"Tea please. And Josiah can have some lemonade," Miriam answered, settling her considerable bulk deep into the cushions.

Martine nodded then went back to the kitchen to fetch drinks. Lovey was grateful that despite its ugliness, the sofa was comfortable and took a seat at its far end. "We missed you at the memorial," Lovey said.

Miriam shook her head. "I liked yer pa just fine, but I'm not fixin' to hang around that bunch iffen I don't have to."

212

Lovey nodded. "I know what you mean. I try to tell myself they mean well, but the truth is I'd rather not spend time with some of them either."

Miriam looked at Lovey in surprise but was spared from answering as Martine walked in bearing a tray of glasses.

"Yer that girl that wouldn't let me name my girl Mary," Miriam said to her.

Martine winced. "I'm sorry for that," she answered. "It was none of my business what name you gave her."

Miriam accepted the apology then shrugged. "Just as well. She was still the mother of God, no matter what her name was."

Martine didn't know how to respond to that, so she simply smiled then left the room.

Lovey waited and watched as Miriam took a long drink from her glass. She could see Miriam's mind working behind her eyes and wondered why they had come.

"I want to thank you for what you done for Josiah," Miriam began. "We been traveling with that group for a while, and they ain't honored him the way they should. We ain't seen a dime before that day, so for that I thank you."

"You're welcome," Lovey answered. "I'm glad I could help."

Miriam turned to her grandson and handed him her glass. "I could use some more ice, boy. Run and ask that Martine if she kin make this a little colder."

Josiah accepted the glass. "Yes, ma'am," he answered then ran off.

Miriam turned to Lovey. "He's a good boy," she said, and Lovey nodded in agreement. "He's a special boy," Miriam continued. "More than most people realize. He's got a message, and I know it comes directly from God. I been tryin' to help him get his message to the people, but it's been hard. People don't always take to kid preachers. They think they're just copyin' their elders. And some I seen, it's true. They just scream like they're preachin', but you can't understand a thing they say."

Miriam paused and listened to Josiah talking to Martine in the kitchen. "Anyway, we came today because we need yer help."

Lovey looked confused. "My help? With what?"

"I can't help him the way you can," Miriam began then paused. Lovey could tell she was struggling with her words. "And I'm not gonna be able to help him for much longer. My breathin' and my insides have gone bad, and I don't know how long I got till they just stop workin'."

"That's terrible," Lovey said. "What exactly is wrong?"

Miriam snorted. "I been this fat for too long. That's what's wrong. But other than the angina, the worst thing is the diabetes and the OHS. But you probably know what that is."

"Obesity hypoventilation syndrome." Lovey nodded. "You really should be on oxygen right now."

"I sleep with it, but we're moving around too much to be draggin' a tank everywhere," Miriam answered. "'Sides, with everythin' else that's wrong with me, it's only a matter of time before the Pale Horse comes for me."

"What about Josiah?" Lovey asked. "Does he know?"

Miriam shook her head. "He knows I'm not in the best of shape, but he don't know how bad it really is. That's why I need yer help. I don't want him by himself when my time comes."

Lovey was confused. "But what about your other family?" she asked. "His uncles and aunts? Surely they'll want to take him when that happens."

"They'd take him in, sure. But they can't help his ministry like you can," Miriam insisted. "He needs someone of faith to make sure his message is heard by everyone. My family won't leave the farm let alone travel out of Merwin for the revival circuit."

Lovey started to protest, but Miriam waved at the air in front of her as if physically dismissing Lovey's objections. "Listen. I know you understand about Josiah. You've been one of the faithful since you were a little girl. I saw you at the church. You came even when it was just by yerself. I know you understand who Josiah is...who he *really* is."

Lovey wanted to discuss Josiah's origins further but said nothing as Martine brought Josiah back in with a fresh tray of drinks and a bowl of ice for Miriam.

"Thank you so much," Miriam said, pulling the ice aside and adding a good handful of cubes to her glass.

Lovey didn't want to continue the conversation in front of Josiah, and it looked like Miriam didn't either. "Can I think about it?"

Miriam nodded. "We're stayin' at the farm till we can find another revival tour. Most don't want kid preachers, and Josiah ain't ready to start his own church."

Josiah smiled. "I've still got some growing to do."

Miriam set her glass on the tray and stood. "Thank you for the tea. Please accept my sorrows on the passin' of yer daddy."

Lovey stood as well. "Thank you. I'll be talking to you soon," she replied, extending her hand.

Miriam shook her hand then pulled Josiah to the door. Before they could leave, Josiah suddenly turned back. "Will you come to the revival tonight? It's not a regular one, but they're gonna let me preach before they leave, since we're not going with them."

Lovey smiled. "Sure. I'd love to."

Josiah returned her smile. "We'll see you there then!" he said then followed his grandmother out.

Martine looked at Lovey as she closed the door behind them. "What was all that about?"

"She came to ask me to help her with Josiah's mission as a preacher," Lovey answered then picked up the tray and carried it into the kitchen.

Martine followed, her expression confused. "Isn't he a little young to be a preacher?" she asked.

"It's unusual but not unheard of," Lovey said. "Most preachers have a sponsor, whether it's a church or an individual. I guess she's asking me to be his sponsor."

"How do you feel about that?"

Lovey thought about the question for a moment before answering. "I don't know how I feel about it. I like his message. Miriam has certainly raised him to do right by the world, and I respect that. I guess I'm not sure how I feel about taking responsibility for someone else's child."

Martine's smile was wry. "Oh, it's not so hard. I think you'll find it to be quite rewarding."

FORTY-THREE

Though the revival tour had ended while Lovey was caring for her father, Ewell Tucker had offered to fill a hole in their schedule by allowing them to return for a Saturday evening. Lovey questioned the wisdom of this since that particular revival group had just been in Merwin and wallets were still empty from their last visit.

Since it was an evening revival, Lovey left early to visit with Ewell, who admitted that several of the preachers speaking that night had stayed near Merwin for reasons other than the saving of souls. Some were shopping for more permanent situations, and since prosperity churches were popping up all over the South, several appeared to have taken a keen interest in Merwin and had stayed after the revival to get the lay of the land. Lovey had been so preoccupied with her father's illness and passing that she hadn't been aware of them until now. They were all going to be there tonight, so she'd have a chance to see who they were dealing with.

Lovey walked out of the church annex to see people driving up for the night's revival meeting. Despite the large tent that remained, it was going to be less of a show without all the bands and singers that had been there previously. She was surprised to see most of the speakers present and wondered if all of them intended to preach. It wasn't unusual for revivals to go into the wee hours of the morning, but with the number of speakers there, they were likely to go into the middle of the next afternoon.

Lovey turned the corner of the building and stopped short at the sight of all the motor homes that ringed the church property. They'd been well hidden before and for good reason. She counted no less than six motor homes, each costing several hundred thousand dollars. Lovey wondered how many people went hungry so their pastor could surround himself in luxury. As she watched, several motor homes discharged well-dressed preachers and their equally well-dressed wives. One woman in particular was beautifully dressed in what looked like an authentic Chanel suit.

Thoroughly disgusted, she made her way back to the tent and saw Josiah sitting on the stage with the other preachers. Miriam sat in the front row surrounded by empty seats, as if people were giving her a wide berth. Lovey sat down next to her and returned Josiah's wave.

"I hope they let him preach tonight," Miriam said with a warning in her voice.

Lovey agreed but said nothing. One of the preachers turned and stared at her pointedly. Lovey recognized him as the man who'd interrupted Josiah's first sermon. She leaned over to Miriam. "Miss Miriam," she whispered, "who's that man sitting in the front there? The one with the black suit."

Miriam looked over then scowled. "That's Pastor Bennett. He's the one that originally invited Josiah on the tour. He just bought a church in North Mississippi and called it the Abundant Life Center or some such nonsense. The only thing abundant about his ministry is his wallet and his backside. We stopped there at the beginning of the tour and damned if his own church had to pay him his honorarium."

Lovey saw the man in a new light. "I saw their motor homes parked along the back of the property. They certainly do travel in style," Lovey said.

Miriam nodded. "Those 're them prosperity preachers. The others use just plain campers or their cars."

Lovey sat back and considered this. She knew the prosperity movement had been around for a long time, but it seemed like when the economy went bad, the promise of quick riches blinded the faithful to the Gospel as Christ had taught.

She knew that the idea that the words we speak determine the blessings God bestows was originally embraced by a preacher named Kenneth Hagin who later clarified his theology to discredit those preachers that had bastardized his philosophy. Hagin's theology of wealth as a redemptive blessing was reinterpreted into the seed-faith message that stated money and material wealth were blessings from God and if they were donated to the ministries of men like Oral Roberts and Jack Coe, God would multiply whatever was given and more back to the donor. Unfortunately, Hagin's criticisms fell on deaf ears, and the prosperity movement spread through the preachers like a virus. They used the improvement in the economy as a sign that God had found favor with their efforts, and everyone flocked to get a piece of the holy pie.

Lovey found the practice especially heinous since it targeted the poor who were so desperate for any means to escape their poverty they were willing to give up their last dime to the church. Tithing demands went way beyond the 10 percent the Bible recommended when pastors insisted their flock attend high-priced ministry-sponsored conferences and buy endless supportive media materials. It was a mind-boggling operation, and the ridiculousness went further when the preachers went on television to testify to the effectiveness of their twisted theology by showing their expensive cars and private jets as evidence of God's favor.

She wasn't surprised when Pastor Bennett took center stage and opened with the notorious quote from the book of John that had sparked the whole movement.

"'Beloved, I wish above all things that thou mayest prosper and be in health, even as thy soul prospereth,'" he began with a thunderous roar.

Lovey glanced at the crowd and was not surprised to see rapt faces throughout.

"What does God want for you, friends? Does he want you to go hungry? Does he want you to go barefoot? Does he want you to live without a roof over your head? Tell me...does he?"

Lovey glanced behind her again and saw heads shaking in the crowd.

"He does not. Because God...loves...you. God wants you to be successful. Didn't the Lord say to Moses, 'But remember the Lord your God, for it is he who gives you the ability to produce wealth, and so confirms his covenant, which he swore to your ancestors, as it is today'? Did he not say in Proverbs, 'Honor me with your wealth and with the first fruits of all your produce, then your barns will be filled with plenty, and your vats will be bursting with wine'? The Lord *loves* you. The Lord *wants* you to have a life filled with plenty. But the Lord loves a cheerful *giver*. The Lord says *your* gifts...*your* blessings...come from him and are to be sacrificed to him, or it is nothing but selfish...personal...gain."

It was a brazen misuse of the Bible, and Lovey had no doubt that the condemnation of personal gain did not extend to the pastor himself. She feared for the parishioners who had been raised to believe that if their pastor said it was so, then it was their sworn duty as Christians to fulfill that promise. She wondered how many in the crowd understood that these passages did not refer to monetary wealth and predated Christ's teachings by over a thousand years.

"Let me tell you a little story," he began. "When I was a boy, I had nothing. I went to school barefoot because my daddy could not afford to buy us shoes. My brothers and I went hungry when my mother couldn't scrape together enough for even a small bowl of stone soup."

Miriam snorted next to Lovey. "What a load of hooey," she said under her breath. Then she leaned over and whispered, "That boy grew up on a farm. He sure as shit didn't grow up hungry. His daddy made a pile of money off them farm subsidies, so I'm pretty sure the boy had shoes too."

Lovey shook her head but didn't answer as the preacher continued his story.

"Do you know why we went without?" he asked then waited until the crowd shook their heads in response. "Because my ma and pa were godless people. They did not follow the scripture. They did not understand that Christ compelled them to give of their gifts before enjoying them. Jesus said that poverty is God's punishment for sins. And they had sinned by not following his word."

Lovey's eyebrows went up. This was an outright lie and deliberate reversal of the Gospel of Luke. She sat in fury as his blasphemy continued.

"But even as a young prophet, I knew," he announced. "I knew the wages of sin would be my tummy going empty...my feet cut by the stones on the road as I walked to school. When I was a little boy, the Lord spoke to me and told me that redemption could only be found in sacrifice. So when my momma and daddy pretended at faith, I practiced it. I took my hard-earned money from picking corn with the migrants on our farm, and I gave it to my pastor, and I told him, 'Pastor? I want to atone for the sins of my father, for they have been visited on me.' And do you know what my pastor told me? He said, 'Son, you have avoided the sin of greed, and God will find favor with you.' And you know what? He *did*."

Pastor Bennett paused, and the congregation took a collective breath. "*He did*, my friends," he continued. "For that one small act of faith, the Lord has rewarded me tenfold...no *thousandfold*. The Lord has blessed me with a fine home. The Lord has blessed me with a beautiful family. The Lord put diamonds on my wife's ears and a Cadillac in my garage because I *gave*. I *gave* all I had before I could *receive* all I have now. So when that widow woman comes up to me and gives me her last two cents, so too will she *receive*." Then he held up his Bible and shouted, "Can I get an AMEN?" And the crowd complied. "I can't hear you, and the LORD can't hear you. I *said* can I get an AMEN?" The response was deafening.

Lovey watched the preacher walk the stage back and forth, ranting into the microphone, working the congregation into a frenzy.

"WHO'S GONNA BE THE FIRST?" he shouted into the mic. "WHO'S GONNA BE THE FIRST TO SHOW GOD THEIR WILLING SACRIFICE?"

Lovey turned and stared in shock as a well-dressed woman jumped up, waving her checkbook, screaming, "I WILL! I WANT TO GIVE TO MY LORD!"

It was a con, plain and simple. The woman who'd jumped up was the same woman Lovey had seen exiting the motor home. No one else in Merwin wore Chanel.

By the time the crowd had divested itself of its last dollar, the furor had died down. People were already tired and needed a break, but the speakers continued. Pastor Bennett was followed by a healer then a charismatic exorcist, and both used scripture to announce long and exhausting altar calls for the purpose of healing and cleansing. Once again, this altar call was met by a group of well-dressed women who were followed by the more familiar faces of Merwin. Lovey marveled at the carefully orchestrated way these preachers coerced people into participating.

And as they had during the earlier revival, the organizers ignored Josiah in favor of more profitable preachers. Lovey despaired of the people hearing Josiah's message before it was too late. They were being told by men they trusted that God wanted their money, and there was no way they were going to let a fourteen-year-old boy tell them otherwise.

Lovey was exhausted by the time they let Josiah take the stage. To see so many people taken in by these shameless grifters was depressing. She barely looked up when he accepted the mic and walked to the front of the stage. His expression was a mirror of Lovey's, both sorrowful and tired. He looked over the crowd silently as the voices fell away.

"'Beware of the teachers of the law,'" he said quietly. "'They like to walk around in flowing robes and love to be greeted in the marketplaces and have the most important seats in the synagogues and the places of honor at banquets. They devour widow's houses and for a show make lengthy prayers. Such men will be punished most severely.'"

He paused to take a breath then continued. "Beware the men who stand here in front of you. They like to walk up here in fancy suits and sit high above you on the stage. They take your money because they tell you that if you don't give them everything, you are a sinner and God won't bless you. They don't pray for you. They're not really here to save you. The money you gave them won't feed the hungry or help the sick. The money you gave them will buy them another car or help them build a bigger church, so more people will come and give them all their money, so they can buy more cars and build

bigger houses, and they'll put walls around their houses, because
they don't want anyone hungry or homeless coming up to their front
door asking for help."

Josiah continued despite the sounds of outrage coming from
behind him. Ewell Tucker placed himself between the other speakers
and Josiah so the boy could finish. Josiah only had one more thing left
to say.

"Such men will be punished most severely." Josiah turned and
stared down the men behind him. "For it is a sin directly against
one's neighbor, since one man cannot overabound in external riches
without another man lacking them...it is a sin against God. You
sinned against God when you took money from these people. You
sinned when you gave witness that your houses and Cadillacs were
blessings from God. You bought those things for yourself with the
money that people like these gave you. They will go hungry so you
can buy your wives diamonds. They will be homeless so you can buy
another car."

Josiah turned back to the crowd, which had fallen silent, and
said simply, "I will pray for you." Then he handed Ewell the microphone and left the stage. Lovey helped Miriam up, and the three left
the tent.

Miriam had made it to the bench just outside the sanctuary when
she had to sit and catch her breath. "Well...it looks...like...we're on our...
own," she panted.

"I'm sorry, Grandma." Josiah looked close to tears. "But I couldn't
say anything else."

Miriam pulled her grandson over and gave him an awkward hug.
"It's OK, boy. What you said...was right...and good. I'm proud...of you.

You can still...preach. I juss...have to stay...put for a little while...till I feel better. Then we'll juss have to find...a way."

Lovey watched Miriam comfort her grandson and made a decision. "I think I can help with that."

FORTY-FOUR

Miriam's health continued to decline, so Lovey and Josiah left her at the Wooten farm with her family, and Lovey took over managing Josiah's ministry. They roamed the South looking for another situation but felt the fallout from Josiah's confrontation when they tried to join another revival tour. Even with Lovey's assurances that Josiah's ministry did not require an honorarium or even a portion of the collection, they found Pastor Bennett had soured many of the churches in the area on Josiah's message. Too many people were so invested in the prosperity nonsense that they didn't want to risk discouraging their flock from making their tithes. Months and months went by without a single invitation. Lovey persisted, dividing her time between homeschooling Josiah and marketing his ministry to any church that would listen to her.

It took one brave preacher, a giant of a man named Brother Balfour Guthrie, who'd been one of the charismatic exorcists at the revival, to break Bennett's curse. There was no love lost between Guthrie and Pastor Bennett, whom Guthrie had fallen out with over the distribution of the collection. Brother Guthrie thumbed his nose at Pastor Bennett and invited Josiah to speak at his church.

Lovey was wary at first, but during their visit to Brother Guthrie's small but well-cared-for church she found that he was not only dedicated to the cleansing of souls but also hosted a soup kitchen and women's shelter. He even opened his sanctuary to the homeless when the weather was cold. His congregation was small but friendly, and Josiah's preaching was met with mostly positive responses.

Brother Guthrie's endorsement opened the door for Josiah to preach at other churches across the South. Though most were either faith healers or exorcists like Brother Guthrie, the offers were trickling in. Lovey found their congregations small and poor, but they embraced Josiah joyfully, and that's all that mattered.

It was at the last stop in their minitour that Lovey noticed a few familiar faces in the crowd. Without realizing it, Josiah was attracting followers.

Josiah had just finished preaching at a small church near Bogalusa, Louisiana, when they were approached by a young man. The young man stopped in front of Josiah, his smile guileless and friendly. At first he looked to be only a few years older than Josiah's now sixteen years, but on closer inspection, Lovey realized he was more likely in his twenties.

"Hey, that was a great sermon, Brother Buckley," the young man said in a strong Alabama accent. "I been tryin' to find y'all for a while now, an' here you are!"

Lovey watched Josiah pull his mask of pastoral responsibility on. He did this whenever a parishioner approached him, and Lovey marveled at his ability to easily assume the role of shepherd to his flock.

"Thank you," Josiah answered and held out his hand. "What's your name?"

"Harley Boyd," the young man answered, giving Josiah's hand a firm shake. "It's nice to finally meet you. I been trying to follow your tour, but it ain't really been announced anywhere."

Lovey reached out and took the young man's offered hand. "I'm Lovey Polk. I'm sorry, but it's not really a formal tour," Lovey answered the young man. "Josiah preaches wherever he's been invited. We usually go back to Merwin when he's not preaching."

"Right, right." Harley nodded. "That's what I thought. Damn shame though—pardon my language—'cause they's others who've been followin' you too."

"Really?" Lovey was surprised.

Harley nodded again. "All kinds of people need ministerin' who ain't got the money to pay them other preachers."

Josiah's expression turned angry. "The Gospel is supposed to be free."

Harley nodded soberly. "That's why they been followin' you. They know who you really are. They know you care about more than their money. So where you think you'll be goin' next, so I can tell them?"

Josiah looked at Lovey, who answered. "We don't have a visit booked yet, but you can tell the others Josiah will be at the First Pentecostal back in Merwin for now."

Harley beamed. "Well that's great! I'll tell the others. It was real nice meetin' y'all," he said then walked away.

Josiah watched the departing back of the young man then turned to Lovey and said, "If any man will come after me, let him deny himself, and take up his cross, and follow me.'" Then he turned to greet the other parishioners walking out of the church.

They returned to Merwin late that afternoon. Lovey dropped Josiah off at the Wooten farm and, seeing Miriam taking some air on the front porch, stopped and got out to check on her. Miriam's blood pressure was up, and her eyes were showing signs of macular edema from her diabetes. Lovey urged Miriam to see the doctor but was waved off. When she offered to treat Miriam herself, she was waved off again. There was an odd smell to Miriam, but Lovey knew better than to ask about it. She knew as she was driving away from the farm that Miriam was giving up.

Instead of going home, Lovey drove the short distance to the church to see if Ewell was there. She was pleased to find him outside mowing the fields that surrounded the church building, so she sat on the front steps to wait until he was done.

Lovey stared out over the fields in front of her and pondered the issue of how to manage Josiah's ministry. Invitations to preach had run out, even from preachers who weren't proponents of the prosperity gospel. Josiah's austerity message had cut deep enough into their tithes that no one wanted to risk their church funding on the boy, regardless of his following and the rumors of his status as the Messiah. Lovey knew she could impose on Ewell for a time, but at some point they would need a more permanent solution.

She was so lost in thought she didn't realize that Ewell had finished mowing until he hailed her from across the gravel lot. "Hey, Lovey," he said, sounding genuinely pleased to see her. "Haven't seen you in a coon's age. You want some tea?"

Lovey smiled at the older man and noted that he looked thin. "Sure. I'd love some," she answered, standing to follow him into the church.

Ewell skipped his office and went to a small kitchenette to grab a pitcher of iced tea and a couple of glasses then motioned for Lovey to follow him back into the sanctuary.

"It's cooler in here," he said by way of explanation, and when they stepped into the darkened room, Lovey agreed.

Ewell pulled over a small table that usually held hymnals and placed it next to the front pew. He poured them each a tea then sat and looked at Lovey expectantly. "So how's our Brother Josiah doing with his ministry?" he asked politely.

Lovey regarded the older man before answering. Up close she could see his previously robust body was indeed sagging from what could only be a sudden weight loss. His skin looked sallow, and pure white showed at the roots of his deeply dyed black hair.

"He's doing well," she answered. "But what about you? Are you feeling all right?"

Ewell gave her a crooked smile. "You noticed, huh?" he asked, and Lovey nodded. Ewell set his glass down and took out a handkerchief to wipe the sweat that beaded his brow. "Sixty years of them cancer sticks finally caught up to me," he said by way of an answer.

"You have adenocarcinoma?" Lovey asked but not really as a question. She was surprised when Ewell shook his head.

"No, the other one. Mezzo-something. The one on them commercials."

"Mesothelioma?"

Ewell nodded. "Yeah. That's it. Doctors asked a bunch of questions about what kind of work I did before I started preachin'. They're thinkin' it's from when I was workin' the factories before I found God."

"The smoking doesn't help either," Lovey said.

"No, it don't," Ewell agreed. "Anyway, you ain't here to talk about me. What's going on?"

"Josiah just finished preaching in Bogalusa, and our invitations have dried up."

Ewell absent-mindedly patted the breast pocket of his shirt, looking for cigarettes that were no longer there. "Well he's certainly welcome here."

"Thank you." Lovey smiled. "I appreciate that, but we can't impose on you indefinitely. We're going to have to figure something else out."

Ewell looked thoughtful. "There's a church near Collinsville that's losing its pastor. And he's had some serious financial problems. The elders have all jumped ship and found themselves another church. I'm pretty sure he's lookin' to sell."

Lovey considered that. "I'm not sure Josiah's ready for his own church. He's only sixteen."

"That he is. But havin' his own church would give him bona fides... make people sit up and take notice. It's something to keep in mind."

"What about you?" Lovey asked. "You really need to take care of yourself right now."

Ewell shrugged. "I figure I've got some time still. And I got a young man coming in to spell me when I'm feeling poorly. He's lookin' for a permanent position, but I'm not quite ready yet."

Lovey was alarmed. "Who's this young man? Does he understand the mission of this church?"

Ewell waved her words away before she'd even finished. "Now don't get yourself all worked up. He's a good sort. Knows his Gospel and knows this church isn't about cleaning out anybody's bank accounts."

Lovey knew she'd have to meet this young man before she'd feel comfortable continuing her stewardship of the church, but she kept silent. Ewell was looking tired from the conversation, and she didn't want to tax him any further than necessary. "I don't want to keep you," she said as she stood up. "Thank you for the tea and for the suggestions. I'll let you know what we're going to do."

Ewell nodded then waved as she let herself out. He remained sitting in the pew, and as she left she heard him launch into a fit of coughing. She could tell by the wet, choking sound of his cough that he was much sicker than he'd let on.

FORTY-FIVE

True to his word, Ewell let Josiah come in as an informal member of the clergy. And as a result, his flock was fuller with the followers who'd come to see Josiah preach. Lovey sat at the back of the small church and marveled at the sight of so many new faces. Harley was there, and he'd brought with him an older woman and what looked like her family. A young woman sat nearby whom, from her lost expression, Lovey assumed had come with Harley and his friends.

The day before Lovey had gone to Collinsville to look at the church Ewell had mentioned. It was a carbon copy of the one she was sitting in but had a great deal of acreage and a few small cabins and larger buildings attached to the property. It looked like it had been intended as a Bible camp, but the listing agent had let slip that the church had let its permit expire at about the same time the church's pastor fell into financial difficulty.

And Collinsville was a nice town. More prosperous than Merwin, it was scattered with fine homes, and the town itself seemed well cared for. The church property was far enough outside town that there shouldn't be any issues with the townsfolk. Most of the churches in town were Baptist, with a couple of Methodist churches sprinkled in. Lovey knew they probably wouldn't pull a congregation from the town, but that was OK. Josiah really needed a home base that he could minister out of that would provide him with enough preaching credentials to warrant his own tour.

Lovey knew she was going to buy the property but still questioned her responsibility to the boy. She believed in his ministry, but she wasn't his mother. She wasn't his anything. And even though Miriam had asked her to sponsor him in his ministry, Lovey knew she couldn't take the place of his own family. It was a dilemma with no clear answer. For once she simply didn't know what to do.

Ewell's protégé had finished his sermon about saints and sinners, and Lovey felt good that when his time came to assume leadership of the church his philosophy would hold to the standards she'd set for Ewell Tucker. And more importantly, the people of Merwin wouldn't be poorer for his message.

Everyone stood as the band started to play "Take the Lord with You," but Lovey kept to her seat in the back. Her mind was troubled with her thoughts, and she wasn't feeling the pull of the music like she usually did. It was a lively song, with the faithful on their feet and clapping, answering the call-and-repeat nature of the song with enthusiasm.

Harley turned around and smiled at Lovey, who returned his smile but demurred when he beckoned her to join him. He shrugged then turned back when Ewell took the stage to sing praises over the lyrics of the song. He might be pushing seventy, but he could still wind up the crowd like a man half his age.

Lovey was enjoying his show when she sensed someone sliding into the pew next to her. She glanced over then startled when she realized it was Silas Pritchett.

"Well look at you," he said, smiling at her. Slight crow's feet crinkled his black eyes, and his black hair had a couple of streaks of silver in it, but otherwise he looked exactly the same. Speechless, Lovey stared at him as he turned back to watch Ewell shake it like an early Elvis.

"I didn't think I'd...we'd ever see you again," she said quietly.

"I'm sorry I've been gone so long," he said as Lovey stared at his profile. "Sometimes life gets in the way of your intentions."

The music ended, and Lovey turned her attention to the pulpit, where Josiah was stepping over to accept the microphone from Ewell. He gazed out over the congregation and waited until the voices fell away.

"'What do you think?'" he began quietly. "'If a man has a hundred sheep, and one of them has gone astray, does he not leave the ninety-nine on the hills and go in search of the one that went astray? And if he finds it, truly, I say to you, he rejoices over it more than over the ninety-nine that never went astray. So it is not the will of my Father who is in heaven that one of these little ones should perish.'"

Josiah paused and looked into the eyes of the people in front of him then continued. "Before each and every one of us are two paths. One path is dark, full of dangers. The other is light, the safest steps that God has put before us. When we go astray, when we leave the lighted path, we stray from God and his plan for us. And even though that path is dark, so dark that we can't see where to step, a light still shines for us. Like a beacon in the night, God shows us a way back to the lighted path. We only have to make the choice to return. But sometimes we don't choose to return. Our journey on the dark path has been so long that we fear stepping into the light. In the light people will see us...will see how far we've fallen. In the light we see ourselves, and we are ashamed. But like that lost sheep, God rejoices in our finding; God celebrates our return. Because he loves us. Because we are worthy of salvation, God leaves that light on for us. We only need to walk to it."

Unlike other sermons where the crowd offered witness when the spirit moved them, the faithful remained silent during Josiah's sermon. His voice fell upon them like a blanket of love and comfort.

"Let us pray," Josiah said softly, and all heads bowed in unison. Lovey put her head down and closed her eyes. She felt Silas's hand move across her lap, and then his fingers entwined in hers.

"Precious Father, Blessed Son, let us never waver from your light. Even through the darkness give us direction to your holy kingdom that we may bathe in the warmth and glory of your love. Amen."

Silas squeezed Lovey's hand then smiled at her when she opened her eyes. "He's really good," he said quietly as the music started to play again.

Lovey nodded, still struck dumb by the warmth radiating through Silas's hand.

"Are you staying at your dad's?" he asked, and Lovey wondered if it was out of politeness or purpose. It had been so long since she had seen him, he was little more than a stranger to her.

"My father passed away," she said.

"I heard about that." Silas's expression turned sad. "I'm really sorry, Lovey."

"Thank you," Lovey replied. "It was expected. But to answer your question, yes, I'm staying there for the time being. I'm looking for a more permanent position for Josiah, and the property available has a house attached, so I'm thinking about moving there."

Silas's eyebrow went up. "You're buying a church? That's very generous of you."

Lovey smiled. "I think the Lord's light is shining on that particular path."

"I'm between jobs right now, if you'd like me to go with you and inspect the property," Silas offered. "Might not hurt to have a second pair of eyes. And Harley there works in construction. He could check out the buildings for you."

Lovey was surprised. "How do you know Harley?"

Silas shrugged. "I've run into him at a few revivals."

Lovey thought about his offer. It couldn't hurt, and it would save her the expense of hiring an engineer. "I'm going back there tomorrow, if you'd like to come with me."

Silas smiled. "It's a date."

FORTY-SIX

The next morning, Lovey stepped out of her father's house to find Silas and Harley leaning against a huge, black four-door pickup truck in front of the house.

"Hey, Miss Lovey," Harley drawled. "I hope it's OK if I tag along. Silas said you might be lookin' at buying some property. I could let you know what kinda shape the buildings are in."

Lovey stepped up to the two men. "It's absolutely OK. The church is outside Collinsville. It has a small camp with cabins and some larger buildings attached. I haven't been in any of the buildings, so the Realtor's going to meet us there with the keys so we can see what we're dealing with."

"Sounds good." Harley opened the passenger's door and held out his hand to help Lovey up. Once he'd settled her, he took the backseat as Silas got behind the wheel. Lovey handed him the address, and Silas put it into the truck's GPS.

The drive to Collinsville was less awkward than Lovey thought it would be, as Harley filled the silence with stories about other revivals he'd been to.

"The worst was this one just outside Gulfport. Oh Lord, I walked in with my paycheck...walked out with nothing but air in my wallet. That collection plate went around like a hooker at a banking convention...oh...uh, sorry, Miss Lovey."

Lovey chuckled. "It's fine, Harley."

Silas pulled off the road and onto the drive that led to the church itself. An older man with a belly that looked like it was in the advanced stages of pregnancy stood waiting by his car as they pulled up and parked.

"Well, hello, Miss Polk. It's good to see you again," he boomed.

"It's good to see you too, Mr. Swilley," Lovey replied then gestured behind her. "These are my friends Silas Pritchett and Harley Boyd. They're here to inspect the property for me."

The Realtor shook hands all around then hitched up his belt. "Well, very good then. Let's take a look."

The property was much larger than First Pentecostal's lot. The small, white wooden church sat at the front, closest to the road, and was surrounded by a flat grass lot bordered by tall hardwoods. A dirt road ran past the church through the trees that hid the camp from the road.

They walked up to where the Realtor held open the front door to the church. When they stepped inside Lovey saw it was an older version of First Pentecostal, with beamed ceilings and hardwood floors. The pews were light oak and looked like they hadn't been cleaned in years. A floor-to-ceiling cross hung on the back wall and was the church's only ornamentation.

"So the church building was built in 1930," said the Realtor, "and it hasn't had any additions put on it, though the HVAC was updated a few years ago. There's a small public bathroom to the right and what we call a sacristy at my church, or where the Bibles and candles and things would be kept, just to the left there."

They looked around, and after a few minutes, Harley looked over at Lovey and nodded. "Dirty as all heck but looks sound," he said, and Lovey agreed.

The Realtor led them back out and suggested they drive to the camp at the back of the property. Though there was a path that cut through the trees behind the church, Lovey doubted Mr. Swilley's stamina, so she nodded. Silas, Lovey, and Harley followed the Realtor's car through the trees then stopped at the first house.

Lovey stepped down from Silas's truck and looked around. Other than the sound of the wind through the branches and the occasional bird, it was dead quiet. Lovey knew from the county map that a stream ran somewhere on the property, but she couldn't hear it at all. The others had walked up to the porch, so Lovey hastened to catch up.

"This was meant to serve as either the pastor's house or a home for the camp director," Mr. Swilley informed them. "The Bible camp only ran for a few years, and Pastor Burdette already had a house in town, so it hasn't been lived in for a while."

The Realtor held the door open for Lovey, who stepped into a small foyer that opened to a small sitting room on the left and a doorway to the kitchen on the right. Like the church, the house showed its age in its furnishings and decay from lack of use. Curtains hung in tatters at the window, and the ancient sofa looked like it had been home to many generations of mice. The kitchen wasn't much better, with an elderly gas stove, an icebox straight out of the 1950s, and sparkled Formica as far as the eye could see. It did have nice hardwood floors, and it looked like the basic structure had held up. Just off the kitchen Lovey could see an old sun porch that was home to an equally ancient washer and dryer.

"We'll definitely need to do some renovations in here, but the bones are good," Harley noted, and Lovey agreed.

At the back of the house, Lovey found two small bedrooms with an old bathroom dividing them.

"What do you think, Lovey?" Silas asked quietly.

Lovey turned and smiled. "I think it'll do just fine."

The other buildings were of the same age and condition as the house. There were a dozen cabins, which were little more than one- and two-room efficiencies with their own bathrooms and kitchens, and a large, barnlike building made of two wings joined at the ends. Further inspection revealed dormitory-type rooms with shared bathroom facilities. Beyond the dorms was a huge field bordered by rises in the land too small to call hills with dense forest beyond. There was even a large underground storm shelter that ran the length of one arm of the living quarters, which was accessible from both the dorm and the field.

In the middle of all the housing sat a large log building that the Realtor led them to next. "This was intended to be the fellowship hall and dining hall. It has a full commercial-sized kitchen that was actually updated not that long ago. Pastor Burdette thought he might rent out the campground and renovated this building so that it would pass inspection."

The interior of the building belied its rustic exterior. The wide plank floors had been refinished, and the walls had been covered with drywall, which Lovey assumed included insulation. The ceiling was high and crisscrossed with heavy wooden beams. A massive stone fireplace anchored one end, while a long counter ran along the other end of the room, dividing off a third of the open space. Through an open pass-through, Lovey could see a gleaming kitchen. Other than a good cleaning, the building didn't need anything.

"There's also restrooms and either office space or smaller meeting rooms for whatever you might want. You could also probably use it as storage. There's a loft space over the kitchen that has a big window. There's nothing in there right now, but it would also be a nice space, though I don't think the window looks at much. Maybe the field or the tops of the trees...maybe nothing."

"This building don't seem to need anything," Harley commented, echoing Lovey's thoughts.

The Realtor shook his head. "No, not really."

"What about water and utilities?" Silas asked.

"Utilities are run in from the county along Cemetery Road, and the property has a well that runs about sixty gallons of water per minute. There's a stream on the property that's fed by an underground aquifer, so you'll never run out of water."

"And what's the acreage?" Silas asked.

"You have two hundred and ninety acres total. Land past the ball field is marked as conservation area, and the other side is a tree farm with a small lumber mill past that. The rest backs to the county's cooperative agricultural extension, so you don't really have any neighbors. Trails were cut through the woods a long time ago. They should still be there, but they probably need to be cleaned up. On the other side of the tree line, you've got a larger maintenance shed for your mowers and other vehicles. That sits on the edge of your property and has its own access from the county road and the church road."

Silas looked at Lovey. "The drive needs to be repaired, and more gravel needs to be brought in to level the road into the camp. It might need grading too. I'd have to do some surveying to be sure."

"I can help with that," Harley offered. "I've done some road crew in my time."

"How long do you think...to do everything?" Lovey asked Silas.

"Property's usable as it is right now. But roads and building renovations? Two months," Silas replied, and Harley nodded in agreement.

Lovey turned to the Realtor. "We'll take it."

The Realtor looked stunned. "Don't you want to talk about the price? Or financing?"

Lovey tilted her head. "The land is worth around four hundred and fifty thousand, and with the number of buildings on the property, I'm going to offer one point five million, all cash, seven-day escrow."

The Realtor cleared his throat then coughed. "Asking price is two point two million, but we can work with that. You really want to close in seven days?"

"Is that a problem?" Lovey asked. "If it's the price, we have other properties we can move on to, if this isn't going to work out. If the closing time line doesn't work, we can do a thirty-day lease to own, but one five is my final offer, nonnegotiable."

"No, no," the Realtor replied quickly. "I just gotta make a quick phone call, but I think we can work with that."

"Great." Lovey smiled. "If you'll give me the paper work, I'll look it over and have it delivered back to you this afternoon."

"Absolutely. I'll be right back," the Realtor cried then dashed out of the dining hall. He certainly moved fast when money was on the table.

Silas and Harley smiled at Lovey. "Do you really have other places to look at?" Silas asked.

Lovey chuckled. "Of course not. Pastor Burdette's total debt is a little over a million dollars, and I know no one has looked at this property in months. He'd be crazy not to take my offer."

Just outside the window, they could see the Realtor on his cell phone talking animatedly while he pulled his briefcase out of his car. They weren't surprised when he walked in and announced, "Looks like we have a deal! I have a blanket lease agreement for you to sign now so I can go ahead and give you the keys. That way you can get started right away."

Lovey read through the single-page lease, signed it, then traded the lease for the keys, which she handed to Harley. "Thank you, Mr. Swilley," Lovey said graciously. "It was a pleasure."

On their way back to Merwin, Silas and Harley discussed the time line for all the work the camp needed.

"We can make that little house real nice for you and Brother Josiah, but what are you gonna do with all them other buildings, Miss Lovey?" Harley asked.

"I'm not really sure yet. I thought I'd ask you if you'd like to take one of the cabins to stay in while the construction is going on, since we're going to need a construction manager."

Harley beamed. "Really? That would be right nice, Miss Lovey. We've been runnin' out of funds stayin' in the motel near here."

Lovey turned and looked at Harley. "What do you mean 'we'?"

"Well, there's been a bunch of us following Brother Josiah," Harley answered then screwed up his face to think. "There's me; Jean and her kids, Micah and Sarah; and Joe Tripple and his brother Emmett. And there's been a girl comin' too...Misty something. She hasn't been stayin' with us though."

"Have all of you been staying at the motel?" Lovey asked, surprised that anyone would go to such an expense to hear Josiah preach.

"Yeah, pretty much, though Joe and Emmett had to sleep in their truck a couple of times when they ran out of cash. We pick up work where we can, but ain't nobody hirin' in Merwin."

Silas had been watching Lovey mull this over. "I picked up Harley at the motel. Do you want me to drop you off first?"

Lovey shook her head. "No, I'd like to go with you."

Silas nodded then turned and headed toward the seedy section of Merwin. Lovey had never been there before but knew it was peppered with run-down buildings housing bars and strip clubs broken up by cheap motels that rented rooms by the hour. Locals referred to the entire area as Milltown, even though the mill nearby had long been closed and the cluster of buildings was as far from a town as one could get.

Silas pulled into the first motel's drive and parked next to a massive, broken sign that read "Brown Motel." Lovey wondered if the name came from the owner or from the motel itself, which had at one time been painted varying shades of brown.

It was a single-story, L-shaped building with an office at one end followed by small, shuttered units. Some of the doors were open, and residents sat in the doorways smoking or drinking. Lovey could hear televisions blaring through the doorways, though it didn't look like anyone was watching them. One woman called out to Silas as they followed Harley to his room.

"Hey, baby," she said, squinting through the cloud of cigarette smoke surrounding her head. "You wanna party with me? I bet I can suck that dick better than she can."

Lovey stopped and glared at the woman. They were a picture of contrasts. Lovey was still crisp and clean despite the blistering heat, her blond hair pulled back in a smooth ponytail. The woman looked like she was melting into the cheap plastic chair she sat in wearing a tiny pair of denim Daisy Dukes that barely buttoned against the rolls of fat that threatened to engulf them. Oddly her breasts were small, covered only by a shocking pink bikini top. The woman's long, thin, brown curls hung greasy and flat, and a massive herpes lesion swelled her lower lip like she'd been punched.

"Shut up, Amy," Harley snapped. "These people don't need to be bothered by trash like you."

Silas took Lovey's elbow and led her away from the woman, who blew smoke at them but left them alone.

Harley knocked on the last door of the units and called out, "Jean? It's me, Harley."

The door opened a crack, and Lovey could see the woman from the revival peeking out. When she saw who it was, she smiled and opened the door wide.

"Oh, Miss Lovey," the woman said sweetly. "It's so nice to see you. We haven't met, but Harley has so many nice things to say about you. I'm Jean Renou, and this is my son, Micah, and my daughter, Sarah."

Jean moved aside and let them enter. The room was spotlessly clean, and Jean's children were sitting on the bed in the corner, reading quietly. Both got up and politely shook Lovey's hand then returned to their books. They looked to be a little younger than Josiah, and Lovey was impressed that they had eschewed the television in favor of their books.

"Please have a seat. Would you like something to drink?" Jean offered, but Lovey declined the refreshment.

"Harley tells me you've been living here awhile. It must be difficult," Lovey ventured.

Jean nodded. "We've been here...three weeks almost?" she answered, looking at Harley, who nodded in agreement. Then she turned back to Lovey. "I guess I'll know when they put another bill on our door. They've been real nice not making us pay in advance because they know we're here for church and not...other things."

"I think it's wonderful that you support Josiah's ministry, but I'm sure you're looking forward to going home," Lovey said.

Jean looked sad for a moment then embarrassed. "We're sort of between homes right now. We lost our first house in the hurricane. Then my husband passed away. The settlement wasn't enough to cover the new house, so we're just trying to figure things out right now."

"I'm so sorry about your husband," Lovey offered, and Jean smiled her thanks.

The room was quiet for a moment while Lovey considered their situation. She glanced at Harley and read the plea on his face. Lovey turned back to Jean. "I have a suggestion that might help solve your problem and maybe help me with one of my own."

"Oh, Miss Lovey. I'm happy to do anything you need," Jean replied. "I can't tell you how much Josiah's preaching has helped me. There's nothing I can do to pay that back."

Lovey smiled. "I'm glad Josiah's message has been comforting to you. It's been the whole point of his ministry, even if others don't agree with him. Since touring is becoming difficult, we are in the process of purchasing a church for him. The church we've found has several buildings attached that need work. Harley is going to be busy with renovating some of the living areas, but there's still a lot of work to be done. I'll need help cleaning the church and the other buildings, and at some point we'll be opening the church for worship, so we'll need someone to help take care of Josiah's visitors and general administrative needs. You'll get a salary, of course, and if you'd like to move from here to one of the cabins that will at least solve the problem of your living situation."

"Oh my...Miss Lovey," Jean replied, tears pooling in her eyes. "Thank you so much! I can't tell you how helpful that is!"

"You're really helping me," Lovey reassured her. "Harley and I will need to go through all of the cabins, so he'll let you know when you can leave here, but it should be soon."

"Oh, Miss Lovey," Jean said and grabbed Lovey's hand. "We are so grateful. You don't even know."

Lovey gave Jean's hand a squeeze. "You're welcome, Jean. I'll see you again soon."

Jean nodded through her tears as Lovey got up to leave. On her way out she stopped by Harley. "Let's meet back at the church tomorrow and finish inspecting the rest of the cabins. Bring Jean and her kids, if they'd like to come."

Harley saluted then smiled. "Will do, ma'am."

Silas followed Lovey outside. Instead of going to the truck, Lovey walked past Amy, who wisely kept her silence, and went into the motel's office. An older man who'd had several hundred too many cigarettes sat behind the counter watching an old black-and-white TV.

"Thirty dollars," he said without looking up. Silas choked as Lovey silently stared at the old man until she had his attention.

"I said it's thirty..." he said again then stopped at Lovey's expression.

"Are you the owner?" Lovey asked.

The clerk shook his head. "No, ma'am."

"You have residents here by the name of Boyd, Renou, and Tripple?" Lovey waited for an acknowledgment, so the clerk nodded. "I will be covering their bill for the remainder of their stay. I'll pay two weeks in advance; then they will be leaving here, at which time you will not charge them for anything. If there is any additional billing, you will contact me directly. Do you understand?"

The clerk nodded. "Yes, ma'am."

"If you're charging thirty dollars then two weeks is one thousand two hundred and sixty, but I'm going to round up to fifteen hundred. I assume that will be sufficient?" Lovey pulled out her wallet and withdrew a wad of hundred-dollar bills.

The clerk nodded again, staring at the cash. "Yes, ma'am," he answered, his eyes never leaving the money. Lovey wondered how much of it would actually make it into the owner's pocket.

"I expect a receipt," Lovey said pointedly and waited while the clerk scribbled one out and handed it to her.

"Remember, you are not to charge them for anything. Have Harley Boyd contact me if there's a problem," she said then took the receipt and left the office.

Silas stepped past her to open the truck's door for her then put out his hand to help her up. Lovey settled herself into her seat then smiled at Silas as he slid in behind the wheel.

"Thank you for bringing me here," she said.

"No problem. I figured you'd want to know," he replied, and Lovey nodded.

"Do you have time for one more visit?" she asked.

"Sure. Where to?"

"I'd like to check on Josiah and see how his grandmother is doing. Do you know where they live?"

This time it was Silas who nodded. Then he started the truck and drove away. Lovey hoped it would be the last time she would ever see the Brown Motel or Milltown.

The Wooten's farm hadn't changed much in the years since Lovey had last been there. The federal-style farmhouse didn't look any better or worse than it had when Lovey had visited it with her father. It was still the same dirty white with the same almost-dead tree in the dirt yard in front.

One of the Wooten women must have heard them driving up and walked out to greet them, her hands wrapped in a faded dish towel. Lovey wasn't sure, but she thought it might be the youngest, Rachel.

She was spectacularly huge and shared Miriam's deep red hair. Lovey knew from Martine that none of the other Wootens had married and none, with the exception of Wade and Miriam, had had children. Lovey also knew that most of them lived on the farm and wondered how so many adults got along in one house.

"Hi, Miss Wooten?" Lovey called out as Silas helped her down from the truck. "I don't know if you remember me, but I'm Olivia Polk. This is Silas Pritchett."

Rachel snorted at Silas's name. "I know who you are. You can call me Rachel. I 'spec' y'all are here to see Josiah?" Rachel's expression had softened at the introductions.

"And Miss Miriam, if she's feeling up to it," Lovey answered.

"Come on in, then." Rachel turned and went into the house. Lovey and Silas followed her in through the door. Rachel led them down a dark hallway to a small room at the back of the house. It looked like it had been a sun porch at one point, but the screens had been replaced by half walls and glassed windows. It was furnished with an ancient hospital bed, a finely carved wooden chair, and an equally fine bureau, which held a smattering of pill bottles, syringes, and exam gloves. An oxygen tank sat unused on the floor next to the bed.

Lovey moved closer and was struck by the overwhelming stench of putrefaction. Her eyes watered from the smell, but in an effort to be polite, she resisted covering her nose. The heat in the room was almost unbearable, as if Miriam was trying to roast herself to death. An old oscillating fan stood in the corner, its meager breeze merely spreading around the smell of rotting flesh and soiled adult diapers.

Miriam lay sleeping on the bed, surprisingly smaller than the last time Lovey had seen her but still large enough that any movement stressed the limits of the bolts holding the bed frame together. Her skin had turned an alarming shade of yellow, an indication of advanced liver disease. Large lesions on her feet were left uncovered and untreated, causing concern in Lovey that sepsis was imminent. She knew that if she looked more closely, she'd most likely find maggot infestation in Miriam's wounds.

"Miriam?" Rachel said softly. "You got visitors. Lovey and that Silas Pritchett boy."

Miriam opened her eyes and peered at Lovey. Her cataracts looked worse than Lovey had originally thought, and she knew Miriam could see very little through the fog that covered her eyes.

Miriam waved Lovey to the chair next to her. Silas took a position next to the fan, trying to stay as far away from the smell as politely possible.

"You give up on my grandson?" Miriam asked, her voice hoarse yet breathless.

"Not at all," Lovey answered. "I've been working on finding a place for him to preach. But the more important question is when was the last time the doctor saw you?"

Miriam shook her head. "Doctor won't come here. He said I gotta come in to see him. Ain't no reason to see him anyway. I'm dyin'. There ain't nothin' he can do for me."

Lovey knew it was true, but she still had to advocate for Miriam's life. "As long as you're still breathing, something can be done. I can have someone here within the hour. You need to be on oxygen, and your wounds need to be cleaned and dressed. You won't have much longer if you don't get some treatment."

Miriam waved her words away. "Honey, I don't have much longer either way. It's done...I'm done. Now tell me what yer gonna do for my grandson."

Lovey knew better than to argue. She avoided sighing because it would mean inhaling an unhealthy amount of the stench coming off of Miriam. "Pastor Tucker recommended that Josiah have his own church to work out of so that other pastors see him as a legitimate preacher in spite of his age. He told me of a church for sale near Collinsville. It has a house and a Bible camp attached. I thought you and Josiah could live in the house. I could have all the equipment you need set up so that you could be close to him while he promotes his ministry."

"We take care of our own," Rachel said from the doorway.

"Go get them some tea," Miriam ordered sternly. Rachel put her head down but obeyed. Miriam turned to where Lovey sat. "Sorry about that. We don't usually take to outsiders, but she's right. Every time we let someone else in, somethin' bad happens to us. 'Sides, there's so much wrong with me that doctors would only make my passin' take longer."

"Should I cancel the purchase on the property?" Lovey asked. "I'm sure your family will want to keep Josiah here with them."

Miriam shook her head. "There ain't nothin' they can do for him. They don't understand who he really is. They can't be true disciples if they don't believe."

Lovey knew Miriam was referring to her belief that Josiah was the Second Coming of Christ. The people of Merwin had made much of the fact that Miriam had believed that she was going to give birth to the Messiah then laughed behind her back when she had a girl. By the time Marianne got pregnant, most people had already written Miriam off as a nut case. But many had believed her; whether out of desperation for a sign of hope or from Miriam's own persistence, Lovey didn't know.

Miriam seemed to read Lovey's thoughts. "I know people think I'm crazy, and I know nobody believes me. But nobody believed Jesus at first either."

Lovey chose to avoid entering into a debate with a dying woman. "Even at sixteen, Josiah is still a minor," she said instead. "And you are his legal guardian. And if you aren't able to provide oversight to his care...for whatever reason, then his guardianship reverts to one of your brothers or sisters. It was one thing when you were traveling with us. If you're not with us, I have no legal right to make decisions on Josiah's behalf."

"Then you give me a piece of paper sayin' you'll take care of Josiah when I die, and I'll sign it."

Lovey shook her head. "It's not that simple—" she began, but Rachel, who had returned with a tray of iced tea, interrupted her.

"Nobody here's gonna go against Miriam's wishes...especially her last wishes. If you're fixin' to take the boy, then we all are just gonna have to be OK with that."

Miriam gave Lovey a satisfied look. "There, then that takes care of that. 'Sides, if yer gonna be takin' Josiah to his own church, Rachel here and the others will keep an eye on him. By the time someone else decides to make it a problem, he'll be on his own anyway." Miriam turned her face toward Silas. "Is that Silas boy in here?"

"Yes, ma'am," Silas answered for himself.

"I didn't forget about you." Miriam affected a sneer. She turned toward Rachel. "Rachel, honey, go get Abel." Rachel darted out as Miriam turned back to Silas. "Do you know who you are?"

"You mean do I know I'm Silas Pritchett?" he asked, a slight smile curling his lips.

Miriam snorted. "Agnes Pritchett never had no kids. I checked. I bet yer birthday is in the beginnin' of September, ain't it? And you were too little when you were born, so it took you a long time to grow like other kids. And I bet you were sickly too, weren't you?"

Silas looked startled. "How did you know all that?"

Lovey watched a knowing smile cross Miriam's face. She looked up to see Abel Wooten step into the doorway. "Oh," she said involuntarily, and Miriam began to chuckle.

"You see it, don't you?" Miriam said, and indeed Lovey did see it.

Silas Pritchett was the mirror image of Abel Wooten, minus twenty years or so. They had the same black hair and deep, almost-black eyes, and even though Silas was thinner and taller, they were clearly from the same family.

"I don't understand. Are you trying to say this is my father?" Silas asked, sounding both incredulous and fearful.

This time it was Abel who answered him, his head shaking sadly. "You're Inez's boy."

Silas shook his head in an unconscious mirror of Abel's. "I don't know who that is. My grandmother never said anything about anyone by that name."

"What did Agnes tell you about yer mother?" Miriam asked.

Silas continued to stare at the face he would wear in twenty years. "Just that she died giving birth to me."

"Well that's true enough. And what about yer pa?"

Silas glanced at Lovey, his face stricken, and her heart went out to him.

"Nothing...just that he died before she did," he answered quietly.

Abel moved over and put his hand around Silas's arm. "Come on, boy," he said gently. "Let's go talk outside."

Silas let himself be led out of the room.

Miriam turned back to Lovey. "Poor boy," she said, shaking her head. "He's gonna need you to help him sort it all out. Josiah too."

Lovey realized she hadn't seen the boy since they'd gotten there. "Where is Josiah?" she asked.

Miriam sighed heavily. "He's probably outside somewhere. Why don't you go see him...let me rest awhile."

"Of course." Lovey stood. "I'll come by later to see how you're doing."

"Sure, honey." Miriam yawned. "You do that."

Lovey left the room and was immediately struck by how much fresher the air was in the hallway. She followed the sounds of dishes being washed to the kitchen, where Miriam's other sister, Dorcas, was cleaning up their unused refreshments.

"Josiah's over in the barn," she answered before Lovey could ask, tilting her head toward the window.

"Thank you," Lovey answered. She went outside and headed over in that direction. She could hear low voices coming from the darkness of the barn. She stepped into the shade then stopped to let her eyes adjust.

Abel and Silas stood just inside where the line of sunlight stopped and the dirt floor turned black. Silas had his head down while Abel talked to him in a low voice, his hand on Silas's shoulder, comforting him.

"Silas?" Lovey called out quietly. "Are you all right?"

When Silas looked up, his face was stricken, his eyes shining with unshed tears. Abel murmured something that Silas answered with a nod. Abel gave him one last pat then gently pushed him toward Lovey.

With his head still down, Silas went to move past her then stopped and took her fingers in his. "I'll wait for you in the truck," he said, his voice breaking. He let go of her hand and walked out of the barn.

Lovey looked over to where Abel still stood. "Give him a few minutes," Abel suggested. Then he turned and stepped deeper into the dark of the barn.

Lovey followed him, wanting to ask about Silas, but froze when she became aware of what was all around them. From floor to ceiling and running the entire length of the barn were exquisite pieces of furniture almost identical to the chair and bureau in Miriam's room. Along the side of the barn were stacks of lumber and various machines that to Lovey's untrained eye looked like medieval torture devices but most likely had created the wooden works of art around her. There were rocking chairs and tables, headboards and footboards for beds, and ornately carved buffets and cabinets. Several bureaus were lined up along the wall in various finishes.

"These are amazing," Lovey marveled. "Did you make all of this?"

Abel turned and nodded. "Ayup."

"Do you sell them?" she asked, running her hand along the smooth, glossy finish of a dining table.

Abel looked embarrassed. "I been tryin', but people round here don't really take to this kind of stuff. They just want that stuff at that Space Place store out on the highway."

Lovey doubted that but didn't want to state the obvious. Most people in Merwin avoided the Wootens at all costs, regardless of what they grew or made. "Is any of this for sale?" she asked.

"Oh, ayup." Abel nodded, looking around. "I reckon all of it is."

"I wonder if you could help me then, Mr. Wooten." Lovey reluctantly took her hand away from the beautiful table and faced Abel squarely. "I've found a church for Josiah to preach out of, and it has several buildings attached that have been sorely neglected. The furniture they left behind is of very poor quality and in terrible condition. I wonder if you would be open to providing new furniture for all of the buildings from your inventory here."

Abel's face was suddenly transformed by a wide smile that caught Lovey's breath. He was strikingly handsome, and Lovey knew in an instant that everything Miriam had said about Silas was true.

"Oh ayup." Abel's tone sounded much more cheerful. "I reckon I can help you there, Miss Polk."

"Would you be able to visit the property and give me an idea of what furniture would work for us? Also, there is a large dining hall that is completely unfurnished, so I may need more tables and chairs than you have here. Oh...and please call me Lovey."

"I can certainly help you there, Miss...Lovey." Abel stepped over and put out his hand. "Thank you so much, ma'am. I know you're gonna be real happy with the furniture."

Lovey took Abel's hand and shook it warmly. "I already am," she said then took out her card and wrote the address of the church on the back. "We'll be there for the next few days, so come out whenever you have time."

"Yes, ma'am." Abel saluted.

Lovey smiled then stepped back out into the sunshine. On her way to check on Silas, Lovey saw Josiah standing next to the truck. Both he and Silas had their heads down, and it looked like they were praying. They both looked up when Lovey approached. She was glad to see that Silas looked better than he had in the barn.

Silas wiped at his eyes. "You ready to go?" he asked, and Lovey gave a nod his way then looked at Josiah, who was smiling at her.

"Grandma said you found me a church?" he asked.

"Yes, and I think you'll be very happy there. But, Josiah, I need you to convince her to see a doctor. I'm going to make some calls and have someone come out tonight."

Josiah's smile faltered as he glanced at the house then shook his head slowly. "I can pray over her, but she's not going to let anyone in to see her," he said solemnly. "She's ready to receive the Lord."

"We should still try," Lovey stated firmly. She climbed into the truck. "Your uncle is coming to the church tomorrow to check out our furniture needs. Can you come with him?"

Josiah nodded.

Lovey smiled. "Then we'll see you tomorrow," she said, waving as Silas drove away.

On their way back to town, Lovey ached to ask Silas about his conversation with Abel but kept silent out of respect for his feelings. They were almost home when he surprised her by speaking first.

"I'll understand if you want to find someone else to help you with the church...after today," he said quietly.

Lovey wanted to pretend not to understand but knew it could hurt more than help, so she told the truth. "I don't know exactly what they told you back there, but it doesn't matter to me...who you are. And I don't think there's any shame in knowing who you really are. There are worse families to find yourself attached to...like mine," she said. "I need your help as much as I need Harley's and Jean's help. I can't do it all by myself."

"You know you and Josiah are a lot alike," he said after a while.

"What do you mean?" Lovey asked.

Silas pulled to a stop in front of her father's house, but instead of getting out or turning off the truck, he stared off at nothing in front of him. "You both want to help people," he answered.

Lovey stared at his profile. Even in distress he was breathtaking, like a fallen angel. "I think the way I help people isn't nearly as important as the way Josiah helps them."

Silas shook his head then got out of the truck to come around and help her down. "No, what you do is more important," he said as he helped her safely out of the truck.

"How so?" Lovey asked, her hand tingling where he was touching her. Silas let go of her hand, and she felt instantly bereft at the loss.

When he finally looked up at her, she could see vast oceans of sorrow in his eyes. Then he smiled at her.

"Josiah just wants to save them from sin," he said quietly. "You want to save them from everything else."

FORTY-SEVEN

Lovey spent the next several hours on the phone trying to find a doctor to treat Miriam. She called every coworker, associate, and protégé of Samuel Polk but received nothing but polite rejections from everyone.

"I don't understand it," Lovey said, slamming down the phone on yet another rejection. "Why don't these people want to help? What is so wrong with the Wooten family that everyone treats them like lepers?"

Martine set a fresh cup of tea down in front of Lovey. "I've never really understood it either, but I didn't grow up here." She took a seat across from Lovey and gave her a sympathetic look. "Your father befriended them, though your mother was a big part of their ostracism."

"Ugh, why would anyone want to malign another human being so thoroughly, let alone an entire family?" Lovey asked. Though she'd known them all her life, she'd never understood the workings of the minds of the people she had grown up with.

"There's just so many rumors about them...you have to wonder, with so much smoke...well you know." Martine's smile was apologetic.

Lovey looked at her. "What rumors? I've only heard the nonsense Verna and Irma made up about Marianne. I've never heard anything seriously questionable about the Wootens."

Martine had the good grace to look away. "Well, you wouldn't have, would you? Your father was a big supporter of the Wooten family. And people wondered about that too, given the rumors that circulated through the town. You know...things like Miriam had an affair with that preacher, Tucker, or that she murdered her husband and burned their house down, killing the boy too. And then there's the rumor that the youngest brother, Wade, was a drug addict. And a true one is that his son has severe mental issues. He had to be let go from his job for beating up one of his coworkers. And then his wife committed suicide, and they blame him for that too."

"But everyone has things like that in their family," Lovey protested. "Things that are true and other things that have been grossly exaggerated."

Martine nodded. "They do," she agreed. "I guess the worst rumor was that the father was using his daughters...like wives...and sometimes they would get pregnant, but they never had the babies. That one appeared to be true."

Lovey looked at her in horror. "How do you know this?"

Martine looked at her sadly. "Your father had a file on the sister who died. He signed her death certificate. Inez had tried to abort early, but it didn't work. By the time the midwife got there, the baby was stillborn. The family did the best they could by her, but Inez died a few days later. Then the father went missing. Some say they killed him; others think he killed himself."

"Oh my God," Lovey whispered. "When was this?"

"A bit before you were born...what's wrong, Lovey?" Martine grew alarmed as Lovey's face had gone pale. "Are you OK?"

Lovey shook her head slowly. "Nothing...it's nothing," she replied then stood. "I'm going to call an internist I know in Jackson. He'll see Miriam."

Lovey made her call and convinced her friend to make the trip by calling in a favor. Though Mark was a great clinician, he had been a terrible student and only made it through medical school with Lovey's tutoring.

When she hung up, Lovey went into her room and closed the door quietly. Now that she understood what Silas had learned earlier that day, she was filled with sadness for him. In a way she was glad to learn of his father from Martine rather than the Wootens or Silas himself. There was no way she would be able to keep the pity from her face.

The next day, Lovey drove out to the new church to meet Harley and Abel. Silas's truck was already there parked next to an old, red pickup that Lovey assumed was either Harley's or Abel's. She could hear voices inside the director's house, so she followed them and found Harley and Silas, shovels in hand and masks pushed up on their heads, discussing renovations amid a pile of rubble in the kitchen.

Harley looked up as Lovey stepped in. "Watch yourself, Miss Lovey. I don't want you to get hurt."

Silas moved over and led Lovey past the more dangerous piles of debris. She was glad to see he looked like he was mostly back to his old self. He smiled warmly at her then dropped her hand when they reached Harley.

"It looks like you got a lot done," she remarked, looking around. The appliances were all gone, and the old cabinets lay splintered and broken in piles on the floor. A huge pile of sparkled Formica sat in a corner, and they stood on surprisingly good wide-plank hardwood.

"There weren't nothin' in here worth savin'," Harley began. He gestured at the wood. "Them cabinets were just thin birch board, and that stove and icebox weren't workin' at all. Me and Silas are gonna go through them cabins, but I'm pretty sure some of that's gonna be junk too."

Lovey surveyed the damage. "I've ordered a Dumpster. They should be dropping it off shortly."

Harley nodded. "I'm right glad you did," he drawled. "I plumb forgot to ask you for that. I called them yesterday, but they needed a deposit...and...well—"

"Oh, that reminds me," Lovey interrupted, pulling open the small wristlet she used to hold her cash and cell phone. "I picked these up this morning." She handed both Harley and Silas prepaid credit cards. "They should work until I get a construction account set up at the bank. Use them for whatever you need; just let me know when they need to be reloaded. I'll have new cards later, but these will do for now."

"Thank you, Miss Lovey." Harley beamed then put the card in his wallet. Silas said nothing but did the same.

"I'm going to go out and make a couple of phone calls. Let me know if you need anything."

Harley nodded then pulled his mask back over his face and set to scraping up the rest of the old flooring. Silas held out his hand and helped Lovey back to the doorway. She wanted to ask him how he was doing, but right at that moment her cell phone rang.

Silas turned back to help Harley, so Lovey pulled her phone out to answer it. "This is Olivia."

"Hey, Olivia." It was Mark, the internist from Jackson. "I wanted to follow up with you on Miriam Wooten."

"Did the family let you in to see her?" Lovey asked. "I know they can be difficult at times."

"Oh, I saw her all right," Mark replied, his tone wry. "She'd passed away before I got there. They had already cleaned her up, but they did let me examine her...or at least they didn't object when I examined her."

"Oh my God," Lovey replied. "I just saw her yesterday afternoon. I knew she was bad but not that bad. Definitely some decline in liver function and possible gangrene on the legs, but nothing that would have taken her that suddenly."

"Well, she *was* pretty sick," Mark admitted. "But I found petechiae in one eye and a hyposphagma in the other. She would need a postmortem, but I don't think the family's going to go for that. They look like they stepped out of the movie *Deliverance*."

"She was OHS," Lovey countered. "And she wasn't using her oxygen. She could have aspirated something or had aplastic anemia along with all of her other problems. That could explain the petechiae."

Mark chuckled. "Whatever gets you through the night, Olivia, but I think she had help. More death by pillow than anything else that might have been wrong with her."

"Did you write a note on it?" Lovey asked, trying to hide the alarm in her voice.

"Hell no!" Mark laughed. "You think I want to get in the middle of this? The woman was sick...no doubt terminally so. There was definite sepsis. If they did help her along, they only spared her a couple more days of suffering. And I have a feeling that with so much wrong with her post would come back inconclusive anyway."

"Thank you for going," Lovey said sincerely. "I'm sorry I wasted your time."

Mark laughed again. "No problem. It's always good to have a reminder of where I'd be if you hadn't helped me. I'll talk to you later."

Lovey ended the call then sat down on the steps of the house. Despite her arguments, she knew Mark was right. And in her heart she knew she couldn't hold the Wootens responsible for what had happened. Miriam had most likely ordered Rachel or Dorcas to help her end her suffering, and they had obeyed. Rachel had admitted they did anything and everything Miriam asked of them. Lovey knew they wouldn't hurt her unless she told them to.

Lovey looked up to see an old truck approaching the camp. She could see Abel driving with Josiah beside him in the passenger's seat. Behind them was an old Chevy Impala driven by a man about her age. His clone sat in the seat next to him, and Lovey wondered if these were the Tripple brothers.

Lovey stood up and walked over as both vehicles parked and the men got out. She went up to Abel first. "I just heard about Miss Miriam. I'm so sorry," she said sincerely.

Abel eyed her suspiciously at first, but then his face relaxed. "It was what she wanted. She was done bein' sick."

Lovey nodded but left it alone. Josiah had already wandered off, so she walked over to where the other two men waited. "Would I be correct in guessing you're the Tripple brothers?" she asked.

Both men gave her identical smiles. "Yes, ma'am. I'm Joe, and this is Emmett." Joe tapped his chest then put his hand on his mirror image.

"I'm not sure that's going to help me," she joked, and the two men laughed.

Emmett leaned toward her and whispered, "The only way to tell us apart is to look for the freckle," he said, pointing to a small, brown dot under his left eye. "I've got this, but Joe doesn't. Find the dot, and you'll know who you're talkin' to."

Lovey smiled. She already liked the Tripple brothers immensely. "Are you here to help?"

"Yes, ma'am." Joe nodded. "Harley told us what you all are doin' here, so we thought we'd give you a hand. Besides, we gotta pay you back for the money you gave the guy at the motel."

"There's no need to pay me back," Lovey began, but Emmett waved her away.

"We like workin'," he said. "Keeps us out of trouble. So there's a semi out on the road with a big, ole Dumpster attached. You want us to tell him where to drop it off?"

Lovey nodded. "That would be great. Thank you."

She watched them walk off toward the church then turned back to Abel. Josiah had wandered down the drive toward the church, so Lovey opted to leave him alone.

"The girls sent along some things you might need," Abel said. He reached into the bed of his truck and pulled out a stack of intricately crafted quilts. "Rachel and Dorcas are real good about takin' stuff apart and makin' these. Ain't nobody askin' to buy them neither, so they'd just as soon give them to you."

Lovey pulled off the top quilt and marveled at the quality. Though it was a simple pattern, it was impeccably made. "These are amazing! But I can't accept these as a gift...they must have taken forever to make, and I know they sell for at least a few hundred dollars apiece. Please let me pay for them," she said.

Abel shook his head. "They mean them as a gift, Miss Lovey."

Lovey pushed the stack back toward Abel. "All the same, I'm going to add a fair amount to the cost of the furniture. What you do with it is up to you. If you think Rachel and Dorcas will be offended by the payment, then use it for the house or for the family. This isn't negotiable," she said firmly.

Abel chuckled to himself then placed the quilts back in the truck. "As you wish, Miss Lovey."

Lovey smiled. "Thank you, and please thank them for me. Now let me show you what buildings we'll need furnished," she said.

Abel pulled a clipboard out of his truck and followed Lovey around. When they were done, they had looked into every room of every building and had amassed an impressive list of needs.

"I can do the cabinetwork for you too," Abel offered. "Yer wood in them cabins is good—those don' t need replacin', but that boy was right to pull out that kitchen. I've got the lumber. Iffen you need it fast, I can get them done for you within the week. They just won't be real fancy like the other stuff."

Lovey nodded. "I like that idea. If we could get the cabins set up quickly, that would be great. I'm sure our new church members would like to move out of Brown Motel as soon as possible."

"Disgraceful things happen in that place," Abel said, his look dark.

Lovey wondered at that but didn't press him.

"You understand about Miriam, right?" he asked.

"What do you mean?" Lovey feigned confusion.

Abel took a moment to think over his words. "There ain't nothin' my family won't do for each other. We ain't never had anyone else lookin' out for us, 'cept your pa and then you. Ain't nobody else even give us the time of day. We always take care of our own."

In a weird way, Lovey understood. There was nothing she wouldn't do for Martine. Lovey nodded. "I guess I understand better than I thought I would. There really isn't...wasn't any arguing with her, was there?"

Abel smiled. "No, ma'am. I'm gonna take Josiah back with me. Boy needs to do some hard work for a change."

"Before you go," she called out as he turned away, "when will Miss Miriam's funeral take place? I'd like to go, if that's all right."

Abel stopped and faced her. "We bury our kin ourselves. We mourn them ourselves. She's already in the ground, if that's what yer askin'. Just take care of Josiah for her. That would please her more than you prayin' over her grave," he said quietly then walked away.

By the end of the week, all the cabins had been cleaned and refurnished, and Harley had made good time on the house and it wasn't long before Lovey and Josiah were able to move into the small house while Harley, Jean and her family and the Tripple brothers took the cabins. With Jean's help, Lovey was able to clean everything that needed cleaning, and by the time Lovey signed the settlement papers, everything was set for Josiah's ministry to begin.

Lovey and Josiah had made several trips into town to make their faces known and spread the word that the church would be reopening. Most of the town's residents were polite, and some even expressed an interest in coming. The church's previous pastor even graciously contacted his congregation and encouraged them to return to the church to support the new minister. Rumors of Josiah's reputation as the new Messiah had already made their way around the area. Lovey was hopeful that at least some of them would come out of curiosity. Luckily they had a built-in congregation with Harley and Silas, Jean's family, and the Tripple brothers.

Sunday dawned gray and dreary. Lovey drove to the church early to make sure everything was in order. When she stepped in, she saw that Jean had had the same idea and was already there straightening the Bibles and filling the pews with bulletins. Micah and Sarah sat in the front pew folding extra bulletins in half.

Lovey put her things down and went to help. The church was small enough that it didn't take them long, and by the time they were done, Joe and Emmett were coming in to set up instruments for the music. It was another stroke of luck that Joe played both the piano and guitar and Emmett played the fiddle. Jean had worked with them on a list of hymns, and, with Lovey's input, they had put together a passable list of traditional gospel music.

Lovey and Jean were standing and listening to the brothers quietly go through the playlist when the door to the church opened. Harley and

Josiah entered, followed by Silas. Lovey could see through the doorway that the sky had turned darker and rain was starting to fall.

"Man, it's gonna start squallin' out there," Harley said, shaking the wetness out of his hair like a dog.

"Harley!" Jean scolded. "I just washed these floors."

"Sorry, Jean." Harley looked contrite then smiled in such a way that Jean couldn't help but forgive him.

Josiah moved to the old wooden lectern and laid his Bible down. Lovey went to give him a hug then looked at him more closely.

"Josiah, are you all right?" she asked quietly.

Josiah shrugged. "I guess so...I'm just worried no one's going to come."

Lovey gave him a gentle smile. "You already have a congregation right here. Even if it takes time to build your followers, you're already off to a good start."

Josiah nodded but didn't look convinced.

As if they understood his struggle, Jean and her children, Harley, and Silas all took their seats in the front pews. Joe and Emmett started to play quietly, as much to rehearse as to give everyone something to listen to other than the rain tapping on the roof.

Lovey gave Josiah another hug and left him to sit next to Silas. She glanced at her watch and saw that they only had ten more minutes until worship was scheduled to start.

After a few minutes, Lovey realized the boys were playing more than just random notes. Jean seemed to notice too. Lovey watched her lean over and whisper something to her daughter. Sarah listened to her mother then nodded. Then, to Lovey's surprise, the normally silent girl walked over and stood near Joe and Emmett. Everyone watched her sway silently, her ear turned to the guitar Joe strummed as if waiting for something. Sarah seemed to hear something in the notes and started to sing. In a clear, high voice, Sarah sang "I Need Thee Every Hour."

A shiver ran right through Lovey. She was so surprised at how good Sarah was that she almost didn't notice the church doors opening behind her. She glanced at her watch and saw that with five minutes to go before worship started, Josiah's congregation was arriving.

Lovey turned and smiled at Josiah, who looked visibly relieved, then settled back to listen to Sarah sing.

When the song was done, Sarah took a seat next to Emmett. Josiah stepped up to the lectern and glanced at the people who had filled his church with a shyness that Lovey had never seen before.

"Good morning," he said quietly into the microphone, and his congregants answered in kind.

"Thank you all for coming in the rain. You know it says in Isaiah, 'Drip down, ye heavens, from above, and let the clouds pour down righteousness; let the earth open up and salvation bear fruit, and righteousness spring up with it. I, the Lord, have created it.' Who knew the Lord would create so much of it," he joked, and his flock chuckled appreciatively.

Lovey felt the crowd relax and knew from that moment that everything was going to be OK.

Josiah took a moment to let the crowd quiet down, and then he began to speak.

"'Be ye followers of me, even as I also am of Christ,'" he began. "It's really just a fancy way of saying let me be your example for I follow Christ's example. Everything that Jesus said and did during his life has been set before us as a blueprint for how we are to live our lives. When Jesus took the lessons he learned from God and set out to teach others those lessons, he compelled us to carry those lessons forth to other lands and to future generations so that all mankind would know his will for us. And as Jesus saved the sick...fed the hungry...and freed the oppressed, so too are we compelled to action, to heal, to provide sustenance, to fight for those who cannot fight for themselves. And as Jesus prayed in the garden at Gethsemane, or on the Mount of Olives, or at the winter stream of Kidron, so too does he want us to pray...for it is in prayer that we discover ourselves...that we examine where we have kept to his path and where we have strayed."

The congregation was rapt as Josiah pulled the microphone from the lectern and stepped away in an unconscious effort to engage his followers more personally.

"'He has shown you, O man, what is good. And what does the Lord require of you but to do justly, to love mercy, and to walk humbly with your God.'" Josiah slowly paced the floor in front of the lectern, his eyes searching the eyes in front of him. He spoke to the congregation earnestly:

"The Lord asks so little of us, yet we still fail him. He asks us to do justly, to be fair...to always be on the side of right. Not our own right, but the right as set forth by God. He asks us to love mercy, to forgive others as he has forgiven us...to set ourselves aside so that we might consider the needs of others. He asks us to walk humbly with him, to not put ourselves and our selfish desires before others and never ever before him. As followers of Christ, we are servants of Christ. As servants we are called to fulfill our whole duty to him.

Some will tell you that a little bit of sin doesn't hurt anyone. A little white lie that spares someone's feelings is actually good. Some will tell you that as long as nobody is hurt, it's OK. Go ahead and cheat that insurance company. They're so big they won't even feel it. They will try to manipulate the Gospel to say that it's OK to give more than God compels you to. Or you will try to tell yourself that it's OK if you don't give up your hard-earned money to the tithe, for it's the *love* of money that's a sin, not money itself.

Let me tell you something. God is not an accountant, but he is a scorekeeper. He doesn't care how much money you make. He cares about how you made it and what you do with it. He doesn't care if you keep it all or give it all away, because money itself is nothing but currency...a tool used in commerce...a tool that we are compelled to use, for we are compelled to do right by the world. He wants us to help the sick, to be there for them, to give them what they might not have, like food, warm clothes, a roof over their heads, and medicine for their illnesses. He doesn't expect you to lay hands like Jesus and heal them, because you can't. No one can.

Those healing preachers don't have the power of Jesus in their hands...they have the power to convince you that they have. Only Jesus was God incarnate on earth. Only he could raise the dead... only he could turn water into wine...only he could make a blind man see. No one else can do that because, unlike Jesus, as preachers we are not God incarnate—we are human. All we can do is teach...feed... help. And that is all God wants us to do. And he knows when we do it.

Let us pray.

Heavenly Father, we pray to you for understanding, that your lessons are not lost on us but that they become as much a part of us as our skin, our hair, our hearts. Help us to see your work in our lives and in the world around us. Show us how to show others. Teach us how to teach others. Save us to save others. In Jesus's name...Amen."

Josiah looked up, and Lovey smiled at the look of relief on his face. Joe and Emmett began to play, and a moment later, without prompting from her mother, Sarah stood to sing again. A tall, curly haired young man stepped up and nodded a question at Josiah, who nodded back indicating the space next to Sarah. The young man took the spot next to her and began to sing the harmony to "Be Thou My Vision."

Lovey closed her eyes and let the music wash over her. She knew she looked like she was praying, and though she hadn't formally prayed to God in a long time, she was grateful in her heart that the people of the town had been open to Josiah's ministry. It might take only one man to speak the message, but it took many ears to hear it. With at least some of the people of the town willing to consider Josiah's message, they were off to a good start. She was also grateful for the love that surrounded him, not just from her but also from Harley, the Tripple brothers, and Jean and her family. They were committed to Josiah and to the fulfillment of his ministry, and for that she would be eternally grateful.

When the worship service ended, Lovey invited their new congregation to have coffee and donuts in the dining hall, where they would have a chance to meet Josiah personally in a space larger, warmer, and more accommodating than the small wooden church.

Jean went with the group to perform the hosting duties, while Lovey stayed behind to clean up the church. It didn't take long to set right the Bibles and hymnals, so Lovey grabbed her umbrella and opened the church door. She was just about to step out when she realized someone was sitting next to the steps where the small overhang almost prevented the heavy rain from hitting the door. Lovey stepped down and looked at the girl more closely. She wasn't sure, but she thought it might be the girl that had followed Josiah as he toured the other churches. Lovey thought her name might be Misty, so she tried it.

"Hello, Misty? Are you Misty?" she asked, but the girl looked away. "Are you OK?"

"I'm fine...I'll be fine," the girl answered but kept her face turned away, which Lovey thought was odd. She didn't know how long the girl had been out there, but the girl was soaked through and shivering. Her long, blond hair was dark with rain and plastered against her head.

Lovey stepped down a little farther and held her umbrella over the two of them. The girl was older than Lovey had first thought. She looked to be a little older than Josiah, and when she turned toward her, Lovey saw that the poor girl's lips were blue and quivering uncontrollably.

"Come with me," she said firmly and reached down to pull the girl up. At first the girl resisted, but Lovey was insistent. "Come on now...or we're both going to be drenched."

The girl let herself be lifted and even leaned into Lovey as they crossed the churchyard to the path that cut through the woods. The rain lessened once they were among the trees, but Lovey kept the umbrella over them. The poor girl didn't need to be any wetter than she already was. They reached the dining hall, and Lovey opened the door and pushed the girl through before closing her umbrella and leaving it beside the door. Everyone turned to look at the girl standing there shivering and staring at the floor.

"Misty?" Jean called out and rushed over.

Harley followed. "Oh man, girl," he said. "You are *wet*. Let me run and get you some towels."

"Thank you, Harley." Lovey smiled then led the girl over to the fire. "That would be great."

Jean fetched Misty a cup of hot cocoa and pressed it into the girl's pale, shaking hands. "Drink this, honey. I'm going to get you something to eat."

Figuring the girl for another lost sheep, the rest of the congregation went back to their conversation. Silas walked up with one of Rachel's quilts, while Harley rushed back with a couple of towels. Misty traded the cocoa for a towel and, with an embarrassment unique to the young, scrubbed at her wet hair until it was mostly dry. Lovey pulled the quilt around her and gave her back the cocoa.

"What were you doing out in the rain?" Harley asked.

Misty looked embarrassed. "I was waitin' for it to stop a little bit before I left," she answered then stopped as a wave of shivering overtook her. "I was goin' to try and get a ride at the highway."

Harley looked incredulous. "Highway's like...what...five miles from here? You were gonna walk that whole way?"

Misty shrugged. "I didn't know where y'all were stayin', so I figured I'd try to get to the next town and see where y'all were gonna be. There's a healer going to be down by Meridian, so I thought y'all might be going that way."

"Oh, hon." Jean had returned with a plate of donuts, which she set down in front of the girl. "We stay here now, at the church. If we knew how to get a hold of you, we would have let you know."

"You're not travelin' anymore?" Misty asked.

Jean and Harley shook their heads. "Miss Lovey bought Josiah this church and invited us to stay in the buildings," Harley said, smiling at Lovey.

Lovey caught his look and knelt next to the girl. "Is there anyone you need us to call?" she asked.

Misty looked away but shook her head. "No, not anymore." Lovey was going to question this, but Jean shook her head slightly.

"You're welcome to stay here, Misty," Lovey offered. The girl was too shy to say anything but smiled her response.

"She can stay with us until we figure out a better place for her," Jean offered. "And she can help me clean. Miss Lovey, I know you like helping, but you're too important to be wastin' your time on easy stuff. Besides, me and Misty can take over the kitchen, so we all start eatin' better meals."

Lovey smiled crookedly. She'd just been demoted from her cleaning job, and it was unlikely she was going to be helping in the kitchen either.

As if he could read her mind, Silas placed his hand on her shoulder and squeezed warmly. With his support, Lovey set aside her pride.

"I think that's a wonderful idea," she said, and Silas squeezed again.

Lovey stood and got herself a cup of cocoa. Silas walked over and stood with her like it was his place in life. Lovey was grateful to have him near. To be honest, she knew she didn't fit in with any of the people there. It had never bothered her before, but now that it was a group that she found she cared about, her outsider status was felt more keenly.

Silas read her mind again and moved closer, his lips almost touching her ear. "You know these people need you, right?" he whispered.

"Jean's, Harley's...even Josiah's circumstances would be much worse if you hadn't taken it upon yourself to help them."

Lovey nodded but didn't answer, so Silas leaned into her and put his arm around her shoulders and pulled her close, the warmth of his body seeping through her damp dress. Lovey felt herself relax and accept what Silas was saying to her. Even if the only thing they really needed from her was her money, she was still necessary to Josiah's ministry. She felt her breathing slow as she watched Josiah detach himself from the others to make his way over to where Misty sat nursing her cocoa.

Misty had devoured her donuts, so Jean left them to get her something more substantial. Josiah knelt before Misty and put his hands over hers where they still held her cup. He said a few words to her, and then they both closed their eyes and bowed their heads. Lovey watched Josiah pray over Misty and knew at that moment that no matter how insignificant she was in his world, as long as she could continue to help Josiah help others, she would be happy.

FORTY-EIGHT

Over the next few months, Josiah's ministry grew in intent. His worship services continued to be somewhat well attended, and with the renovations completed on the buildings, they were able to expand his outreach ministry to help feed the hungry families in the area and host a free market where people could "shop" for things they needed among donated items.

As Josiah's message got out, more and more followers continued to show up hoping to find refuge at the church. Silas called them Josiah's disciples, and it wasn't long before Zion Pentecostal had grown into its own little community.

With little to do, Lovey applied for a volunteer medical license so she could practice in the state. Once it was approved, Lovey converted the meeting rooms at the back of the dining hall into a small clinic where she could take patients who couldn't afford care anywhere else.

To stay in keeping with the people she met with on a daily basis, Lovey donated all of her more expensive clothing to Jackson's Dress for Success program and opted for more modest outfits from the local stores.

Days at Zion fell into a rhythm, with followers and families in need coming and going. Lovey had to set an informal rule that only members of Josiah's church could stay on the property, and while they were there they were to attend worship services and work there in some capacity.

A section of the ball field had been converted to garden plots, and Abel graciously donated his time to show the residents how to grow food. A couple of the women who'd joined them had experience working in commercial kitchens and restaurants, so with the addition of farm-fresh produce, their meals improved tremendously.

Zion was shaping up to be an ideal community with outreach as a shared goal. Along with her clinic, Lovey took great pride in their free market. With the help of the other churches in the area, she was able to amass an impressive inventory of clothing, toys, and household items. Visitors were given vouchers from the area churches and local offices of health and human services to come and purchase clothing for their children or items for their homes.

Though their numbers weren't huge, everyone managed to make themselves useful. Lovey hoped that in time they would be able to make Zion completely self-sufficient.

Even with the garden, Silas and several other members often needed to make trips into town for the things they couldn't grow or make themselves. Despite Lovey urging him to join them, Josiah usually begged off on the pretext that he had to settle down for some prayer and reflection. He was spending more and more time in prayer, and Lovey worried that he might be struggling with something. He'd taken the large window room above the kitchen as his private space, and it was there that she found him.

The room was completely unfurnished, with bare wooden floors, plain, white walls, and, above them, an unfinished beam ceiling. The room's only feature was a large floor-to-ceiling picture window that overlooked the untouched section of the field behind them.

Josiah knelt in front of the window, his head down. Lovey noted that in the short time since they'd moved to Zion, he'd become a man. All of his previous boyishness was gone, and his face had grown into the mirror image of the Wooten men. Lovey couldn't see Joe Buckley anywhere in his son, except in the blue of his eyes.

"Dinner will be ready soon," she said quietly.

Josiah looked up, then back at her, and nodded before turning back to the window to pray.

Lovey left him alone, resolving to come back later with a dish of food if he didn't come down.

As she helped with the dinner preparations, Silas came into the kitchen to stand next to her at the large stainless-steel counter that stood in the center of the room. She was absurdly pleased to see him, despite the fact that she was up to her elbows cleaning up potato peelings.

"That's a nice look for you, Lovey." Silas smiled as he picked a potato peel from her sleeve. "Never knew a woman could look so nice wearing vegetable scrapings."

The other women in the room smiled knowingly at each other as they went about their work. Lovey blushed to her roots then brushed at her faded print dress. "Oh," she laughed. "Well, that's what I get for not putting on an apron."

"Why don't you go change for dinner, and I'll finish this up for you," Silas offered.

Lovey looked down and saw she'd managed to stain the front of her dress. She pushed her hair away from her face with the back of her hand then reached for a towel. "Thank you, Silas," she murmured, then, after a final check on the other women, left the kitchen.

In her room at the cottage, Lovey unbuttoned her dress then went to her closet to find something else to wear. She was surprised to see that Silas had been there before her, for hanging on the back of the door was a beautiful, sky-blue dress wrapped in plastic. Lovey checked the label and knew immediately that Silas must have sent away for the dress, for it was too fine to have come from any store in Mississippi, let alone Collinsville. She gently removed the plastic and donned the gift. In the mirror she saw a much different woman than the one who had taken to wearing discount-store shirtwaists. The blue of the dress perfectly matched the blue of her eyes. Lovey felt almost beautiful. A glance at her watch brought her back to earth, however. It was time to serve supper. Lovey quickly ran a brush through her hair then ran out.

Back at the dining hall, she was surprised to find the kitchen nearly empty of both women and food. Only Jean was left, piling hot dinner rolls onto a massive tray. Lovey moved to take the tray, but Jean, after a quick glance at Lovey's new dress, waved her away.

"Go on, you," Jean admonished. "All's done in here. Why don't you go and eat some hot food for once." Embarrassed, Lovey thanked Jean, who replied by shooing her out the door.

In the dining room, Lovey was not surprised to see that the only empty seats were right next to Silas. Almost shyly, she moved across the room and blushed when he jumped up to pull out her chair, his eyes shining. As she sat down, Silas leaned over and whispered in her ear, his voice catching. "You look beautiful." Lovey stared down at her lap, unable to stop smiling and unaware that many of the women in the room were also smiling.

Josiah had managed to come down and led the room in a prayer then sat down on Lovey's other side.

Lovey was so wound up she could hardly eat the delicious beef stew the women had prepared. She glanced over and saw that Silas was hardly eating his meal too.

"I was wondering if you would like to take a walk later," he said quietly.

Lovey nodded, unable to answer.

Dinner was a quiet affair, with Josiah lost in his thoughts and Lovey and Silas lost in each other. When it was done, Lovey offered to help clean up, but Jean shooed her away again, pushing her toward the doorway where Silas waited holding an old blanket. She felt weirdly shy stepping out the door with him.

It wasn't quite dark yet, so they took the path that led farther into the woods. The men had cut a wide swath clearing the path, so access to the stream was easier and unencumbered by branches and poison ivy. When they were out of sight of the camp, Silas reached over and took Lovey's hand. It was a warm night, but Lovey could feel goose bumps rising on her arms.

When they reached the stream, Lovey was surprised to see that the men had built a deck on the bank. Silas laid the blanket over the wood and sat down with his legs dangling over the side. Lovey took off her shoes and sat beside him.

They sat silently and stared at the moon that hung full and heavy just over the tops of the trees. In the distance they could hear Emmett firing up his fiddle and what sounded like Joe on a banjo.

"Can I tell you what I love most about you?" Silas asked in a voice quiet and reverential in the dark.

Lovey turned and smiled at him. "Sure."

"You're economical with your words," he said, surprising her.

"Do you mean to say I don't talk enough?" she joked.

Silas smiled back at her. "Sort of. I guess I mean I love that you appreciate silence. You don't seem to need to fill it with nonsense conversation."

"You know, they say that people who are meant to be friends can just sit, not speaking at all, and feel completely comfortable," Lovey said just to fill the silence.

Silas moved his hand over and twined his fingers with Lovey's. "Is that what we are? Friends?"

"I guess...I mean...I don't know. What do you think we are?" Lovey wasn't sure she wanted to have this conversation. Relationships were a problem she'd never been good at solving.

"Do you remember the revival, when you first got sick?" Silas asked, and Lovey nodded, her face red with embarrassment at the memory.

"I sat near the Wootens because I knew you were going to sit there. And I was going to talk to you after the revival, but when you started bleeding, I knew I needed to help you. I felt like, right at that moment, I was supposed to be there...even if it was just to carry you."

Lovey stared at him, her expression somber.

Silas looked away, his eyes distant with the memory. "I already knew who you were, and I knew from the first time I saw you that you were supposed to be my girl."

"You knew that at the revival?"

Silas shook his head. "I saw you long before you ever saw me. We were just kids. You were with your dad, making a visit to the Hollis's house. I think it was for the baby. Your dad was looking at the baby anyway. And you were drawing in the dirt with the other kids so they wouldn't be scared. You were so beautiful and so...different from anyone else in Merwin. You were...bright...and shining..." Silas gave a sad chuckle. "The exact opposite of me."

Lovey was surprised. "I remember that day. The baby had a bad cough that my father thought might be whooping cough. He didn't want the other kids near, in case it was, so I took them outside. But they lived out in the middle of nowhere. What were you doing there?"

Silas shrugged. "My grandmother...I mean Agnes, delivered the baby and knew she was sick, so she sent me to deliver some medicine for them. When I saw you and your dad, I knew the baby wouldn't need the muck Agnes made."

"Why didn't you come up then?" Lovey asked.

Silas smiled derisively. "I was only twelve. I wasn't brave enough."

They sat silently for a while, and then Lovey had to ask the one question that had been bugging her all this time.

"Silas? Why didn't you ever come back to see me?"

Silas looked at her, his expression worried. "I did...a couple of times, but you were away at college, and then you were away away...far away."

"But when I came back to Merwin before my last surgery, you were gone."

Silas looked away. "It was my time to go try to be somebody. I needed to deserve you, Lovey. I needed to be someone good enough, important enough, to deserve to be with you."

Lovey's expression turned sad. "I don't have that kind of value," she said quietly. "I can't even give you what a normal...healthy woman can."

Silas smiled at her, his eyes warm. "I disagree. I know we can't have children together, and that's OK. I want to be with *you*. Nothing else matters to me."

Lovey was moved by his sincerity. Suddenly shy, she turned away. Silas shifted so that he was facing her and pulled something out of his pocket. Lovey turned to see him holding out a piece of paper.

"What is it?" she asked then reached out to take the paper. She unfolded it to see a permit application for a wedding license. She looked up in surprise.

"I want to marry you, Lovey," he said then opened his palm. In it lay a ring, a simple, satin-finish band with a perfect, white diamond. Silas reached over and took Lovey's hand. She held her breath as he slid the ring onto her finger. It fit perfectly.

"It's beautiful," she breathed.

"I hope it's OK," Silas said. "I wanted to give you something more personal than a store-bought ring, so I made this."

"You made a diamond?" she asked stupidly, and Silas laughed.

"No, I bought the diamond. I made the rest of the ring though."

Lovey looked down at the ring that now graced her thin finger.

Silas smiled at her. "You didn't answer my question."

Lovey looked up and gave him her own smile. "You didn't ask me a question."

Silas moved over and took Lovey's face in his hands. Her eyes went wide as he moved closer.

"Lovey, will you marry me?" he whispered.

"Yes."

Lovey tried to remember to breathe as his lips came down on hers.

FORTY-NINE

Lovey and Silas were so consumed with each other that they didn't notice the air changing around them. The weather had turned wet and cold, and the general mood in Zion had declined, especially Josiah's. If she'd looked more closely, Lovey would have seen Josiah withdrawing from the community, spending less time in the church and more in front of his window. He'd taken to preaching long, rambling sermons in front of the fire in the dining hall. At first they were consistent with his earlier lessons of love and compassion. But over time they began to change. They became more prophetic, but from his demeanor, the future was equal parts bleak and fearsome.

These sermons were followed by conversations with whoever happened to be sitting with him. It wasn't until Lovey noticed the growing audience that she realized she'd been living in a lovely dream.

The reality was that Josiah's message was changing, and she needed to understand why. She could hear the group gathering in the dining hall, so she left her clinic and took a seat at the back to listen. She'd come in midconversation but managed to catch Misty's question, which took her aback.

"When does God stop loving you?" Misty asked, and the room went quiet. She rarely spoke but could often be found near Josiah when she wasn't helping Jean. Lovey thought Misty might have a little crush on Josiah but had written it off as nothing, especially since Josiah hadn't seemed to notice.

Instead of answering her, Josiah asked a question of his own. "Why would you think he's stopped loving you?"

Misty struggled with her words. "The Bible says that you musn't have sexual relations with both a woman and her daughter. That it's wicked. But whose sin is it? Because God told Moses he would punish the sinners...that they would be driven out of their lands because they had defiled...well I guess themselves."

Josiah seemed to consider her question. "The sinner is the one who broke God's law, the one who lay with both mother and daughter. Then the mother sinned when she didn't keep her husband to the marriage bed but let him lie with the daughter. The daughter sinned if she invited the father to her bed."

Lovey watched Misty's face go pale. Jean moved over and whispered something in Misty's ear, but the girl just shook her head as she fought back tears. Josiah watched the exchange with something like sorrow on his face, but instead of comforting Misty, he left her to Jean and changed the subject.

"Some of you have asked me why we don't do altar calls here at Zion. It's because we are not faith healers. But if you have need of spiritual healing, we can start laying on hands and praying for you."

Lovey approved of this. In her work in the clinic and out in the field, she'd found there was great power in human touch. People were so emotionally and physically disenfranchised from each other that they no longer gave hugs or even shook hands when they met. When Josiah glanced at her, she smiled and nodded. He gave her a rare smile in return then went back to his flock.

Late the next morning, Lovey was sitting in her clinic making notes on the previous day's patients when Jean came in pulling a reluctant Misty behind her.

"Come on," Jean said to her, pulling the girl past her and pushing her toward Lovey. "She's not going to bite you."

"Is something wrong?" Lovey asked.

Jean pushed Misty down into the chair across from Lovey then sat in the chair next to her.

"It's OK," Jean said quietly, putting her arm around the young woman. "She can help you...I promise."

Misty still wouldn't answer, but Lovey got the feeling it was due more to embarrassment than stubbornness. "Are you sick?" she asked.

Misty shook her head but wouldn't look at Lovey. Jean was losing her patience with the girl.

"Hon, either you tell her or I will, but she's gonna have to know either way," Jean said.

Misty shook her head again, and Jean threw up her hands. "Misty's worried she might not ever get pregnant," Jean blurted.

Lovey was surprised. She wasn't sure what she'd expected, but it definitely wasn't that. "Do you want to be pregnant?" she asked gently.

When Misty finally looked at her, Lovey saw she was trying not to cry. She understood the young woman's pain and felt an old, familiar pain wrap its fingers around her heart. More than anything she wished she could have her own child.

"I've been going to healers to make me better," the girl said softly, "but now I'm feeling poorly...like pains in my stomach, and I ain't had a period in a long time."

"What's a long time?" Lovey asked. She knew she needed to palpate the girl's belly but was hesitant to touch her until Misty felt more comfortable with her.

Misty shrugged then wiped at her eyes. "I was never regular, but I never went this long without it coming. Few months maybe?"

Jean nudged Misty. "Tell her what you told me. She needs to know what's wrong so she can take care of you."

Lovey's gaze went back and forth between the two women, but she kept quiet. Misty was as skittish as a cat even on her best days; the last thing Lovey wanted to do was scare her off.

"I been followin' the healers because I can't have a baby," Misty began. "I got married real young because I was pregnant, but I lost the baby. Robbie said I wasn't any good to him if I couldn't give him babies, so I kept tryin', but I couldn't get pregnant again. So he left."

Misty glanced at Jean who nodded for her to continue. "We had a real nice trailer, but when Robbie left I didn't have any way to pay for it. There was a family near Union who needed help taking care of their babies, so I went to stay with them. They were real nice at first, but the wife got mad at me. She was real holy and told me that I was a sinner and that the stain of my sin would stain her family too unless I repented and bathed in waters of righteousness. So I did. I thought maybe God would find favor with me if I did what they asked."

Misty paused for a long moment. Jean gave Misty time to gather herself then reached over and took the girl's hand as if to reassure her. Misty took a deep breath and continued. "They had this big pond in their yard but a fake one, like people make to put fish in. They had me walk down to the pond, and then they told me I had to take my clothes off in front of them. I didn't want to, but I knew they'd make me leave otherwise, so I did it. Then the wife made me follow her into the water with the husband behind, reading his Bible. When we got to where it was deep, she pushed me under the water. It was real cold. She would let me come up for air, and then she'd push me down again.

"We were in there a real long time, but when we were done she said I was still dirty because I let the husband put his eyes on my nakedness. I could tell he liked lookin' at me because he had a...he got hard. The wife got real mad and called me a word, but I don't know what it means...*want*...something with *want*."

"Wanton?" Lovey asked, her heart aching for the girl.

Misty nodded. "That's it. She said, because I was wanton, that I would always be a sinner and that I couldn't stay with them anymore or I would make them all sinners. So I thought if I could get healed Robbie would come back. I started going to all the healers, but some wanted money, so I sold my car and hitched rides when I could. I finally fetched up at Brother Guthrie's, and he let me stay for a while. That's when I first saw Josiah."

"You know Josiah's not a healer, right?" Lovey asked.

Misty nodded. "I know that's what he says. But I heard Josiah's the second son. God has sent him back to judge us this time. I figured if there was anyone who could do miracles, it was him."

Lovey didn't want to add to the girl's disappointment so she left that one alone. "Did a doctor ever tell you why you can't get pregnant?"

Misty's face flamed red with shame. "I got hurt real bad when I was younger. My mother's boyfriend...he did some things...he let his friends do it too. Anyway, I had to go to the hospital, because they hurt me real bad, and I heard the doctor there say that my insides were too messed up. When Robbie got me pregnant, I thought it was a miracle, but when the baby died...well...I knew God was punishing me for being a sinner."

Lovey finally understood Misty's earlier conversation with Josiah. "Misty, you're not a sinner because of what your mother's boyfriend did. He's a sinner...and a criminal...but you're not. Why would you think that?"

Misty looked up at her with tears in her eyes. "Because I didn't say no."

"Even so," Lovey said quietly. "You were too young to make a decision like that...too young to know what they did was wrong. I'm not sure what I can do about the damage—I'm not that kind of doctor—but I can try to figure out why you aren't menstruating. Are you OK with me examining you?"

Misty nodded, so Lovey handed her a sheet. "If you'll take everything off below the waist and lie down, I'll take a look, OK?"

Misty nodded again, so Jean and Lovey stepped out of the room to give her some privacy. "I just feel so bad for her," Jean said quietly. "Can you imagine wanting a baby so bad?"

Lovey gave Jean a sad smile. "I can."

After another minute, Lovey knocked on the door and entered. The exam only took a few minutes, but Lovey could tell Misty had an extraordinary amount of scarring on her cervix and on her vaginal walls, either from damage or infection or both. The fact that Misty had been able to get pregnant at all was pretty remarkable. Lovey didn't have an intrauterine sonogram to determine how far the scarring went but was fairly certain it extended into Misty's uterus. Everything else seemed normal, however, and Misty was likely to have her cycle any day now.

"You do have a lot of scarring, probably from the assault, but I'm not feeling any masses or fibroids, so you should be fine," she said as she pulled off her gloves.

"What about having a baby? Can I still do that?" Misty asked, her voice hopeful.

Lovey covered her legs with the sheet and helped her sit up then sat across from her. "I'm not a gynecologist, but with the extent of the scarring on your cervix, it is surprising that you were able to get pregnant the first time. And I can't determine why you miscarried without the right equipment. You would need to see a fertility specialist for that."

"I went to one of them after Robbie left, and he told me there was nothing he could do," Misty answered. "But the Lord can do anything. He could heal me if he wanted to."

Lovey didn't want to argue faith with Misty, so she shrugged instead. "We'll just have to pray then, won't we?"

Misty gave her the first smile she'd ever seen from the girl. "Thank you, Miss Lovey."

Lovey had to put her personal feelings aside. Her talk with Misty had brought up old anger and regrets that a little bottle of pills taken before she was born had affected her life so profoundly. She felt her resentments bubbling up, and if she didn't resolve them once and for all, they would consume her.

A few days later, still bothered by her conversation with Misty and all the feelings it had brought up, she found herself wandering through the cold rain as if it could wash away her sorrow. Habit brought her to the church. Worship would be starting soon anyway, so she let herself in and found Josiah already there. He usually waited near his pulpit, but today he was sitting in one of the pews staring at the plain wooden cross in front of him, his face pensive.

Lovey hesitated for a moment then sat down next to him. "Everything all right?" she asked quietly.

Josiah turned and looked at her with a sad smile on his face. "I'm fine, Lovey. I was just...listening."

Lovey couldn't think of any response that wasn't insipid or banal, so she said nothing, choosing instead to sit quietly and offer him her silent support. Josiah continued to stare ahead at nothing. She closed her eyes and listened to the silence that had filled her ears. She didn't know how long they sat that way, but after a time she felt Josiah shift next to her. Lovey opened her eyes to find Josiah staring at her.

"Lovey?" he asked quietly.

"What is it, Josiah?" she asked.

"I'm not who they think I am," Josiah answered.

"What do you mean?"

"The one they seek is not yet here...'Do not be afraid for I bring you good news of great joy. Today in the town of David a Savior has been born to you; he is Christ the Lord.'"

Lovey stared at him in confusion then realized what he was saying. "You're the angel...the messenger."

Josiah gazed at her sadly then nodded. "I am but a servant. I can't give them salvation."

Lovey stared at Josiah as a deep and penetrating sadness filled her heart. Miriam's whole life had been dedicated to the prospect that she would give birth to the Messiah. Marianne's life had been sacrificed for it. Even though Lovey knew intellectually that this was born out of desperation for relevance or religious delusion, a part of her respected the magnitude of their faith. Too many people living at Zion were there in the hopes that it was true.

"Josiah, you have to tell them..."

"I have told them."

"Lyrical language and poetry probably weren't the best way to do that."

"Do not be afraid. You have found favor with God."

Lovey was taken aback. "What do you mean?"

Josiah held her hand in both of his. "There will be a mother. Out of extraordinary circumstances, a child will be born."

Lovey wondered if Miriam's delusions were being made manifest in her grandson. She shook her head. "I'm—"

"No, you have been a faithful servant of the Lord, but you have no womb, Lovey."

Lovey pulled her hand away to put her fingers to her eyes and tried to shake away the turmoil in her head. Then she stilled and dropped her hands. "Misty."

Josiah nodded. "'Whoever then humbles himself as this child, he is the greatest in the kingdom of heaven. And whoever receives one such child in my name receives me.' There will be miracles today, Lovey."

Lovey stared at the cross in front of her and thought for a moment, though a question had come immediately to mind. Then she turned and looked into Josiah's eyes, where she saw, with his sadness, an immense love that enveloped her and gave her peace.

"Is this real?"

Josiah reached over and again took Lovey's hands in his own and looked into her eyes. "God does have a plan for everyone, and he has a very important one for you. You are going to be a mother, Lovey. As you were to me...you are going to be a mother to the most extraordinary child the world has ever seen."

Lovey shook her head and stared at him uncomprehendingly. "I don't understand. How is that possible, even for Misty?"

"From the moment of creation, God's plan has been in motion. And despite man's every effort to thwart that plan, it is his will that will prevail." Josiah's voice was firm.

Lovey hardly recognized the man sitting before her. "And what is his will?" Lovey asked carefully.

"That is another question." Josiah smiled. "But one I will answer." Josiah dropped her hands to lay his gently on either side of her face. "He is sending a child...a second child to save all the world."

"Save it from what?" Lovey whispered.

Lovey stared as Josiah's face crumpled and his eyes filled. He struggled to regain his composure, but a tear escaped and traced its way down the sharp lines of his face. Josiah sighed. "From itself."

Lovey had moved to comfort him when the door behind them opened. Lovey turned to see Harley and the others coming in for worship. She put on a smile and stood while Josiah wiped at his eyes.

Though the people of the community came to Sunday services, all of Zion was present for daily worship. Their numbers had grown enough that they were able to fill at least the first few pews of the old church.

Josiah stood before them, his eyes clear of the tears he'd shed earlier. "Joshua said to the people of Israel, 'Choose for yourselves this day whom you will serve, whether the gods your ancestors served beyond the Euphrates, or the gods of the Amorites, in whose land you are living. But as for me and my household, we will serve the Lord.'

"After Moses led the children of Israel out of slavery, they wandered for years, for decades, but still Moses persevered. When he descended from the mountain and saw that his people had taken up worship of the golden calf, he ordered its destruction and took his faithful farther away from Egypt but closer to their home. When they were set upon by the Amalekites, Moses sent Joshua to lead the army of the Israelites so that he could raise the staff of God to ensure their victory. And when his arms tired, Aaron and Hur came to help the old man by holding the staff high in Moses's own hand. When Moses died in sight of the promised land, Joshua took up the mantle of leadership and told them to make that choice, to be deliberate in their decision of who they would serve, who they would worship, but to know that anyone who stood with Joshua would be serving the Lord.

"Families are born of blood...mothers and fathers having children who in their time have their own children. Generations born of a single bloodline. But families are also born of circumstance, of shared ideas,

of sameness of faith. Without mothers or fathers...brothers or sisters...
we can all still be part of a family. Zion is a family. We have mothers and
fathers, sons and daughters, brothers and sisters...not born of blood but
of shared love for the Lord...and a hope to build a new kind of family."

Josiah stepped away from the lectern and took the microphone
with him. "I am going to offer everyone the opportunity to receive individual prayer and blessing through an altar call, but before I do, I want
to offer Misty the chance to come first."

Lovey glanced over at Misty, who looked startled for being singled
out then stood and shyly stepped forward toward Josiah, who had
reached out to her.

Josiah set down the microphone, but his voice still carried throughout the small church. "Our sister Misty came to us broken of heart and
body, in despair that she might not ever have a child again," he said
gently.

Misty's face crumpled, and tears spilled from her eyes.

"But she persevered in her service to the Lord, and he is pleased. The
Lord loves Misty...we...love Misty." Josiah was now speaking directly to
the weeping girl. "He has heard your prayers, and he has answered."

Lovey watched as Josiah stepped up to her and placed one hand
over her womb and the other around the girl's shoulders. She held
her breath and watched Josiah pray over Misty, who looked at him in
wonder.

"'Before I formed you in the womb I knew you, and before you were
born I consecrated you; I have appointed you a prophet to the nations,'"
he prayed quietly, and Misty gasped. Then she fainted.

FIFTY

Josiah's mood improved following what people were calling his "miracle" with Misty. His sermons were once again about love and commitment to Christ's teachings, and his congregation grew again. Winter became spring, and the chilling rains cleared away to reveal a world made clean.

Though Lovey remained doubtful of Josiah's ability to heal Misty, she knew that she *wanted* to believe and hoped that was enough for God. And she hoped for Misty's sake that God would indeed send her a child. Her heart sank when Misty came into the clinic looking pale and shaken.

"What's wrong?" Lovey asked as she helped Misty onto the exam table.

"It's like before but worse," Misty said. "I ain't had a period, and I feel sick and dizzy all the time." The girl began to cry. "I thought Josiah could fix me...make it better with the Lord, but I'm too dirty...too...broken...to fix."

"Here, lie down, and let me check," Lovey said and helped Misty lie back. She palpated the girl's abdomen then frowned. She stepped over to the cabinet and opened it. "Can you give me a urine sample? I want to check for blood."

Misty got up and took the specimen cup from Lovey then stepped into the small bathroom. She returned a moment later with a cup of dark urine.

"Well I can tell you right now you need to be drinking more water," Lovey said as she accepted the cup from Misty. She placed it on the counter and dropped in a litmus test then, for good measure, dipped an HCG test strip as well. She turned back to see Misty sitting on the table holding her stomach, her face still pale and drawn.

"Water's been tasting bad...everything's been tasting bad." Misty groaned. "I'm dying, Miss Lovey. The Lord has found me wanting, and he's punishing me. I know it. I'm dying."

Lovey turned away to check the test strips. Her breath caught in her throat, and a maelstrom of emotions started swirling around in her head.

"You're not dying, Misty," she said quietly through the catch in her throat. "You're pregnant."

Misty burst into tears behind her. Lovey fought to get her emotions under control then put on a smile and turned to comfort the girl.

The news of Misty's pregnancy was met with great joy throughout the community, and no one bothered to question the girl about her baby's paternity, accepting it as a miracle rather than the extraordinary act of nature that Lovey knew it to be. As if in agreement with Lovey's internal conflict, the rains returned, and Zion was once again caught under a deluge.

With the abrupt weather change came an unfortunate spate of ill-nesses and an uptick in visitors to Zion's free clinic. By the end of the month, just about everyone had come down with one kind of sickness or another. Lovey was just finishing up with several cases of the flu, a mysterious rash, and a run-of-the-mill ear infection when she heard the roar of engines accompanied by the popping-corn sound of tires on gravel. Lovey stepped outside to see a trio of trucks coming to a stop in the center of their little village.

Visitors were unusual enough that people came to their doorways or from their jobs to see who had arrived. Lovey knew one of the men was a Wooten the moment he stepped down from his truck. Like Abel, he was an older version of Silas, with the Wooten black hair and black eyes, but where Abel lived a hard but clean life on the farm, this one looked like he'd been ridden hard and put up wet. He was shorter than Silas and thin to the point of emaciation, with his skin stretched tight over his chin and cheekbones. Random tattoos marked his arms and neck, and while old meth scars pitted his face, his eyes were clear and taking in everything around him.

There were four other men with him who looked like they had taken the same path as their leader. One had the look and mannerisms of someone with either cerebral palsy or a traumatic brain injury. He struggled to climb down from the truck and almost fell trying to push the door shut. When he turned toward her, Lovey noticed his right arm was significantly contracted and his right leg dragged when he walked.

"Looks like we got ourselves a bustling metropolis," the leader sneered.

Lovey stepped out to greet them. "I'm not sure if you could call us a metropolis, but we're certainly bustling," she replied then held out her hand. "I'm Olivia Polk."

Her visitor glanced at her hand then weakly touched the ends of her fingers, his expression a moue of distaste. "Wade Wooten. Where's my nephew?"

Lovey was about to answer when Josiah came up behind her. "I'm here, Uncle Wade," he answered, though his tone sounded anything but happy to see his uncle.

Wade, though, made a great show of greeting his nephew. "There's Jojo! Let me look at you. Damn, boy, you're a man now!" Wade gave Josiah a big hug then stepped away with his hand still clamped around the boy's neck. "Why don't you show me and my boys around? We got a lotta plans for your little place here."

Josiah stepped away. "Uh, Lovey should be the one to show you around, Uncle Wade. It's really her church. She's the one that paid for it."

Wade turned his black eyes back to Lovey. She'd seen that look many times before.

"Oh, well then, *Lovey*. How about a little tour then?"

"We'll do it," Lovey heard behind her. She turned to see Silas and Harley coming up to their little group, with Joe and Emmett close behind them.

Wade started to chuckle. "I can tell just by lookin' at you who you are. You're Inez's dead baby boy." Wade stretched out his hand toward Silas, who pointedly ignored it.

Wade shrugged then put his hand down. "We'll since we're all bein' neighborly, I'll just make the introductions." Wade swept his hand behind him in a grand gesture. "These two fellas are Davis and Jackson." Both men nodded but kept their position behind Wade. "This one here is my buddy Arlen. Him and me go way back, and that one there is Willie.

He had an accident that made him a retard, so you're gonna have to talk real loud and real slow, or he can't understand." Wade leaned back and put his mouth up to Willie's ear. "AIN'T THAT RIGHT, RETARD?"

Willie winced slightly but nodded. Lovey spotted the tension around his eyes and doubted very seriously that Willie had a hearing problem.

Wade turned back to Lovey, who made her own introductions. When she was done, Silas kept his spot and pointed out each building and gave a short, curt summary of its purpose.

"And that's it. Thanks for coming," Silas finished.

Wade threw up his hands. "Oh now, we ain't here to take in the sights. We're here to watch over our boy Josiah here."

Josiah looked uncomfortable at the prospect. "I'm fine, Uncle Wade. I've got Lovey and Silas and all the others here to help me."

"Yeah, but they ain't family, Jojo," Wade replied, making a big show of shaking his head. "They ain't gonna have your back like me."

Their exchange was interrupted by the man standing directly behind Wade, the one he'd called Jackson. Lovey hadn't noticed before, but he was holding his hand against his chest. She could see blood seeping from under the makeshift bandage.

"Wade," he said quietly, "leave it for now. I gotta get this taken care of."

Lovey stepped forward and held out her hand. "Are you hurt? I can look at it for you."

Jackson pulled his hand closer and glanced at Wade, who nodded. "It's all right," Wade said. "My brother told me Miss Polk here is a bona fide doctor."

Jackson looked doubtful but let Lovey pull his hand out. When she turned the palm up, she saw a deep laceration across his palm.

"Had a flat on the truck. The wrench slipped and got me," he said by way of explanation.

Lovey looked up at him. His eyes were clear, and he was missing the meth scars that dotted Wade's face. "This is pretty bad. If you'll come with me, I can get you fixed up. OK?"

Jackson looked at Wade, who nodded again, then let Lovey lead him into the clinic.

In the privacy of the exam room, Jackson was surprisingly polite, thanking Lovey for helping him. Lovey smiled but said nothing as she pulled on gloves then examined the wound on his hand.

"The cut is deep," she said. "I can clean it for you, but since it's on the palm of your hand, it's going to need stitches to stay closed. I can do them for you here, but you'll have to come back to have them removed. Is that OK?"

"If that's what it needs, then go ahead. I'm not useful if I can't use my hand," Jackson answered.

Jackson watched as Lovey set about cleaning the wound. She pulled over a needle and a bottle of lidocaine. "Have you ever had stitches before?" she asked.

Jackson nodded.

"I need to give you a little anesthetic first. Do you know if you're allergic?"

Jackson shook his head. "Naw, I'm good."

Lovey prepped her needle. "It's going to pinch. OK?"

Jackson went a little pale at the sight of the needle but nodded. Lovey smiled. "It helps if you don't stare at it." Jackson looked away and only flinched slightly when the needle went into his hand.

"There. We'll give that a few seconds," Lovey said before pulling out a suture kit from the cabinet behind her.

"You know Wade's not all that bad," Jackson said quietly. "He puts on a big show, but he's had it rough."

"I've heard he's had some...issues," Lovey said.

Jackson shrugged then looked away as Lovey prepared to suture his wound. "We all have issues. Wade's are just a little more serious. He was doing rig work when one of his crew sparked the pipeline and caused a blowout. The families were really hard on Wade, saying it was his fault for giving the orders even though he was really only doing what the engineers told him to."

"Did you and Wade work together?" Lovey asked.

"Yeah. Wade was on the rig when it happened, but I was in Biloxi on leave. I was due back the day after the accident." Jackson's voice went quiet. "My buddy died...I was supposed to take over for him." He stared out the window, his face pensive.

"I'm very sorry about your friend," Lovey said then tied off the last stitch. "You're done. I'm going to bandage it for now, and I need you to keep it clean and covered until I look at it again. Have you had a tetanus shot within the last five years?" she asked, and Jackson nodded. "Good, then I'm going to give you a ten-day supply of antibiotics, and I need you to take all of them. Are you allergic to any medicines?"

Jackson shook his head again.

Lovey handed him a small pile of packets. "Take all of these. The instructions are in the packet."

"Thanks. How much do I owe you?" he asked as he took the packets with his uninjured hand.

"We're a free clinic. You don't owe anything." Lovey smiled.

Jackson didn't return the smile. "Then can I ask you for another favor?"

Lovey's smile faded, and her face mirrored his seriousness.

"Wade came here because he...we don't have anywhere else to go," Jackson began then looked over to the doorway where Josiah and Silas had appeared. "We went to his family's place in the basin, but his brother Jacob wouldn't let him stay. Said he's too much of a problem. Then we come to the farm, but Abel and the other one..."

"Caleb?" Lovey offered.

Jackson nodded. "Yeah, that one. They said the same thing. I guess Wade did some things long ago that got them worried about having him around."

"I can tell Wade's had some...issues...in the past. Could that be why?" Lovey asked delicately.

"You mean the drugs?" Jackson asked. Lovey nodded. "We all had some problems. Mine was the drink. It got worse after the...accident. Arlen and Wade did meth. Wade met Davis in rehab. He had a heroin problem. Willie just showed up at one point. I'm not even sure where we found him. Anyway, we've all been clean for long enough to matter. Wade might be a dick, but he's not a user...not anymore."

Lovey looked over at Silas, who shrugged, then at Josiah. "Well, Josiah? What do you want to do?"

"'For the Son of Man came to seek and to save the lost,'" he answered. "We can't turn them away when they come to us."

Lovey looked at Jackson, who regarded her in turn. Though Wade made her nervous, Jackson had been up front about their situation. She appreciated his honesty, and she felt his sincerity. Wondering if she was making a mistake, she took a deep breath and smiled.

"Welcome to Zion."

FIFTY-ONE

It wasn't long before Lovey regretted her invitation. Wade's presence brought an unfortunate influence into the community. Despite Jackson's words, he behaved as if his relationship with Josiah conveyed some level of ownership over the property, and he could often be found holding court in the dining room where Josiah had once preached to the community. Jackson and Davis often helped out around the camp, but Wade seemed to feel his status as Josiah's uncle exempted him from working, consenting only to running errands into town.

At some point he and Arlen had picked up a handful of groupies that Lovey had forbidden from staying on the property. They often arrived during the afternoon and sat with Wade and his friends, drinking and eating the community's food. One girl in particular, Tamara, looked too young to be courting the likes of Wade. Lovey couldn't be certain, but she was pretty sure the girl was only sixteen. She was heavyset, with a pretty face and a mass of badly permed hair. Lovey was certain the girl was spending her nights at Zion and resolved to put an end to it before she brought trouble to the community.

She'd been seeing patients all morning and was taking a short break when she walked out of the clinic to find the group parked in front of the fireplace. Wade had a roaring fire going despite the relative warmth of the day. He lolled in Josiah's armchair in shirt-sleeves, with Willie and Arlen sitting alongside him. Wade and Arlen were idly fondling the girls perched on the arms of their chairs, while Willie sat alone and unattended, an unfortunate audience to the other men. He was the only one who looked up when Lovey entered the room.

"You know there are plenty of things to do around here," she said. "Everyone else earns their right to be here."

As a unit the group turned and stared at Lovey. Wade opened his mouth to reply, but it was Tamara who answered.

"Why don't you talk like us?" she asked, though the question sounded more like a challenge.

"Don't you know?" Wade answered. "Lovey here's a educated woman. She ain't trailer trash like the rest uh y'alls."

Tamara squealed her protest and gave Wade a flirtatious jab. "I ain't ever lived in a trailer." Tamara pouted then leaned her plump breasts into Wade's arm.

"Now *Lovey* here," Wade continued, ignoring the girl. "You know she ain't ever set foot in a trailer, let alone lived in one." Wade eyed Lovey speculatively. "She's quality. Seems like she and me should get together. We could make this place something special."

Lovey's eyes narrowed along with Tamara's. "Zion was special long before you got here, and it'll continue to be so long after you're gone," she said quietly.

"Zion could be great...strong," Wade countered. "Like that one place, what's it called? Jericho...that's it."

"Do you even know your Bible?" Lovey asked. "Jericho wasn't something to aspire to...even children know God commanded Joshua to kill the entire city for having fallen into sin."

Wade scowled. He didn't like being corrected, much less by a woman. "Shit...nothin' wrong with a little messin' around." He pulled Tamara across his lap and let her purr against him.

Lovey shook her head. "Nothing wrong with a little bestiality...or sacrificing children to false gods...no, nothing wrong with that."

Wade smiled. "Exactly. We could party like Jericho, baby. We'll be king and queen. You and me. We could have lots of fun together."

Disgusted, Lovey turned to leave the room and bumped into Silas, who caught her. "What was that all about?" he asked, anger in his tone.

"Nothing," Lovey answered. "It was nothing."

Silas scowled over her shoulder then pulled her away. "What did he say to you?" Silas insisted.

Lovey shook her head. "He's just baiting me into a confrontation... being an ass because he has nothing better to do."

Silas took her hands in his and took a deep breath. "Would you and Josiah like to go into town with me tomorrow? Harley and I have some errands to run, and it would be a chance for you to get away from all the craziness here."

Lovey smiled and nodded. "I'd like that."

Lovey awoke happy the next morning. The prospect of a trip anywhere with Silas made her smile, and she knew Josiah needed to take some time away from Zion to clear his head and regain a little perspective.

After breakfast they followed Harley to Silas's truck and climbed in for their little trip. Josiah's mood lightened considerably the farther they drove from Zion. Lovey made a silent promise to make sure he got out more. He sat in the back with Lovey, his head resting against the window. His eyes were closed against the sun, but from the small smile on his face, Lovey could tell he was happy.

Lovey glanced out her window at the landscape rolling past them. "Where are we going?" she asked.

Harley beamed a smile at Silas then sobered his expression and turned back to reply. "Uh...we need to pick up some stuff in Meridian."

It was a short drive, but Lovey was glad to escape the confines of the narrow backseat when Silas stopped in the middle of the small city. It wasn't until she looked up that she realized they were standing in front of the courthouse.

"Why are we here?" she asked, confused.

Silas was about to answer when Abel walked up with a slight, balding man dressed in an ill-fitting suit.

"Hello, Mr. Wooten?" the man asked, reaching out and shaking Silas's hand. "Are you all ready?"

Lovey stared at Silas in confusion. "I don't understand...who is this? Why did he call you Mr. Wooten...what's going on?"

Silas turned and took Lovey's hands in his. "This is Gene Dillard. He's a justice of the peace. I know this probably isn't what you were hoping for, but if you're OK with it...well...I thought we could get married...today."

Lovey fought the tears that came to her eyes. Speechless, she nodded instead then pulled Silas into her arms.

"I love you, Olivia," he whispered into her ear. "I love you so much I don't want to wait another day."

Lovey nodded into his chest, still unable to speak. When she pulled back she laughed and wiped at her eyes.

Silas's expression was concerned. "Are you OK with this?" he asked. "We can have a proper wedding if that's what you want."

She shook her head. "No...this is perfect...wait...no." Lovey's expression turned stricken. "Martine isn't here."

Silas smiled this time. "She's waiting inside."

When they stepped back out into the sunshine, Lovey was a married woman. Though Silas had arranged for the justice of the peace to sign their paper work, it was Josiah who actually married them. Abel, Harley, and Martine were there as witnesses, and even though the ceremony only took minutes, Lovey was the happiest woman on the planet.

Harley and Josiah left with Abel, who also took Martine with them.

"Where are we going?" Lovey asked as they drove off.

"We have a little bit of a drive in front of us, but we're going someplace...quiet."

They indeed drove for a while, and it was late afternoon when they reached an old asphalt road that cut through a thick forest of trees. Silas turned onto the road, and day instantly became night under the canopy. They followed the road for a few minutes then slowed when a tall, thin man stepped out of the dark and onto the road. Silas stopped, and his doppelganger stuck his head in through the window.

"You know where you're going, right?" he asked quietly, and Silas nodded. Then he held his hand out to Lovey. "Jacob Wooten...I'm not sure if you remember me, but I just wanted to say congratulations."

Lovey smiled and shook his hand. "Thank you so much. I'm very pleased to meet you."

Jacob returned her smile then pushed himself out of the window. "Welcome to the Wooten family," he said then waved them off.

Silas drove the winding road through the trees. The asphalt ended and turned to gravel, and as the gravel turned to dirt, they drove into a clearing, where Silas stopped. In front of them a small but perfectly kept cabin was perched right over the water.

Silas pulled a pair of small suitcases out from under the cover on the back of his truck, leaving Lovey to wonder how long he'd been planning this surprise. Then he took her hand and led her up the ramp and into the cabin.

It was simple but clean inside, and Jacob had lit a fire in the wood stove that stood in the corner. A small kitchen sat to the right, and an opened door to the left revealed a small bathroom. The rest of the cabin was open, with an old iron bed covered with a beautiful, red-and-white wedding-ring quilt on one side and a sofa and small dining table on

Servant

the other. Lovey could tell by the quality of the furniture that Abel had provided the furnishings and Rachel and Dorcas had made the quilt. Everything faced a wall of windows that overlooked the bayou.

Silas set the suitcases down and reached out. Lovey immediately stepped into his embrace and melted into his arms as his lips came down on hers. Though she wasn't a virgin, it had been a very, very long time since she'd been with a man.

Silas pulled back and held Lovey's face in his hands. "I'm sorry if this wasn't what you were hoping for," he said quietly. "It's just that you do so much for everyone else that I wanted to do something just for you."

Lovey smiled up at him. "It's perfect...everything is perfect."

Silas kissed her again, and she shivered as he moved one hand up to pull out her ponytail and the other down the length of her back to rest at her waist. She wrapped her arms around him and pulled him closer, the length of their bodies pressed against one another. Silas's lips moved over hers then left a trail of heat down her neck as he pulled at the buttons on her dress. Lovey took her turn unbuttoning his shirt then pulled it off his shoulders, revealing a chest thin but muscled and tan from hard work.

Silas let her dress fall then pulled her over to the bed, pulling the quilt aside and laying Lovey gently down before covering her with the full length of his body. With a practiced deftness, he reached between them and unsnapped the front clasp on her bra. Lovey was suddenly shy and uncertain about her body. Though she'd never had children, her body had aged and wasn't as toned and trim as it used to be. She covered herself self-consciously and turned her face away.

"Don't do that. You are so beautiful. Don't hide that from me," he admonished her quietly then moved down to take her nipple between

325

his lips. Lovey moaned from the feeling of his tongue slowly pulling it into hardness. She could feel the heat growing between her legs, and her back arched in pleasure as Silas gently sucked her nipple between his teeth.

Lovey moaned again as he pressed into her. She could feel the extent of his arousal against her hip and ached to feel his naked skin against hers. She reached down and unbuttoned the top of his jeans. Silas growled against her neck then helped her push them down. Lovey reached down and caught his erection as it sprang free from its confines. Silas hooked his finger in her panties and pulled them down then moved up to run his thumb along the length of her slit. Lovey shuddered as waves of pleasure moved through her body. She shuddered again when he put his fingers deep inside of her, finding that tiny universe of pleasure, sending her off into a wave of an orgasm.

Lovey pulled him close and wrapped her legs around him, forcing him up against her. "Oh God, Lovey," he groaned as he pressed into her. Lovey lifted her hips to receive the full length of him.

Silas pushed into her, slow at first then faster and faster, their hips meeting in a desperate need for release. Lovey cried out as another orgasm ripped through her just as Silas shuddered with his own. Spent, he dropped next to her and gathered her in his arms, his face buried in her hair. She could feel the pounding of his heart in sync with her own.

"I have loved you for so long, Lovey. And now you're finally mine," he panted, tightening his grip around her. Tears sprang to her eyes, and she shifted in his arms so her cheek lay against his chest.

"I love you too," she whispered and felt him press a kiss to the top of her head.

Their heartbeats slowed as they both fell asleep.

With the cabin surrounded by trees, it was the sound of birds calling in the early morning rather than the sunrise that woke them up. Lovey kept her eyes closed to better savor the feeling of Silas's warm body pressed against the length of hers. He'd molded himself to the contours of her back, his arm draped over her, his hand cradling her breast. She could feel the chill of the morning on her cheek but was perfectly warm underneath the quilt. She didn't dare stir in the hopes of drawing out that perfect moment for as long as possible.

She knew he was awake when he planted a kiss on her shoulder. She shivered from the intimacy of the gesture. Mistaking her shiver for being cold, Silas drew the quilt over them and pressed his body harder against hers. She could feel his arousal growing against her and smiled to herself. Silas sensed a change in her wakefulness and moved his hand from her breast to the cleft between her legs. His fingers parted her then moved slowly along the length of her. Lovey's sharp intake of breath spurred him further, and he gently increased the pressure until a delicious itch began to build deep within her. As her orgasm crested over her, Silas pressed himself into her from behind, the full length of him sliding in with ease. So great was his need that it was only moments before he too was shuddering from his climax. Lovey lay still, relishing the feeling of his warmth filling her even as he grew soft. It wasn't long before she was asleep again.

It was full morning when she awoke again, this time to the smell of breakfast. Silas was just setting the table when she pushed herself off the bed. Every part of her body ached from the previous night's exertions.

"Good morning, Mrs. Wooten." Silas smiled. "I hope you're hungry."

"Starving," Lovey replied, wrapping the quilt around her nakedness. She crossed the room and sat down before a plate steaming with eggs, French toast, and bacon. A huge mug of coffee beckoned.

"So you're Silas Wooten now?" she asked.

Silas sat in front of her and picked up his own mug. He sat silently for a moment as if considering his words. "After Miriam showed me who I really was...I didn't feel like it was fair to keep the name of a woman who essentially kidnapped me," he replied. "I don't know if my life would have been any better, but Agnes wasn't the best of parents. I'm not even sure why she kept me. It was Abel who convinced me to take the name of the family I was born to."

"So you're sure you're a Wooten?" Lovey joked and took a bite of her eggs.

Silas smiled back ruefully. "Well the possibility exists that I could belong to some other black-haired, black-eyed family with the exact same face, but I seriously doubt it. Why? Would you rather have been Lovey Pritchett?"

Lovey shook her head. "No, I've always been partial to the Wootens. Besides, Olivia or Lovey Wooten sounds better than Lovey Pritchett."

Silas's expression turned serious as he reached over and took Lovey's hand. "You know it doesn't matter what we call ourselves, right? If you wanted me to be Silas Polk, it wouldn't matter to me."

Lovey squeezed his hand. "You're right; it doesn't matter. We'll be Wootens. It feels right."

Their time at the cabin was short, and though Lovey knew they needed to get back to Zion, she wished they could stay there for at least a little while longer. Josiah was in good hands with Jean, Harley, and the Tripple brothers, but Wade's presence in Zion made her uneasy, and she'd feel better keeping an eye on him herself.

With their responsibilities waiting for them back home, they reluctantly left the cabin, and, after thanking Jacob for his hospitality, they set off for home.

It was late afternoon when they got back to Zion, and Lovey was pleased to see that the place hadn't burned down to the ground in their absence. Everything looked normal, and they were greeted warmly as they drove up.

Silas parked next to the cottage, and Lovey suddenly wondered about their living arrangements. Josiah had been staying with her but might find quarters cramped with another adult. As if in answer to her unspoken question, Harley and Jean stepped out just as Lovey walked up. They carried boxes of clothes and books Lovey recognized as Josiah's.

"Welcome back, Mrs. Wooten!" Harley called out. "We figured Josiah could come stay with me...give you and Silas a little more room."

"Are you sure that's OK?" Lovey asked. Josiah was her responsibility, and she didn't want to impose on anyone. She could see signs of stress around Harley's eyes and wondered if it might be better to keep Josiah with her.

"It's fine," he reassured her. "It'll be nice to have the company."

At that moment, Jackson drove up in a small John Deere utility vehicle Lovey had never seen before. He stopped in front of the cottage and got out to help Jean with the box she was carrying.

"Load it up, and I'll drive it over," Jackson offered.

Lovey stared at the cart. "Where did that come from?"

"Guy at the mill is getting rid of all his stuff before it closes," Jackson replied. "Got a real good deal on it. Thought it might help having wheels around here rather than trying to drag things around in wheelbarrows."

"It's a good idea," Silas murmured to Lovey. "Saves wear and tear on the road...especially with the trucks."

Lovey concurred, but her mind went in another direction. Jackson's news about the mill was unsettling, since several of the residents of Zion had found work there, including Jackson himself. "The mill is closing?"

Jackson rubbed at his face. "Yeah, it's for sale, but no one's interested in it. It's not a big producer, and the owner's lookin' to retire anyway. I got maybe two more paychecks, and then they're done."

"Let me reimburse you for the cart," Lovey offered.

Jackson gave her a rare smile. "That would be great, Miss Lovey," he said then drove off with Jean and Harley and all of Josiah's things.

Lovey turned to Silas. "I'm going to go check on Josiah," she said quietly. He gave her a quick kiss then turned to carry their luggage into the cottage. Lovey set off toward the dining hall first. She was halfway there when she crossed paths with Tamara. Lovey glanced at her then turned back and stopped the girl. Tamara's usually overmade face was completely devoid of makeup, and a massive bruise colored her eye and cheekbone.

"What happened?" Lovey asked. Her fingers went up to examine the girl's face, but Tamara jerked her head away.

"I made Wade mad," she said sullenly then burst into tears.

Lovey took the girl by the arm and led her into the clinic. "Tell me," Lovey ordered as she sat down in front of Tamara.

"I have this thing...in me...and I sometimes say shi—I mean things that I shouldn't. I can't help it. I know it's the devil in me, but...anyway...Wade got real mad when I wouldn't shut up...so he smacked me." Tamara looked up at her beseechingly. "But it wasn't his fault. I totally deserved it."

Lovey was incredulous. "Tamara, nobody deserves to be assaulted," she began, but Tamara shook her head.

"It ain't like that," she protested. "I've done had the devil in me for a long time...like that girl in that movie. He makes me say bad things, and sometimes he makes me do them too." Tamara looked up at her. "You ever see that movie? About the little girl that had the devil in her?"

"You mean *The Exorcist*?" Lovey asked, amazed at the direction this conversation was going.

"Yeah, that's it. You know that was a true story, right? And...like...the priest in the movie, well, he was a real priest, and when he was tryin' to help that girl, the devil gave him a heart attack, and he died...for real."

"Tamara, the priest was played by an actor named Max Von Sydow. He didn't really die. None of that was real," Lovey said slowly.

Tamara shook her head. "It was real. They even say it was real. Ain't no way a girl's head can turn around like that unless she's evil. It's 'cause the devil was in her. And if the devil can get inside that little girl when she didn't even do nothing wrong, then he can get in me too."

Lovey stared at the girl. "The movie was based on a true story about a boy who lived before I was even born. But the movie itself is fake...make believe...to tell the story. And not even the exact story."

Tamara gave Lovey a sympathetic look that Lovey found spectacularly ironic.

"But never mind the movie, why do you think you have the devil in you?" Lovey asked to end the pointless argument.

"I just know it. I can feel him sometimes making me say bad things and do bad things."

Lovey was concerned about the strength of Tamara's conviction but didn't know what to say to convince her otherwise. "Let's see if we can get the swelling down on your cheek. This looks recent. Did it just happen?" she asked as she reached into the freezer.

Tamara nodded then accepted the cold gel pack and held it gently to her face. "It's my fault. I was running my mouth while Wade was busy cleanin' up that room outside. He told me to shut up, but I didn't listen."

Lovey looked at the girl. "What room outside?"

"You know...the one with the door in the ground. Wade and Arlen been cleanin' it up," she replied. Tamara took the pain-killers that Lovey had handed her and stood up to leave. "I gotta go back there...I'm s'posed to be helpin'. Wade's gonna get mad at me again."

"Come back and see me if the pain gets worse," Lovey called out as Tamara darted out the door. She almost called the girl back to question her further, but nothing Tamara said would make any kind of sense. Lovey wondered why they would care about an old storm shelter but decided not to look a gift horse in the mouth. At least Wade was doing *something*. She decided to go see Josiah instead.

When she didn't find him in his prayer space, she walked over to the church and found it empty too. Wondering where he might be, Lovey followed the drive toward the maintenance shed then took the path through the woods. She found Josiah on the deck by the stream, where he sat by himself staring at the water below his feet.

332

Lovey walked over and sat next to him. "Hey, Josiah," she said quietly. "We're back."

Josiah looked over at her with a smile that was genuine if a little sad. "I'm glad you're back. This place doesn't feel the same when you're not here."

"I'm sorry about that. It was a bit of a surprise." Lovey felt terrible. She'd been so consumed by Silas that she had neglected Josiah entirely.

"It was a good surprise," Josiah reassured her. "Silas really loves you...and I want you to be happy."

Lovey put her arm around Josiah who, despite his size, leaned into her like a little boy. "Are you OK?"

Josiah shrugged. "It feels like things are changing around here. It's not like it was in the beginning."

"You mean because of me and Silas?" she asked.

Josiah shook his head. "No, that's always been there. You just made it official. It's just that...there's almost too many people here, and it doesn't feel like they're here for the same reasons as before."

"I can ask them all to leave if you want, Josiah." Lovey hugged him close. "Anything you need...that's what we'll do."

Josiah gave her a crooked smile. "I believe you would do that too...even though it goes against everything you've worked for." He looked back down at the water flowing beneath his feet. "But too many people here don't have anywhere else to go. We can't send them away."

"It'll be warm soon, anyway," Lovey offered. "People will start to leave on their own, and things will go back to normal. And I promise not to go away again."

Josiah nodded then laid his head on her shoulder. He was a man now, but Lovey felt that surge of love for the boy he'd always been to her.

"'But the child's mother said, "As surely as the Lord lives and as you live, I will not leave you." So he got up and followed her,'" Josiah said quietly then wrapped his arms around Lovey's waist and held her tight.

FIFTY-TWO

It was much as Lovey had predicted. As the days grew warmer, most of the more temporary residents of Zion moved on to find stable work or better living situations. The Tripple brothers were among them, having secured work outside the state, and Lovey felt the loss of them keenly. She had hoped that Wade and his friends would move on too, but they remained stubbornly ensconced in the community.

Jackson and Davis managed to stay useful and, when the mill closed, found work with the county, while Arlen and Wade continued their work renovating the storm shelter. As much as she detested Wade Wooten, his status as Josiah's great-uncle and now Silas's uncle/brother couldn't be denied, so she let him be. Willie, on the other hand, was so invisible that it wasn't until he asked her for a ride into town that she remembered he was there.

Lovey was in her clinic getting some paper work together when Willie shuffled up to her doorway.

"Miss Luhvee?" he mumbled behind her.

Lovey turned to see him swaying crookedly, his right arm pulled tight against his chest, his left leg splayed at an awkward angle. She'd never heard him speak before and noted a profound speech impediment.

If she didn't know better, she'd have thought he was talking through a mouthful of marbles.

"Oh, Willie." Lovey smiled. "I didn't see you there. What do you need?"

"Kin yoo gib me a rye ta town?" he asked, his face turned away.

"Sure," she answered. "What do you need from town? Is it something I can get for you?"

Willie shook his head. "I jush nee a rye."

Lovey shrugged. "OK. I'm leaving in a couple of minutes."

Willie nodded then turned and shuffled out the door.

By the time Lovey was ready, Willie was already sitting in the passenger seat of her car. Silas walked up just as she was about to get in. He raised his eyebrows in question then tilted his head in Willie's direction. Lovey shook her head and shrugged it off.

"Be safe," he whispered then kissed her gently.

"I will," she promised. She got in and drove away.

The trip into town was not long enough for her to start any kind of conversation with Willie, so they rode in silence. Once they got to the center of town, Lovey parked in front of the drugstore and got out. She went around to Willie's side to help him but found him already on the sidewalk.

"Do you know where you're going?" she asked, and he nodded. "OK then. I have an appointment at the bank, but it won't take long. I'll be back here in about forty-five minutes. I'll wait for you if you're not back by then, OK?"

Willie nodded again. "Tink yoo," he said then shuffled toward the drugstore.

Lovey watched him go then turned and walked into the bank.

Her appointment went much more quickly than she'd originally thought, so Lovey walked back toward the drugstore to see if Willie was ready to go. She went in to pick up some things she needed for the clinic then stepped back out and looked around in case Willie had come back. When she didn't see him out front, she started to go back toward the bank but stopped when she heard the sound of his voice coming from around the corner. Lovey stopped and listened for a moment, her ear cocked. It was definitely his voice, but his speech impediment had miraculously cleared. She moved closer to the corner and listened.

"Yeah. They've already hit the shows in Philadelphia and Jackson, and they're talking like they're going to hit Southaven Tri-Lake next. No...I still haven't determined where the money is coming from. I'm almost certain we can rule out Olivia Polk. She's been hostile to our presence since we got there. I'm sure if Wooten weren't the kid's uncle, she would have had us out on our asses long ago. The kid? He's been going off the rails a bit with his preaching, but I don't think he knows what's going on either. Yeah, I'll follow up with that. Problem I'm seeing now is they're talking about connecting with our target, who's been traveling with the local white-pride group. They've been ordering some of the bigger straw purchases, but I haven't seen any faces. I'll let you know if any of them show up at Zion. Right...will do."

Lovey stepped forward and stood directly behind Willie, who turned then jumped back with a comical squeak when he realized she was there. His weight shifted slightly, and his arm came back up to his chest.

"You know," she said. "The interesting thing about brain injury is how inflexible the resulting condition can be. For instance, if your brain is injured so that you've lost mobility in your right arm, it's fairly unlikely for it to suddenly switch to your left arm." Lovey reached over and tapped his left hand, which he had inadvertently pulled up to his chest. "And it's even less likely that your previously unusable right hand would be able to hold a cell phone, let alone operate one."

Willie dropped his arm and stood and stared at Lovey.

"So, who are you, what are you, and why are you pretending to be disabled?" she asked just as his cell buzzed.

Willie raised his miraculously fully functioning hand and answered the phone. "Hey, I'm hot right now. I'll call you back," he said then hung up and slid it into his jeans pocket. They stood and stared at each other for what seemed like an extremely long minute.

"You're not going to tell me who you are, are you?" Lovey asked. She wasn't surprised when Willie shook his head. "Then what's to stop me from outing you to Wade and Arlen?"

"Because that would make things infinitely worse for you and Josiah," Willie said quietly. "And I know you don't want that to happen. We need to see this through to the end, or it could get a lot worse for everybody."

"Worse how?" Lovey asked but Willie just shook his head and refused to answer. "Then I take Josiah and leave," she countered.

Willie shook his head again. "And leave behind everyone else? Silas? Harley? What about Jean and her kids and all the others?" Willie rubbed at his face.

"But if we're in danger...I can't leave anyone in harm's way. How can I ensure everyone's safety if you won't tell me what I should be looking for? What if something goes wrong?" Lovey objected.

Willie shook his head. "Nothing's going to happen. Wade's small potatoes...a link to something potentially more serious...yes...but still just a link. I need him to find the bigger guys, so I need everything to stay just as it is right now."

Lovey considered the man in front of her for a moment. "Then I need you to do something for me. Whatever happens, whatever you have to do, keep the others out of it and keep them safe. Josiah, Harley, Jean...all the kids, I don't want them hurt. If you work for who I think you work for, then you already know all about me. You know what resources I have at my disposal, and I'm sure you don't want me to have to utilize those resources. Do we have a deal?"

Willie paled at the threat but nodded. "Deal."

Lovey looked at the other man, wondering if she could trust him. He was actually quite good-looking now that he'd dropped the act. His eyes blazed with intelligence, and she wondered why she hadn't noticed it before. "Why the disability act? Why not just be normal?" she asked.

"There's something about being disabled that makes people look away. It's a way to be relatively invisible. And it's a way to get inside...to be adopted by a group."

"Huh, play on their sympathy," she commented, and Willie nodded. "But Wade doesn't seem like a particularly sympathetic guy."

"No, Wade isn't," Willie agreed but didn't elaborate.

Lovey stared at him for another moment. "But Jackson is," she said. Willie nodded. Lovey turned away then stopped and turned back. "Is your name even Willie?"

Willie gave her a half smile. "Sort of. My grandmother called me Willie."

Lovey stared at him a moment longer. "By the way, you might want to make sure you're dragging your right leg all the time. You tend to go back and forth," she remarked then turned and walked to her car.

Willie assumed his pose and shuffled after her.

When they were almost home, Lovey slowed the car. "If you need a quiet space where you won't be overheard, come to the clinic. The walls are soundproofed for privacy."

Willie looked over at her. "Wade's going to wonder what I'm doing there, especially after all this time."

"Right now you're faking spastic diplegia, which can cause pain in your lower extremities, and under normal care your arm would require physical therapy. Tell him whatever you want, but physical therapy takes time...enough time to communicate with whomever you need to without having to drive all the way into town."

Willie thought about this then agreed. "Yeah, that'll work."

"Tell him we're doing speech therapy too, so you can start to sound at least a little bit more normal," she said sarcastically then pulled into the driveway of the church.

Willie snorted but said nothing.

Now that she knew the truth about Willie's presence in Zion, she was noticing more about the day-to-day activities in the camp. It grated on her that there was nothing she could do about Wade and Arlen and whatever they were doing there that warranted federal scrutiny. She was glad that even though Josiah had moved in with Harley, their cabin was closest to hers and both were closest to the way out if they needed to leave quickly. She went in search of Jackson to suss out if he was part of whatever Wade was doing or an unfortunate casualty stuck out of loyalty. She just needed to come up with a good reason for approaching him.

With his county work, Jackson wasn't due back in Zion until dinner, so Lovey cornered him after their evening meal.

"Jackson?" she called out just as he was about to leave the dining hall. "Can I talk to you a second?"

Jackson looked surprised but stopped just inside the door and waited for her to catch up.

Silas followed Lovey over and stood quietly behind her. It felt good to know he never questioned her decisions and always had her back. Lovey looked at Jackson and wondered how he'd ever hooked up with a troublemaker like Wade.

"I know you've been working with the county...with the maintenance crew?" she asked. Jackson nodded. "I was wondering if you've ever come across something the church could use...like a van or a bus. Something we could have on hand to take groups out."

Jackson scratched at his chin and looked thoughtful. "I might know of something," he replied. "There's an old school bus for sale on the other side of town. I think it was decommissioned from the county and someone was using it for their church group or whatever. I'm not sure what kind of shape it's in, though it wouldn't take much to fix it up."

341

"Do you have time in the next couple of days to take me to go look at it?" Lovey crossed her fingers Silas wouldn't object, but Jackson did it for him.

"I'll take care of it, Miss Lovey." He smiled. "It's on my route, so it wouldn't take nothing to just stop by and check it out. I'll let you know what I find."

It was Lovey's turn to smile. "Thank you, Jackson. Let me know how much they want, and I'll make sure you get the cash for it."

Jackson beamed, and Lovey knew for certain that whatever Wade was doing that had Willie and his agency investigating him, Jackson had nothing to do with it.

True to his word, Jackson indeed took care of it and had the bus towed to Zion the next day. Lovey followed the truck to the maintenance shed, where Jackson was having the tow-truck driver drop off the bus. It looked to be in good condition, but Lovey worried about why it needed to be towed in rather than driven.

"Hey, Miss Lovey." Jackson smiled then waved at the tow-truck driver as he took off. "What do you think?"

"I think it looks great," Lovey replied. "It's exactly what I was thinking of, but does it run?"

"Engine just needs a little work. It runs but not perfectly. Nothing I can't fix. Inside's clean, and body is in great shape, automatic transmission, and it even has air. They wanted five but took three grand for it."

Lovey looked skeptical. "How long until it's safe to drive?"

Jackson shrugged. "I've got to pick up some parts, and I want to paint out their name but...a week maybe? It drives right now, but it'll give you fits. It needs some work on the starter and a new carburetor. But that's it."

Lovey smiled. "Come by the cottage so I can give you a check and an account card to cover expenses."

Jackson nodded. "Will do," he said, turning to the bus. Lovey was about to leave when he turned back. "Miss Lovey?"

Lovey stopped. "Yes?"

"Thank you," he said with great humility. "You've been right kind when you didn't have to, and I just wanted you to know that I really appreciate it."

"You're a part of this community, Jackson, a part of the family. As the Wootens say, 'We take care of our own'...and you're one of our own," she replied.

Jackson looked at her, his face serious. "I just want you to know... whatever happens...I got your back, Miss Lovey."

Lovey's smiled faltered as she took in his words. "Thank you, Jackson. And I have yours."

Jackson and Lovey regarded each other for a moment then, with a short nod of agreement, turned and went their separate ways.

FIFTY-THREE

Willie availed himself of the clinic and kept Lovey as much in the loop as he could without jeopardizing his investigation. Lovey had already guessed that Wade and Arlen were either buying guns or drugs but couldn't figure out why or where they were. There weren't any weapons in the storm shelter. No one new had come to stay at Zion, and so far they hadn't had any unusual visitors either. Though she tried to stay vigilant, Lovey was soon distracted by Misty's advancing pregnancy.

After the initial shock that Misty had been able to get pregnant in the first place, Lovey was consumed by thoughts of who the father could be and whether or not Misty could carry the baby to term.

Though she'd never been pregnant herself, Lovey had treated enough pregnant women in her time to know that every pregnancy was different. Some were easy, with little to no complications, and others were fraught with every misery an expectant mother could face. Misty's was definitely turning out to be the latter.

She had managed to get the girl to at least a couple of visits with a local OB-GYN who declared Misty fine and doing well, though Lovey had her doubts. She'd just given her a once-over and finally managed to talk Misty into taking a trip to the hospital for a sonogram to check the status of the fetus. But despite all of her efforts, Misty still insisted that the baby was a holy miracle and the Lord wouldn't let anything happen to it. Though she appreciated the girl's devotion, Lovey was still concerned that even so near the end, something could go terribly wrong.

As Misty left the clinic, Lovey turned and stood at the window watching the youngest residents of Zion walk through the trees at the end of the drive where the county school bus would pick them up. At least they would be safe from harm for the day. She wished Josiah hadn't received his GED already, or he'd be safely ensconced in a high school, surrounded by staff and students. She was full of anxiety now that Wade seemed to be done with whatever he had done to the storm shelter. If idle hands were the devil's playground, Wade was a prime candidate for mischief.

She could hear him back in the dining hall expounding on whatever nonsense had filled his head at that moment. Tamara's voice rang out over the others and sounded angry. Lovey stepped out of her clinic but stopped short at the doorway to listen in on the conversation.

Tamara was in full rant mode. "Ain't no way I'm gonna let my man have another wummun and call her his wife. If I can't have another man, ain't no fuckin' way I'm gonna let him have another wife."

"But it's God's will, dumbass," Wade responded. "If God wanted me to have more than one wife...well, then who am I to go against his will? Solomon had lots of wives, and so did David, and they're the big shots."

Lovey was stunned to see Josiah sitting with them and wondered at his presence. She looked at him pointedly but was surprised to see him react with sadness rather than righteous anger or his usual need to educate. But he still answered appropriately.

"'Let deacons each be the husband of one wife, managing their children and their own households well,'" Josiah said. "Men who had multiple wives were charged with their care and protection; they were not solely for pleasure. But we are taught to live as Christ lived, above lust... above carnal knowledge. We are to serve our fellow man, not ourselves."

Wade turned to correct his nephew but spotted Lovey in the doorway and called out to her instead. "I suppose you're here to tell me that I'm wrong, aren't you?" Wade sneered.

Lovey's eyes narrowed. "Though the Old Testament speaks of men having several wives...and concubines...and Jesus didn't condemn it, we have grown...evolved beyond the time when the Bible was written. Our understanding of the world has grown exponentially, and so should our understanding of God's will. With all we know now, it is clear that plural marriage is a misogynistic construct put forth during a time when men denied women rights and considered them to be property. The richer the man, the more property he had. Animals, crops, slaves...and wives."

"So you would break the laws in the Bible because you don't like them," Wade said to her, his eyes narrowed, his tone challenging.

Lovey looked at him coolly. "I would deny those laws I don't consider to be from God. In fact, the only laws I feel are genuinely 'from God' are the Ten Commandments. All the rest are deliberate misinterpretations or misrepresentations by men driven by their own bigotries. Fundamentalist thought is very dangerous. It denies the existence of two millennia of evolution of the human condition. It steadfastly adheres to laws written by men with their own prejudices and agendas inserted as God's truths. And you break these laws daily, but polygamy is the one you would choose to follow?"

Wade was taken aback. "I ain't broken none of the Lord's laws."

Lovey gave him a small smile. "You already have...several, in fact. As I recall you had a ham sandwich for lunch yesterday. That's forbidden. And those tattoos you display proudly are an affront to God for, 'Ye shall not make any cuttings in your flesh for the dead; nor print any marks upon you.' And you're clean-shaven; that's forbidden too. And don't you have a son?"

Wade's eyes narrowed. "Yeah, so?"

Lovey shrugged. "If you were married to his mother yet you are engaging in sexual relations with other women, then you are committing carnal sin...essentially adultery, despite being divorced. Even looking at another woman with intention, like you've been looking at Tamara, is adultery."

"I ain't talkin' about dumb shit like that. 'Sides, what's that got to do with havin' more than one wife?" Wade demanded.

"It's got everything to do with plural marriage," Lovey answered. "You can't pick and choose. If you follow one, then you follow all of them. If one seems dumb or unnecessary, then you have to consider that the rest are likely dumb and unnecessary as well. You have to determine what is truth and what is false prophecy. In terms of polygamy as a right, God did not create one man and multiple women."

"What's that supposed to mean?" Wade challenged.

From his expression, Lovey could tell he knew he was losing the battle but still insisted on asserting his superiority as a man, despite his intellectual inferiority.

Lovey sighed. "So that even you can understand, in the creation story itself, God created one Adam and one Eve. Not Adam and Eve and Eve and Eve and Eve."

"There," Tamara chimed in. "Just like I been sayin'."

Lovey smiled at the thought that the person she had the least in common with was the one that agreed with her.

Wade caught Lovey smiling at Tamara and stood up, abruptly casting the other girl aside. "Fuck this shit," he said, his tone both angry and defensive. "I got better things to do than listen to this nonsense."

Lovey stepped aside as Wade pushed past. She looked after him then turned to see a scowling Tamara coming up behind him. There was a fresh bruise under her eye, and Lovey's eyes went right to it.

Tamara caught the pity in Lovey's gaze, and her expression turned mulish.

"Tamara?" Lovey asked quietly, afraid of spooking the girl.

"Mind your own fucking business," Tamara muttered and moved past her.

Lovey turned and caught Josiah's eye. He looked deeply despondent, and Lovey didn't know if it was because of Wade or because of her. She suspected both.

FIFTY-FOUR

Suddenly things stopped making sense.

It was like watching a damaged film. Time would speed up then stop suddenly in random places, disorienting Lovey. She could feel her heart racing and her body going cold all over. Her fear that there was nothing she could do to set things right was paralyzing.

It started when the stranger showed up. He looked relatively normal, like a beefy high-school football coach, but Lovey knew the minute she saw him that something was seriously wrong with him. He drove up in a truck that looked like everyone else's with three others, who similarly lacked anything overtly threatening but still left her deeply unsettled. Later she would realize that it was their expressions that gave them away. Normal visitors to Zion were happy or grateful to be there, and their faces reflected their hope of finding some kind of sanctuary. But these men wore blank faces, their eyes soulless and disinterested.

Lovey wasn't surprised to see Arlen come out to greet them then take them around the back of the dorm building. When she realized Willie had gone into town with Harley, time stopped and her mind went blank. She had no idea what to do.

Then, yearlong minutes later, they left and time resumed its normal course. When Willie returned, Lovey practically ran to him to tell him about the men, but he scowled and shook his head slightly before turning away. Lovey stared after him, feeling helpless. Panic was setting in, but she was powerless to fight it.

Silas did his best to comfort her, but her mind wouldn't settle down long enough to thank him for his effort. She wanted desperately to tell him about Willie and Wade but at the same time knew that he would want to act on it and would force Wade and his friends to leave. Lovey wanted to keep Silas as far away as possible from anything that might happen.

The next morning was a Saturday, and Willie insisted that Lovey take the few residents of Zion to the movies. Time started moving more quickly than Lovey could keep up with. Harley and Jean saw her distraction and ran interference, gathering everyone together. Jackson drove up in the bus and stopped it near the dining hall, so everyone could load up. In no time the bus was full, so Silas offered to drive Josiah and Misty while Lovey rode the bus with Jean and Harley and the children.

Wade, Arlen, and Tamara were nowhere to be found, but Lovey told herself to be grateful that the men from the day before weren't there either.

Time resumed its normal pace as the bus made its way off of the church property with Silas right behind. Lovey checked that he was there then turned to respond to Jean's enthusiasm. She was almost back to normal by the time they made it to the movie theater in Meridian. But everything froze when she stepped off the bus and realized that Silas wasn't there.

"Where are they?" she said to herself then startled when Jackson answered her. She hadn't realized she'd spoken aloud.

"Silas turned back halfway here," he said mildly. "Maybe Misty changed her mind about comin'. She wasn't feelin' so hot earlier."

Lovey felt a strange disconnect as her world completely shifted. Without answering Jackson, she pulled her cell phone from her bag and frantically dialed Silas's number. It rang and rang then eventually went to voice mail. She tried several more times before Jackson put out his hand to stop her.

"He's in a dead zone if they're back at Zion," he said gently.

Lovey stared at him, the blood draining from her face. "I have to go back," she whispered.

"They'll be fine," he reassured her. "They'll probably just drop Misty off then turn around to come back here."

Lovey shook her head slowly. "You don't understand. Something's wrong. I have to go back."

Jackson looked confused. "What do you mean 'something's wrong'?"

Lovey turned and looked all around her as if a solution was suddenly going to present itself. "Willie made everyone leave. He wouldn't do that if something bad wasn't going to happen." Lovey's fear was so great that she couldn't articulate what she was really thinking. She was blind to everything but her desperate need to get to Josiah and Silas. The air seemed too thin around her, and she fought to catch her breath.

"Give me your keys," she said to Jackson and held out her hand.

He shook his head politely. "No offense, Miss Lovey, but there's no way you're gonna be able to get that bus back to Zion. It's not like driving a car."

"I need your keys, Jackson...please," she pleaded, her voice breaking.

Jackson rubbed at his face then ran his fingers through his hair, leaving it standing on end. "Shit," he said quietly then stared at the doors the rest of Zion's family had disappeared through. "Wade's gone and fucked something up, hasn't he?"

Lovey didn't trust herself to answer calmly, so she simply nodded.

"Fuck all," Jackson muttered. "Come on then. I'll take you there."

Lovey threw her arms around Jackson and gave him a quick hug. "Thank you, Jackson."

"Shit," he replied, embarrassed. "You wouldn't be in this mess if it weren't for me. Get in."

Time started moving all over the place as they made their way back to Zion. Jackson broke as many traffic laws as humanly possible, and for once providence was on their side. Not a single cop was working on their route from Meridian back to Zion.

When they pulled into the drive, time had stopped, and Lovey held her breath. It was as she had feared; the men from yesterday had left their trucks near the dorms, even though nobody ever parked there. Silas's truck was parked near the dining hall, and it was there that Lovey went first.

As soon as she stepped into the dining hall, time began skipping again. Single moments of clarity punctuated the mass confusion that followed.

Simultaneously, Lovey heard glass shattering, shouts and shots fired outside then a woman screaming upstairs. She didn't know which way to turn at first until a second cry, full of pain, called her up to Josiah's room, where she found Misty lying on her side on the floor, with Josiah praying over her.

Why is she here and not in the clinic? Lovey asked but realized as the world shifted again she'd never said the words aloud. She turned and realized Silas was talking to her, though his words were little more than a babble of confusion underscoring the roar in her ears.

From outside she could hear someone shouting, but only a gray mist was visible through the big picture window. Lovey didn't know it was smoke.

Lovey's brain shifted again, and all she could see was a mother in distress. "Silas," she interrupted. "I need my black kit from the clinic and some towels." Her order was punctuated by what sounded like fire-crackers. Jackson fled the room.

Silas pushed Lovey down onto the floor then ran after Jackson. Lovey crawled over to Misty and gently eased her legs apart. The baby was already crowning, but there was so much blood. Misty cried out as another wave of pain ran through her body.

Lovey heard a commotion in the doorway. Jackson had returned to check on them, a rifle in his hands, and Silas moved past him to drop Lovey's kit and a pile of linens from the clinic and kitchen next to her. Then both men ran out the door.

Lovey swabbed Misty's perineum as the girl cried out again. Misty was pushing desperately, but the baby's head was stuck.

Josiah continued to pray but stared at Misty as Lovey prepped her for an episiotomy.

Lovey made the incision along the perineum, a volley of gunshots and screaming in the distance.

The room began to smell of smoke.

Lovey barely heard the sound of glass breaking as Misty's baby slid out into her hands. Lovey wrapped the baby in a towel, gently wiping the vernix away. Black hair and solemn blue eyes regarded her calmly.

"She's beautiful," Lovey said then moved up to put the baby in Misty's arms.

Josiah was staring at Misty, his face drawn in shades of infinite sorrow. Lovey looked down. Misty was staring off, a pool of blood spreading from beneath her head.

Lovey was staring at Misty, her mind unable to process what she was looking at, when Silas ran in. He wordlessly pulled Lovey and Josiah to their feet then pushed Lovey toward the door. Silas turned to grab the still-staring Josiah as the window behind them completely shattered.

Josiah looked at Lovey and shook his head, speaking though she couldn't understand the words. Lovey stared at him, trying to understand, her expression turning to horror as a red bloom opened in the center of Josiah's chest. Lovey's heart felt the pierce of the bullet that had hit him, and she glanced down, certain she too wore a red bloom. Oblivious to the child in her arms and the bullets spraying the wall next to her, she reached for the child that was slowly falling at her feet.

She barely felt it when Silas wrapped his firm hand around her arm and pulled her from the room as Josiah fell to his knees behind them. She could only see the light leaving Josiah's eyes as Silas pulled her away from the boy she'd promised to keep safe.

The world shifted again, and she and Silas were running toward the woods with the baby.

Lovey looked back to see the dorms completely engulfed in flames. Tamara stood in front of the fire screaming at nothing, firing a gun at nothing, her demons fully consuming her in their need for gratification.

Silas pulled Lovey deeper into the trees. Deep in the woods the gunshots seemed farther away, quieter.

Finally Silas stopped. They were at the end of the driveway, past the maintenance shed. The road in front of them was deserted.

Lovey looked down to see the baby, the image of every Wooten ever born, gazing up at her. Tears began streaming down her face, landing like raindrops on the baby. Lovey gave in to the grief that she had failed him. She'd failed all of them. Josiah was gone.

Silas dropped the rifle he'd been carrying and put his arms around them.

The forest behind them was finally quiet.

FIFTY-FIVE

Despite Willie's best efforts, too many people died that day. Misty was killed by a stray bullet through the large picture window, as was Josiah. Arlen and Tamara were also killed during their standoff with the ATF and FBI agents who were raiding Zion for the cache of weapons Wade and Arlen had hidden in the walls of the storm shelter. All but one of the men who'd come to buy the guns were also killed. Their leader had managed to escape but was apprehended later trying to carjack a soccer mom with a van full of kids. He was shot while resisting arrest.

Willie, whose real name was Bill Ryan, survived with a minor injury, but Jackson did not. His body was found lying on the ground near the school bus, riddled with bullets, all of them from Tamara.

Wade was the final casualty. Deep down in the storm cellar, surrounded by an arsenal, he had put a gun to his head and pulled the trigger just as the federal agents swarmed Zion. Lovey knew that despite all his big talk, deep down inside, Wade had been a coward.

Rain was starting to fall when Lovey finally saw Willie to the door. It was more a courtesy call than anything else...a formal apology from the US government and a token gesture of clemency for Lovey and Silas. The gesture was unnecessary. Lovey's army of attorneys had built a wall around her that had proven impenetrable, not that the government was that interested in her in the first place. They had wanted a man named David Hobbs the whole time. He had been building an army, and Wade had been supplying his guns. Willie reassured her that everyone else at Zion was considered innocent and no charges were to be brought against them.

Lovey had already made arrangements to move Harley, Jean, and the other members of Zion to Maryland. She then had the church and camp demolished. The only thing that remained was a large wooden cross standing at the spot where Josiah had died. Lovey made sure that Josiah was buried at the Wooten farm as was Wade. And even though Misty and Josiah had been killed by the agents that had been firing on the camp, pursuing it further wouldn't bring them back. She accepted the government's formal apology then let it go. As far as she was concerned, it was done. Willie was satisfied.

After he left, Lovey closed the door behind him then pressed her face against the cold wood. She had failed everyone...Marianne, Miss Miriam, and, most importantly, Josiah. She had failed to keep him safe, and her grief consumed her, eating her very cells like a cancer. Tears filled her eyes as her body convulsed in silent sobbing. She wanted to scream out her anguish, to let the fire of her rage and self-loathing burn her to ash, but she couldn't. There was a child now.

Somehow Josiah had known. Lovey had long felt bereft of God's love, her heart hardened with the knowledge that she was not among the favored in his eyes. But Josiah had given her means to her salvation, and a tiny sliver of hope pierced the shell that had formed around her. She was being given a chance to redeem herself. She could not fail again.

After another minute, Lovey was composed enough to return to the sun-room at the back of the house, where Silas sat with the baby watching the birds fishing off their dock. She felt her heart ache at the sight of the precious face that looked so much like Marianne's...so much like Josiah's. Too many had given their lives in the hope that this tiny baby would be the world's last chance for salvation...mankind's champion against evil. Such an awesome responsibility lay on her tiny, little shoulders. Lovey smiled through her tears when Silas looked up at her.

"I think she wants her mother." He smiled.

Lovey stared at him for a moment. Misty was dead.

Silas reached out and took Lovey's hand and pulled her closer. She could feel his warmth flowing from his fingers into hers, melting the ice she was certain had replaced the blood in her veins.

"Come here, Mommy," he said quietly. "Your baby wants you."

ABOUT THE AUTHOR:

K. Wiley Sider lives in Ellicott City, Maryland with her husband, two beautiful daughters, and two deeply spoiled dogs.

Other titles by K. Wiley Sider:

The Things That Fall Away
Solitary
Servant
Boy Toy, Book One of the Dead Husbands Series

Learn more about the author at:
www.kwileysider.com
www.facebook.com/kwileysider

And on Twitter at:
@kwileysider

www.ingramcontent.com/pod-product-compliance
Lightning Source LLC
Chambersburg PA
CBHW072321280626
47159CB00027B/252